VAGRANT SOULS BOOK 1

THE SHATTERED ORB

SAMUEL E. GREEN

Also by Samuel E. Green

Vagrant Souls
Fall of Mundos
The Shattered Orb
The Dragon Soul
The Infernal City (June 2017)
Mountain Guards (July 2017)

Sovereign Sands
Daughter of Sand (June 2017)
Princess of Thieves (August 2017)
Queen of Serpents (October 2017)

With Dylan D. Oscar

The Everlasting Throne
Book of Elements
Sorcerer's Oath (June 2017)

Cover art by Alberto Besi

Cover design by www.designbookcover.pt

Print Layout and Maps by Novelarium.com

Printed in the United States of America

ISBN: 9780648067306

Valor Forge Press
PO BOX 30
Quinns Rocks, WA 6030
Australia

www.SamuelEGreen.com

My dear wife,

You endured the long nights and early mornings
So I could write stories about magic and mysteries.

KRISTNES

MOUNT STOWUM • MUNDOS

SCORCHED
LANDS

KOGTAR

KRANAK-UR

THE SEPULCHERS

DUKGARRD

KILYN
UNIVERSITY

ISLE OF SULITH

EASTERN
SEA

THE FIVE KINGS

MYRAR

LAGAR

VAGRANT SOULS BOOK 1

THE SHATTERED ORB

SAMUEL E. GREEN

Valor Forge Press

1

HIROC

HIROC knelt behind a boulder, wishing he'd brought a weapon to Tyme's Hill. *Acolytes of the Holy Order of Aern don't fight with weapons*, he could hear Ealstan say. Poor advice now.

Six dead warriors, their own spears protruding from their bodies like tent poles, lay outside the gate at the bottom of the hill.

Thunder boomed. Rain fell from the dark clouds.

Swallowing his fear, Hiroc bounded over to the gate. The warriors were certainly dead, all lifeless eyes and gaping wounds. Whoever had murdered them had done so swiftly and with little effort. Taking a sword from a dead warrior's scabbard, he turned away and climbed the steps.

At the peak of Tyme's Hill, stone pillars twenty feet high encircled the holy ground. Blue wards marked the sandstone of the outer circle. Normally they ebbed with power, but now they were dull. The altar was within the inner circle, along with the golden hands that housed the Guardian Aern's orb. The hands were empty.

Hiroc gasped as he rushed over to the altar.

Shards of broken crystal lay in a pool of bloody smears on

the altar's capstone. An intermingling of blood and water ran down the dark stone and pooled at Hiroc's feet.

The rain intensified.

The sound of crunching gravel made Hiroc look up. A lumbering figure, wider than an ox and taller than two men, lurched toward him. It wore black robes that seemed to swallow the little light coming through the storm clouds.

Hiroc rolled sideways as a giant foot crunched stone. Leaping upright, Hiroc gripped his sword in both hands. The thing charged, splashing mud with each tremendous step. Hiroc jumped aside at the last moment, and the thing crashed into a stone pillar, producing a sound like splitting earth. The pillar toppled sideways onto the next. Hiroc could only watch as the entire circle of pillars plummeted.

When the dust faded, the creature turned again to Hiroc. In desperation, Hiroc hacked at its feet. The sword glanced off its skin. A backhand sent Hiroc sprawling. Losing the sword, he tumbled, wrapped in his acolyte robes. He staggered to his feet and freed himself of the tangled cloth. Just a foot away was the edge of Tyme's Hill and a drop that would have surely killed him.

A deafening roar set his teeth on edge.

The monster stomped the ground like a bull, dropped its shoulder, and charged.

Hiroc had no weapon. Behind him, a deadly drop. Quaking, he gripped his ring so hard, the sharp edges of the sigil drew blood. He rattled off a litany of Guardians and old gods, starting with Aern and ending with Wodan, hoping that one might save him.

He wasn't sure what particular god's name had spilled from his lips when lightning forked across the sky. The air boomed. A lightning bolt hammered into the giant, throwing it from its feet. Another boom sounded as the creature slammed into the ground.

Astonished, Hiroc breathed a sigh of relief as blue fire

enveloped the creature.

For a moment it was still.

Hiroc kissed the ring. If he only knew which god had saved him, he'd be forever in their debt.

A grunting noise drew his attention back to where the giant had been. It was no longer lying on the ground. It now stood, a tempest of writhing flames. With a snarl, it cast aside its burning robes. The creature's hardened muscle was etched with scars. Its pale skin bore no burns from the heavenly fire.

Hiroc's heart skipped a beat as the creature moved two steps forward. A deadly grin formed on a head knotted and wrinkled like an ancient tree. Hiroc inched backward until his right foot almost slipped from the edge. There was nowhere to go.

He cried again to a dozen different gods.

Nothing.

Had he forgotten one?

"Taste of my vengeance," it said. Before Hiroc could begin another litany, the giant gripped his neck with a hand the size of a buckler, lifting him from his feet. "Indham and all its people will suffer for their slight against the gods."

Hiroc kicked, thrashing his legs. The kicks glanced off the creature's hardened stomach. He wretched, breath evading him like a thief.

His vision blackened.

Then, suddenly he was on his knees, gasping for air.

Something roared. A blinding light burst above him, showering him in golden sparks. When the light faded, someone stood next to him.

It was not the giant, but Saega the augur in his faded habit. His wrinkled left hand grasped a fox-head staff, its tip smoking from recent use.

"Acolyte Hiroc," Saega said, helping Hiroc to his feet. "Are you harmed?"

Quivering, Hiroc shook his head. All courage had faded.

All he could see was the empty hands where Aern's orb should have been. "The orb is shattered."

"Indeed," Saega said, his wispy white hair plastered to his scalp from the rain. "But the creature fled. It could not remain when I summoned the forces of holy magic."

Hiroc thought to question how an augur had come upon holy magic, but his mind went elsewhere as he traced the line of blood to the ancient altar. Upon its surface lay the broken shards of the orb. It was the one thing that protected Indham, and it had been shattered.

2

FRYDA

FRYDA straightened, not wanting to miss what was likely to be the best match of Summertide. She was squished between two women. Fat chins pressed against fat necks as they sneered down at her. But Fryda didn't care. She wasn't going to miss this for anything.

The crowd around her was made up mostly of Fatherless, warriors, and a smattering of priests and acolytes. They sat on wooden trestles surrounding a circular patch of dirt that was outlined in white paint. The stadium seated two hundred, and most of the seats were filled. Fryda was—as far as she could tell—the only Daughter of Enlil in the audience. If Mother Edoma learned of Fryda's presence at the tournament, it would be dishwashing for at least a month.

Oswin and Alfric were the remaining pair of contestants after months of grueling matches. They were Fatherless, a polite term for the children of the caravans of people who had come from north of Babon's Pass eighteen years ago with little more than the clothes on their backs. Because they were born outside of Aernheim, they normally would have been forbidden from becoming warriors. But not today. The winner of the duel would be able to enter the barracks.

Alfric bowed to a chorus of cheers. He was handsome, as attested to by the women beside her—although they did whisper about his scars and how they marred an otherwise striking face. Fryda had long grown used to the three slashes extending from Alfric's forehead to his chin. She thought they added character.

Oswin somersaulted into the arena. He pranced about like a dancer as women swooned. Fryda had to stifle a chuckle. He cartwheeled before parrying an imaginary attacker with his practice sword. When the crowd had finished applauding, he bowed.

Fryda knew that Oswin wanted to become a warrior because he needed the money to treat his ailing daughter, Whitney, who was sick with devil's fire. Few employers wanted a Fatherless, and those who did paid meager sums. The luckiest of the Fatherless were able to work within Idmaer's Spire, but that had its shortcomings, too—Idmaer was a short-tempered man who expected perfect obedience.

Alfric came over to Fryda and kissed her lightly on the cheek. Mere months ago, she had started dreaming of what it might be like to marry him. She was twenty now, four years past the age of marriage, and he was eighteen. She still had time to marry Alfric. He just had to ask and she would happily be his wife.

Mother Edoma would allow Fryda to leave before she took her vows. If Alfric became a warrior, he would be able to live and work in the town. So there was more than just Alfric's future on the line today, but their shared future, too.

The women sitting beside Fryda snickered. They whispered, "cursed" loudly enough for her to hear. Despite her yellow robes that showed her for a Daughter of Enlil, most everyone knew she was a Fatherless. Feeling her face flush, she drew her hood closer over her head.

"You don't have to hide," Alfric said, his hands meeting her own. Gently, he pulled her hood back.

Fryda tried to keep frowning, but it was impossible with the way he looked at her. Not wanting Alfric to see, she looked down and adjusted her hair pin.

He shot a deadly look at the two women beside Fryda before lifting her chin and meeting her eyes. "You have no reason to be ashamed."

"That's easy for you to say," she said, turning away again. "Look at all your supporters." Most of the people in the audience wanted him to win. Although he was a Fatherless, he was unusual in that most people liked him.

Alfric gave her a smile, as he always did before a duel, as though he might die. She had called it an attempt to manipulate her, but deep down, she feared that it just might happen. Injuries were infrequent, and deaths even more so. But even practice weapons could kill if someone was hit hard enough.

Fryda had thought the concept of a tournament to become a warrior ridiculous. But she wasn't a man, and men possessed an irrational desire to prove themselves.

The bell sounded. The stadium silenced as Alfric and Oswin met, bowed, and then stepped back four paces.

"Keep yourself grounded," Fryda whispered, even though she knew he couldn't hear her. "He'll try to attack you from the side." She had said those very things during their training session that morning. He could be hardheaded at the best of times, so she offered a small prayer. Four points were all he needed in order to win.

In just a few short minutes, it seemed like the gods had answered her prayers. Alfric had scored three points, all of them direct blows to Oswin's chest. Oswin had two points. Gone was his previous joyfulness. He scowled as he wiped sweat from his forehead.

Alfric's face was scrunched in determination. Fryda could just imagine what might be going through his head. He would be trying to justify winning. He and Fryda had argued earlier that week about fighting in the tournament. Oswin, after all, needed the employment more.

When Alfric stood for the next round, Fryda knew he was ready to win.

Alfric and Oswin met in the center and bowed before the bell rang. Oswin leaped backward as Alfric lunged. With his longer arms, Oswin used his free hand to grab Alfric's shirt. Eyes wide with desperation, Oswin pulled his sword over his head and drove its pommel onto Alfric's head. Alfric crumpled.

The bell rang.

Oswin had won the point.

Fryda jumped to her feet. "That was dirty!"

Alfric rose groggily, clutching his head. There was blood coming from the wound.

The warriors whispered among themselves. One stepped forward, a warrior by the name of Sigebert. "The point stands. But any more of that and we'll have to disqualify someone."

A healer attended to Alfric, dressing the wound and then wrapping his head with bandages. Fryda wanted to go over to him but couldn't. Alfric needed to stay focused.

The match started again. Alfric's moves were more aggressive, as though Oswin's foul play had infuriated him. It made him vulnerable. His swings held too much power and were wider than normal. He was overcompensating because of the wound.

Oswin slipped inside Alfric's reach and brought his sword down. In a flash, Alfric blocked the attack. The two swords met each other again and again. They pivoted sideways, dancing in circles. Neither gained the upper hand. Both men heaved, their shoulders rising and falling with exertion. A guttural roar exploded from Alfric's mouth as he charged Oswin. Ducking below a wide swing, Alfric dropped his back foot and rammed his shoulder into the other man's stomach.

The force of the blow floored Oswin. Before he could

stand, the match was over. Alfric slapped Oswin lightly on the cheek with the flat of his sword. It was a move that made the crowd uneasy, but not for long. They soon erupted into a fit of applause and cheering.

"Winner!" Sigebert yelled, barely audible above the din. He stepped out from the table and walked to the playing field.

Tears wet Fryda's cheeks. Alfric had done it. He had won the match.

Sigebert grabbed Alfric's arm and raised it into the air in celebration. But Alfric was frowning. He stared at Oswin still kneeling where he had lost.

The crowd dissipated, likely displeased with the victor's poor attitude.

Fryda ran out from the stands and hugged him.

"You did it," she said. "You're going to be a warrior."

Alfric forced a smile and nodded. Looking again at Oswin, he started walking toward him.

Fryda wondered what Alfric might do to the other man for fighting dirty.

The warriors weren't likely to intervene. Their corrections were typically violent anyway. They'd probably be pleased to see a fight that drew more blood than the sword match.

Alfric grabbed Oswin's arm and dragged him to his feet. Oswin's eyes were red-rimmed.

"No hard feelings," Alfric said as he clapped the other man's hand.

"You were the better man."

"You can take my job as porter at Idmaer's Spire once I'm admitted into the warriors," Alfric said. "The High Priest pays well, but you'll have to work hard."

Oswin's mouth dropped. When he'd recovered from his shock, he clapped Alfric's hand again. "I only fought dirty because I couldn't let Whitney waste away without her tonics." He sighed. "As much as I like sparring, I didn't want to become a warrior. I've never been comfortable with killing things."

Alfric smiled. "Then I'm glad we both got what we want."

Thunder rumbled and the clouds opened with rain.

Alfric and Oswin walked over to Fryda.

"You heard all that?" Alfric said to her.

She smiled. "You did a good thing." Lightning flashed above them. "I don't like the look of this storm."

Alfric grasped the pendant hanging on his chest. "Let's get inside." He frowned before grinning again, the scars twisting. "We have a win to celebrate."

"No celebrations for you lot," a warrior said. "I couldn't help overhearing. This storm has the Council concerned. Everyone is to return to their homes . . . or wherever it is you Fatherless spend the evening."

3

EDOMA

EDOMA, Mother Superior of the Daughters of Enlil, fastened her toolkit to her belt. It was filled with chisels, brushes, hammers, and various other utensils required for the catacombs. She wasn't looking forward to descending into the depths of Enlil's Temple today, but she never really was. The allure of the mysterious catacombs had worn off years ago.

But she wasn't one to give up so easily.

"Mother," Mildryd said as she came into the room. Normally she wore a smile, but today she was frowning. If she weren't so old, Edoma might have considered Mildryd for the next Mother. Mildryd enjoyed her duties as librarian in the temple's substantial library, but she led the other Daughters well and normally handled most things herself. Whatever concerned her now had to be important. "The novices are fearful of this storm. They think Aern has finally come to strike us Daughters down."

"Foolishness. It's just a little rain." There had always been antagonism between the Daughters of Enlil and the Holy Order of Aern. It was true—many who had been devoted to Aern had begun praying to Enlil, but Enlil wasn't a jealous god. She wished she could say the same for Aern. The new gods, who were called Guardians, sought single-minded worship. The old gods, however, were beyond fickle vices such as jealousy, which was why Edoma had devoted herself to Enlil and not Aern.

"It's more than rain," said Mildryd. "Lightning forks across the heavens. The thunder sounds like the gods doing battle."

Edoma rolled her eyes. Mildryd had a penchant for exaggeration. She was likely just feeding the novices' fears.

With a brief word of thanks to Mildryd, Edoma left her room and went into the Novice Hall. Women clad in yellow robes were nestled together like litters of newborn pups.

"You expect to become Daughters, and you're scared of a storm?" she called out.

A novice stood, a plump girl who'd been the orphan of a wealthy noble from Winhurst. "They say Aern has grown angry. What can *we* do against him?"

The temple walls shook. The novices whimpered. Edoma wrinkled her nose at their lack of faith. Enlil might not be visible like Aern was within an orb, but that was because he wasn't trapped within a crystal prison. "Who are *they?*" she asked.

The plump novice bowed her head. "The acolytes of the Holy Order."

Edoma barked a laugh. "Of course they would say that. They would say anything to make you think Aern is greater than Enlil."

Edoma spotted Fryda leaning against the far wall. She appeared unaffected by these stories. Edoma called to her, and she sauntered over.

"You don't think the same as the others?" Edoma asked, trying to ignore the torn hems of Fryda's robes and the way her hair fought free of its braid.

"It's like you said, the priests will say things to make us feel less than them. I don't like storms much, but I'm not about to lose my mind." Fryda glanced around at the other novices, who were still clutching each other. Unlike the other novices, she was Fatherless. She had stumbled through Indham's gates when she was two years old, and she had been one of the oldest to survive the mind disease that afflicted so many others. All the adults had died.

"While I'm gone, make the novices see sense," Edoma said.

Fryda nodded. "I'll do my best, but I can't promise anything." Despite being Fatherless, the other Daughters looked up to her, even those who had taken vows. If she couldn't calm the other novices, no one could.

Suddenly, pain lanced through Edoma's core. A vision came to her of the altar at Tyme's Hill, the golden hands empty, and the shattered remains of Aern's orb.

The vision faded, leaving Edoma lightheaded. Unable to stand, she fell onto Fryda.

"What is it?" Fryda said. She called out for a healer.

Edoma steadied herself, the pain subsiding.

The paroxysm was less of a shock than the vision. She had felt a similar pain while she had been eating dinner in the hall, but she thought it was just a pang of old age. The vision that had flashed before her eyes was new. It could only mean one thing—Aern's orb had been destroyed.

It couldn't have been long ago, and it was likely the reason for this storm.

There was only one person in Indham who might have the means of committing this sacrilege.

Without a word to the novices, and still wearing her tools, she ran to the Basilica.

4

IDMAER

FROM atop the spire, Idmaer gazed at the tumultuous heavens. Thunder rumbled and lightning slashed across the firmament, illuminating Indham with azure flashes before relinquishing it to the darkness again. Since the First Priest had brought the Guardians into the world, Aern had guarded the region against such storms. But now, without his protection, unbridled heavenly power rained from the sky. Beyond Indham's walls, a single thread of lightning split the air, and a tree exploded into flames and splinters.

After hearing Hiroc's recount of the empty altar, Idmaer had struggled to breathe. According to Hiroc, the gods had responded to his prayers and struck the giant with lightning. At Idmaer's insistence, Hiroc had sworn not to mention a word of this to anyone. The last thing Idmaer wanted was to discover that Hiroc was Talented. Saega had come soon after and seconded the account.

Idmaer had contemplated going to the altar, but the storm was confirmation of the story. Besides, the journey to the altar would take a few hours—hours he didn't have. He needed to inform the right people to stop the wrong people from finding out what happened.

14

Only now was Idmaer breathing normally again. Of his fifty years, thirty of them had been as a priest, but all of them had known Aern's protection. Now Aern was gone. Stripped from the altar by something with enough power to render a Guardian defenseless.

Idmaer turned toward Tyme's Hill. On most nights it could be seen from his spire, but tonight it lay hidden behind the thick fog.

Idmaer closed his eyes as the roar of destruction washed over him. No human sounds punctuated the leaden evening. At first, children had scuttled out from their homes to play in the rainfall, but the viciousness of the storm drove them back inside. The tradesmen and merchants had been smarter. They closed shop as soon as the first raindrop hit their thatched rooftops. There were over six thousand people living in Indham. Another thousand or so came and went while on their pilgrimages. Every one of them would be devastated to the point of panic if they learned what had transpired today.

Something would need to be done to hide the truth from them.

Careful of the slick stone, Idmaer walked down from the parapet and entered his study. Water dripped from his cloak as he laid it on the rack beside Hiroc, who hadn't moved from the chair in front of the fireplace.

Idmaer gripped his braid in both hands and wrung it out, then did the same with his graying beard. He draped a dry cloak over his shoulders and kneaded his numb hands. A slight extension of his hand toward the fire and the spire responded. The bricks shifted like living organisms until the fireplace was three times larger. Pleased with the spire's response to his command, he brought more firewood to the furnace, and the flames licked them up.

Hiroc shivered uncontrollably. The roaring fire seemed to provide him little comfort. Idmaer pulled the dry cloak from his shoulders and covered Hiroc with it, pushing the corners underneath his collar.

"It's gone," Hiroc said. After recounting what had happened at Aern's altar, they were the only words he would speak, and he continued saying them again and again. It was possible that he'd said them even while Idmaer was out on the observation deck.

Only eighteen years old and Hiroc had witnessed what so few ever would: an altar without its orb. Edoma, Idmaer's estranged wife, had come from a region whose orb had been shattered. She had refused to speak of it. Idmaer had always thought that much of the difficulties of their marriage had been caused by whatever trauma remained from that past event.

Idmaer could only hope that the night's events hadn't broken Hiroc beyond repair. Hiroc without his confidence, a brashness impervious to all, was like a woodsman without his ax, a priest with no god. Idmaer poured two goblets of firewine and forced one into Hiroc's hand. But he didn't drink, nor did he stop staring vacantly into the fireplace.

In Hiroc's visage was the fear that would proliferate through Indham unless this event was kept secret. The rest of Indham was ignorant of the storm's true nature, but an event of this magnitude would loosen tongues and ignite every gossipmonger from here to Wostreheim. Even the Council couldn't learn the entire truth.

Wulfnoth was tracking the giant now. It should be a simple task for a man as skilled as he was. After all, a giant should be easy to find. But what would they do when they found him? A man who could shatter a carcaern orb wouldn't be captured easily.

Idmaer left Hiroc and stepped into the hallway. Torrential rains buffeted the spire, causing it to shake and sway.

Idmaer retrieved a silver bell from his pocket and rang it. A moment later, Alfric approached the hallway. He rubbed his eyes as if just waking from a deep sleep. The smell of ale on his breath suggested he'd been drinking on the job. Had Idmaer not adored the lad, he might have scolded him.

Alfric wasn't the most ingenious porter, more suited to attracting the eyes of women than performing the menial tasks Idmaer required of him. But employment provided better hope than the bottom of an ale mug. A good portion of the Fatherless were employed in one fashion or another within the spire—one of many decisions that had earned Idmaer detractors through the years.

Alfric looked at Idmaer with half-open eyes and stifled a yawn.

"When Wulfnoth returns, have him sent to my spire," Idmaer said. Wulfnoth was the only man he trusted to go to the altar. Someone would need to clean it, gather the orb shards, and not speak a word of it to anyone. The families of the dead guards would also need to be told a story. "Then call the Council. We must find the reason why Aern has been weakened so greatly."

Alfric's eyes shot open, dispelling any trace of sleepiness. "Aern has been weakened?"

"How else do you explain these storms?" Idmaer said as if this was the only sensible explanation.

Alfric smiled for a second, and then frowned. "That is terrible."

The slight smile didn't go unnoticed. Idmaer had planned on the lad detecting a morsel of information that would be valuable to the right people.

Alfric chewed his lip. "There's something else I must talk with you about."

Idmaer didn't have the time, but he decided to hear Alfric out anyway.

"I won the tournament," said Alfric.

"Then you're to be a warrior." Idmaer smiled. Despite the atrocity that had happened earlier that day, this was a proud moment.

"What I wish to ask you is whether Oswin can take my position as porter. He is a reliable worker. It would mean so much to him if you—"

Idmaer raised his hand. "Say no more. It will be done. Have Oswin come along tomorrow. You can teach him the processes."

With a thank you, Alfric bowed and hurried out. It wouldn't be long before every person in Indham believed the poor weather was because Aern had been weakened. It was a superb misdirection. Had the situation not been so dire, Idmaer would have been pleased with himself.

Idmaer returned to his room.

The rain had not been able to remove all the blood from Hiroc's robes. His knees were stained scarlet. Whether the blood was from the Guardian or the Guardian's killer, Idmaer didn't know. He struggled to believe that a god existed within a carcaern orb. Regardless, their protection had been removed.

Hiroc nodded slowly, raised the firewine to his lips, and drank until the goblet was empty. Wine trailed down his chin, but he seemed oblivious.

"I was too headstrong," he said. "I should never have gone to the altar alone today. The others stayed inside because of the storm. I called them cowards."

"If you didn't go, then others would have found the altar defiled. Better you than them, I say."

Hiroc dropped his head into his hands as if to weep. When he looked up, his eyes were dry.

"You are right," he said. The terror had vanished. "What must I do now?"

"Still your tongue. The rest of the acolytes cannot know what happened to Aern. We will also need to forbid all pilgrimages to Tyme's Hill."

"This seems like a lot of trouble for a lie."

"It's the only way," Idmaer said. "It is too difficult for men to believe Guardians can be killed." A bard had been executed for speaking of broken orbs and godless altars. Idmaer had been listening to the bard's tale when Idmaer's father, the late High Priest Rowe, had stormed into The Flaming Monkey with a dozen armed warriors and had the bard arrested. It wasn't long after that he was hanged. The bard's stories were stamped out before the crows had picked the flesh from his bones.

"It doesn't seem right to deceive the Council."

"Do you wish to be hanged from the gallows?" Idmaer didn't care to tell Hiroc the story of the bard, but it was a reasonable question nonetheless.

Even though Hiroc might not have known where the question had come from, he shook his head vigorously.

"Neither do I."

5

EDOMA

WARRIORS filtered in and out of the multi-leveled buildings in the Basilica Quarter. They questioned acolytes and priests who rubbed their eyes and stifled yawns. The Holy Order had strict rules about when to sleep and when to wake, but there would be no sleeping tonight. The sounds of crashing thunder would see to that.

Saega's home was a standalone chalet located next to the acolyte commons. Candlelight flickered through the window. Edoma went to the door.

"What's your business here?" a voice called out from behind her.

Edoma turned and saw Bertram, the warrior who captained the town watch. "Excuse me!"

"Mother Edoma." Bertram bowed at recognizing whom he had just challenged. "My apologies. There has been an incident. Idmaer has ordered us to search for anything suspicious."

"Suspicious? What does he mean by that?"

Bertram shrugged. "I'm not sure. But those are the orders."

"You best be about following them."

"Yes, your grace." Bertram bowed again and left.

Idmaer had every bloody warrior searching the town. A mage who could shatter an orb wouldn't be easily found. Unless that mage was on the other side of this door.

Edoma banged on the door with her staff. The door opened.

"Edoma." Saega grinned as if this were an ordinary house call. He seemed older tonight, hunched over his fox-head staff.

"Just what are you playing at? Acting like this isn't the worst night of your bloody life."

"You felt it, too?"

"Is there any other reason I'd be outside your home at this hour?"

"Well, you're not the first person to knock on my door this evening," Saega said. "Would you like to come in?"

"That depends." Edoma frowned. "Did you do it?"

"Of course not," Saega said.

Edoma saw a dark patch on Saega's tunic and leaped back. "Then why are your garments soaked?" Her instincts brought her hand to the hammer at her belt. "There's blood on your tunic."

Saega looked down. "I'd better explain myself. Come inside."

Edoma didn't move. She lifted the hammer from its slot.

"Blood and bones, Edoma. Let go of that hammer and come in from the rain."

No, he couldn't have done it. We both swore an oath.

Edoma finally put the hammer back and followed Saega inside.

In recent years, Saega had embraced the southern lifestyle, with all its excesses. Priceless tapestries covered the walls, illuminated by a hundred candles. Most likely there were more candles and expensive ornaments in Saega's storeroom than the entire town. Most notable was the absence of his wife, Bodil. Without her, the room seemed somehow empty.

"I went to Tyme's Hill tonight," he said.

Edoma's eyes widened. Perhaps she had been too quick to come inside his home. "You swore an oath!"

"Edoma, please. We both threw our grimoires into the furnace." They'd done so after taking their oaths. Without the grimoires, they couldn't turn on the oaths even if they wanted to. Saega couldn't have done it. He handed her a bowl of broth before sitting on the couch beside her. "Something ill was afoot. I noticed the ravens circling Tyme's Hill three days in a row."

She sighed, loudly enough for him to stop talking. He wasn't really an augur. He could no more read the ravens than she could read Kristnesian. Still, she apologized and let him continue.

"A dark cloud gathered over the hill this morning. So I took Agnerod's Touch and ventured to Aern's altar. There I found the acolyte Hiroc fighting a giant. It was only Agnerod's Touch that prevented the giant from killing us both." He laid the staff over his lap. Edoma had a matching staff. She had never named hers, though. He had done so after reading about the two staves the First Priest had lost in the wilderness. It was impossible to know whether they were the actual staves of legend since they would have to be thousands of years old. Edoma and Saega had taken them from a band of orcs in the Scorched Lands. Even though they'd both sworn not to use magic again, they'd allowed themselves the use of the staves.

"A giant?" she asked. "Could it be another northern mage?"

Saega shrugged. "He fled before I could make him out. Maybe the giant was merely a servant. Maybe he was the shatterer. I do not know. By the time I assisted Hiroc, the giant was nowhere to be seen."

"The guards?"

"All dead."

"So if it wasn't you," Edoma said as she tried to settle into the goose feather cushions, "who was it?"

22

"Of course it wasn't me. What would I have to gain from fulfilling our mission now? We abandoned it twenty years ago. I like my life in Indham, even if it's gotten a little sad in the last few years."

Edoma couldn't believe he would look for sympathy in their present circumstances. She pressed on with the topic at hand. "There must be other mages who've taken up our oath. But why now?"

"I'm surprised it hasn't happened sooner."

Edoma sipped from the broth, allowing the warmth to calm her nerves. She couldn't help feeling terrified. If another northern mage had come to Indham, that meant they might have finally been discovered.

"There was nothing in the scrying crystal," Saega said.

Edoma shot to her feet. "You used the crystal? What happens if the others see you?" She sank back into the cushions, defeated. It didn't matter if the other mages knew where they were now. The orb was shattered. Their mission was fulfilled, even if it had been completed by a mage other than them. "Then there's no trace of the mage who shattered the orb?"

"None at all. You're welcome to try for yourself."

Edoma shook her head. The last thing she wanted to do was taste the allure of the other-realm. "How is that possible? Could the murderer somehow be masking himself?"

"Maybe," Saega said. "Or maybe it wasn't a mage who did it."

A rapping came from the door, and Saega went to answer it. He used the staff to keep himself upright. Usually, he walked with such ease. Had the giant harmed him?

A few moments later, he returned. Before he sat back down, he fought through a coughing fit. He wiped spittle from his mouth. For the first time, Edoma noticed deep wrinkles etched into his face. He had been old when she'd met him. He was ancient now.

"Idmaer is calling a Council meeting at first light," he said. "I'm interested to see what he makes of this event. The talentless are so intriguing when they try to explain magical happenings."

Talentless. The word was a terrible way to describe those without a magical propensity. Edoma caught herself scowling.

"Idmaer is the worst of them," Saega continued. "He thinks he knows of magic. He hasn't been called by the gods, nor has he developed enough devotion to be granted their magic. His father passed the spire down to him. Some say he's an *atheist* now." His sneer turned into a look of surprise, as though he had said something he shouldn't have. "Sorry. You two aren't still . . ."

"No," Edoma said. "Certainly not." Not wanting to remain in the awkward situation another moment, she thanked Saega for the broth and went to the door. Bodil's headdress hung over a hook, even though she had left him for another man two years ago and died a year after that.

Edoma turned and looked at Saega with pity. A terrible thing had happened—the worst possible thing—and she had come to his house in the middle of the night to accuse him. The man had done much for Indham. He'd given High Priest Idmaer counsel for years. When Edoma had needed a friend, Saega had been there.

"I'm sorry I accused you," she said.

Saega waved his hand. "Nothing to worry about." He hobbled over to the door and glanced down at her tool kit. "You've been searching the catacombs for years, and you've yet to find the tomb. Don't you think you should try something different? Why not bring someone along with you?"

Edoma smiled, glad to be talking about something other than Aern's orb. "I doubt your old lungs would handle the dust."

"I have my magic," Saega said.

"That you do. But we've sworn not to use it." The magical

staves they'd obtained in the Scorched Lands were one thing, but blood magic was something else altogether.

"I fear that oath will be broken soon. You'll have to make wards again, you know."

Edoma's smile faltered. She hadn't thought that far ahead.

Grasping the runestone around her neck, she wondered how she would use magic after so long. She remembered simple wards of healing, but nothing beyond that. She had never been anything more than an apprentice mage. The little she remembered didn't include wards of protection.

With this distressing thought in mind, she left Saega and traipsed through the muddied streets back to Enlil's Temple.

6

IDMAER

"KING Beorhtel has refused to give us sanctuary in Wostreheim." Idmaer held up the letter that had arrived by raven that morning. It had been two days since the orb was shattered. "'A single foot into my territory is trespassing. Anyone to do so will be filled with arrows. No one is exempt,'" he quoted, "'not even you, High Priest Idmaer.'"

In his haste, Idmaer had organized a Council meeting for the morning after Aern's orb had been broken. But that had been foolhardy. He needed more time to gather his resources. So he had postponed it. Many of the Council members had been pleased. Most considered the meetings tedious and the time better spent attending to their tasks.

He had planned on presenting the Council with a way out—a mass exodus to Wostreheim. But with the letter he now held in his hand, that was impossible. It meant he would have to present the Council with his alternative plan. To do that, he needed the support of Wulfnoth the tracker and Saega the augur.

Idmaer had called them to his spire. Now they stood before him. Saega was warming his age-spotted hands by the fire. Wulfnoth scowled at his hirsute image reflected on a

26

polished shield mounted on the wall.

The two were Idmaer's trusted advisors. But they hadn't always been. He'd inherited his previous advisors from his father's rule. Soon after Idmaer took office, the men were replaced. None of them had approved of Idmaer's secret marriage to Edoma—an unclean northern wench, they had called her—so he had them banished. That decision, along with marriage to a foreigner, had been the first in a long line of "mistakes" that had ostracized him from Indham's Council and its people. Luckily, the High Priest of Aern was as much an office of kingship as it was sacerdotal. So his rule was total.

"We're on our own," Saega said, his eyes vacant.

"How many years have you talked of alliances with Beorhtel?" said Wulfnoth. Mud was spattered over his tunic. Bags sat beneath his eyes. He had been searching for signs of the giant for two days straight now. It was probably the longest time he'd been sober in years. "We sold him bloody dragons, and this is how he repays us?"

"He already paid for the dragons," Saega cut in. "And quite highly."

"Beorhtel refuses us because he can. We have nothing to offer him." Idmaer sighed. He was angry, too, but he couldn't see how complaining would help matters.

Wulfnoth grimaced. "The gods give him the plague. I never liked that bloody king." He still wore the green outfit of a warrior even though he had retired years ago. The garment was a little snug around the waist and bore scuffs and stains from spilled food and drink. Even from a few feet away, the stench of ale wafted from him.

Saega coughed into his hand. When he looked up, his eyes were swollen and rheumy. "I spoke with Edoma. She knows the orb is shattered. Unsurprising, considering what happened in Mundos. I thought it important to tell you, particularly if you were thinking of lying to her about it. She won't tell anyone else."

"That's good to know," said Idmaer. He would have lied to her had he not known. And that would have led to trouble. In saying that, he avoided most conversations with Edoma. Mostly because he feared his conscience might finally succeed and he would admit everything. He wasn't ready for that. Especially now. There were bigger things to worry about than his past sins.

Idmaer trusted Wulfnoth with his life, Saega less so. Idmaer had sought Saega's advice often, more than any other man, but he'd started to question his motives. It wasn't that the man was untrustworthy. He was just watchful. Beady eyes always roaming as if he might discover something he could use against you. He'd never openly opposed Idmaer, not even with the dragon trade. But he had been friends with Durwin, the man Idmaer had sent to the chopping block. That wasn't enough to incriminate Saega, but it had made Idmaer more cautious. Nevertheless, he needed the man's advice and assistance now.

"When you were in Mundos," Idmaer said to Saega, "how long after the orb was broken did the wraiths come?"

Edoma and Saega had told Idmaer little about their flight from Mundos. All Idmaer knew was that they had been scholars in Mundos's library. They had fled through the Scorched Lands and come to Indham. Much of what they had told him was vague. Even when he had been married to Edoma, she had spoken little of her past.

Idmaer suspected they were hiding things, but he hadn't wanted to press the issue. For one thing, they each carried magical staves, written with runes of power. They had said they'd found them while traveling through the Scorched Lands with Jaruman. A dying man had given the staves to them and asked nothing in return except a decent burial. Idmaer suspected that wasn't the whole story. After all, they'd crossed a land few survived.

"We had dozens of mages," Saega said. "They provided

wards that kept the wraiths out. For a time. Two years later, the wards were broken, and the wraiths came in their clouds of flame. I don't know exactly how much time Indham will have. Winhurst is directly beneath Babon's Pass, so they'll be the ones to suffer the wraiths first. Our time will come soon after."

Idmaer swallowed. He didn't like that a whole city might die to give them time to stall. But it was a necessary evil. "When Winhurst's warning beacons are lit, we'll know the wraiths have come." Not that it would matter much. If they hadn't left Indham by then, they were doomed anyway. "We must ask Hurn for help. We will be safe in Eosorheim."

Eosorheim was the region to the east. Its forest lands were mostly uninhabited by humans. Once, many people had lived within its boundaries. But that had been before Hurn had estranged himself from other men. It had also been before he'd declared revenge upon Idmaer. That message had come in the form of a vial of poison, accompanied with a letter. The letter told Idmaer to drink from the vial, for that would be better than Hurn's planned vengeance.

After some thought, Idmaer wondered whether Hurn was responsible for killing Aern. But Idmaer had once been a friend of Hurn, long before their enmity began, and he knew that Hurn wouldn't doom an entire region of thousands just to avenge the slight of a single man.

"I had a feeling this was what you dragged us here for," Wulfnoth said. "I thought about it myself. Hurn isn't likely to agree. Not after what you sanctioned."

"I realize that." Idmaer's mind had been playing over the various ways he might convince Hurn to help them. Most fell short. There was, however, one that might just work. "It'll take two men who were friends with him. Men who never wanted the dragons to be sold."

"Sigebert and Cenred," said Wulfnoth, guessing immediately.

29

"They despise me, but that just might mean Hurn will listen to them. I'll need your help if they're to agree."

"I can try," Wulfnoth said. "But what happens when they learn that the orb is shattered?"

Idmaer had been waiting for this question. "They won't learn of it. At least not until we've come up with a solution."

"Do you think it's wise to lie to the Council?"

"I think it's necessary."

"I don't mind bending the truth," said Saega. "The Council need not know what has happened to Aern. The truth is far worse than any lie we might tell. A giant shattered Aern's orb and removed his protection from Aernheim. We have no choice but to tell them otherwise."

"I'm not pleased with it," Wulfnoth said, "but I see your point."

"If the people learn the truth," said Saega, "there'll be chaos. Soon, maybe even tonight, the wraiths will come and rip Indham's children from their beds. Mothers will tear the flesh from their infants' bones. What then?"

Idmaer nodded. "They will try to escape from Aernheim on the very night they discover Aern no longer protects them. Those who go south to Wostreheim will become target practice for King Beorhtel's soldiers. And if thousands go east to Eosorheim? Hurn will take it as an assault on his forest lands. A smaller group will succeed where a large one would fail."

Wulfnoth stiffened. "So you're suggesting Indham should be saved while the others in Aernheim perish to these monsters?"

"I'm saying we keep things quiet. We'll send a small party into Eosorheim to ask Hurn for refuge. Should he accept, then Indham's people will go first. We'll see about getting others through the boundary after that."

"He's not simply going to say yes," Wulfnoth said.

Idmaer threw his hands in the air. "Do you have a better

idea? It's the best we have."

Wulfnoth chewed his cheek. He seemed unable to disagree. *Good.*

"In the meantime," Idmaer continued, "we'll send ravens to all the major towns and cities within Aernheim, writing of Aern's apparent weakness. That will give reason for the storms and why the pilgrims cannot visit Tyme's Hill. If the entire region starts to panic, the roads will be blocked off, giving us no hope of retreating into Eosorheim."

Idmaer paused at that. By not informing the other places of what had really happened to Aern, they would be ill-prepared for the coming wraiths.

He walked over to the window. It was small and rounded, but at a single command, the bricks shifted until the entire wall vanished. Now, Idmaer could see across the horizon unhindered. The nearest village looked no bigger than his thumb. How many people lived there? One hundred? Two hundred? Would they become hosts for the wraiths as all those in Mundos twenty years ago?

It didn't matter. Those elsewhere in Aernheim would have to find their own means of protection. Idmaer was only responsible for Indham.

7

EDOMA

EDOMA remained in the hall after the Council meeting had concluded. Saega sat beside her, staring into a mug of ale.

During the meeting, the two warriors, Sigebert and Cenred, had agreed to go to Eosorheim to request Hurn's aid.

"Aern is gravely ill," Idmaer had said. "We will ask Hurn for refuge inside Eosorheim while we seek a way to make Aern well again. It is just a precaution. There is nothing to worry about."

Edoma's stomach churned at remembering the smug smile Idmaer had worn while he spouted his lies. Without blinking an eye, he had promised that the wraiths would never enter Indham. How could he make such an empty promise?

"The way Idmaer stood before the Council and lied made my blood boil," Edoma said to Saega. "You lied, too. And you forced poor Hiroc to lie as well. Was that your idea or Idmaer's? Ah, forget it. I don't want to know."

"It's for the best," said Saega, his soothing tone setting her on edge. "You saw what happened in Mundos after the people learned that Mun's orb had been destroyed."

There had been chaos. The lords had calmed them

32

eventually, after the mages had constructed wards to protect against the wraiths. But many lives had been lost in those initial riots. She still thought Indham's Council would be able to take the news where the regular folk of Mundos hadn't.

"Besides, it's a good plan," Saega said. "I was thinking of it myself."

"Hurn isn't going to let us inside Eosorheim. He's more than capable of stopping us. King Beorhtel might have an army guarding the boundary, but Hurn has magic greater than anything you and I have even thought of."

Even in Mundos, when Edoma was learning the basic history of magic, Hurn had been legendary. It was unknown exactly how old he was, but some said he had lived while the First Empire was in its infancy. A man who was thousands of years old had plenty of time to learn the kinds of magic that could destroy armies with a single empowered rune.

What if that magic had been used to kill Aern?

"Do you think Hurn could be responsible?" she asked.

Saega raised an eyebrow. "He would certainly have a motive." He rubbed the back of his neck. "But it cannot be. The man I fought was a giant. Hurn has no giants in his employ—he despises them. I need not remind you of the millennia-long feud between dragons and giants. Hurn would be no friend of dragons if he employed giants."

Edoma had to agree. There were still dragons within Eosorheim, and Hurn wouldn't antagonize them. He was also a just man, deep down. He would only take his vengeance out upon Idmaer. Maybe he had even forgiven Idmaer since he had taken no steps toward retribution since the poison vial.

If not Hurn, then who? The lack of an answer to that question infuriated her.

"You said before that the murderer might not have been a mage," Edoma said, speaking her thoughts aloud. "Even if that's true, then he still needed a grimoire. There is a grimoire inside the First Priest's tomb." The histories wrote that all grimoires found their beginnings in the First Priest's grimoire. Although difficult, a person without magic could use the grimoire. It would require incredible sacrifice, but it could be done.

"Maybe if the catacombs have been touched," she continued, "we might have a clue as to where the giant went or who he was." Wulfnoth had said during the Council meeting that there was no trace of the giant. Strange, considering Wulfnoth was renowned for his tracking skills.

"Finding the murderer won't bring Aern back," Saega said.

"But it'll mean justice."

Saega shrugged. "What is justice? I'm sure knowing that he has doomed thousands of people to a terrible fate is weighing heavily on his conscience. Finding the man who did this means little now. I have other matters to attend to." He coughed over his hand and hid it in his pocket. Edoma was sure she had seen a dark patch of blood on his palm.

"Are you not well? I can heal you." She hadn't used healing wards in years, but she could do so now. Especially since she would soon use magic again for protection wards.

Saega raised his hand, but not the one he had coughed on. "Nothing to worry about. Take one of the Daughters to the catacombs if you must. I fear you're far too old to be going down there alone. You might find yourself unable to haul yourself back up the shaft." He laughed, a wheezing sound like he was breathing through a tiny hole.

Edoma examined Saega. It was unlike him to be ill. Time affected everyone, of course. But why now, when she needed him more than ever?

* * *

Edoma eased herself down the shaft for what felt like the thousandth time in two decades. The pulleys creaked from

34

her weight, which had grown substantially after twenty years in Indham. She had stayed for much longer than she originally planned after falling in love with Idmaer, and the birth of her twins had made the stay permanent.

Now, her days were spent trying to decipher the runes covering the sibylline halls beneath the temple.

Fryda's ropes creaked above. Edoma had dragged Fryda from the barracks where the warriors trained. She had been watching Alfric. Fryda had protested, thinking that Edoma had caught her shirking her novice duties. After Edoma told her that they would be going into the catacombs, she couldn't leave fast enough.

Edoma was certainly glad to have Fryda along with her. She questioned why she had never taken anyone else into the catacombs before. She hadn't wanted anyone to discover what secrets the catacombs might hold. Not because she was selfish or wanted them for herself, but because she knew even the slightest knowledge of the arcane arts could corrupt the most virtuous.

Edoma reached the bottom of the shaft and unclipped herself from the harness. Shortly after, Fryda landed lightly on the ground.

"It's a little dark," Fryda said in jest. It was too dark to see her face, but Edoma knew she would be grinning.

The darkness was no hindrance as Edoma found her way across the corridor to the sconce and lit the torch. The domed entrance flickered into dazzling colors as the light touched the wall paintings and floor mosaics.

"It's beautiful," Fryda said. The colors reflected on her face, which, as Edoma had surmised, was peeled back in a full-toothed grin.

"There was a lot of dust before I came down here." After the long, lonely, and grueling hours with the smallest scrubbing brush known to man and a bucket of water, she uncovered a small square of the beauty beneath the dust and debris. The days had stretched into months, and then years, and she'd never allowed herself to appreciate the beauty truly. The quest to find the tomb of the First Priest, hidden somewhere within these vast catacombs, prevented that. "It took many hours. There's still a long way to go, but it's a start."

Fryda wasn't listening. She was too busy darting from one wall to another, reciting the epic tales represented in the paintings. At first, Edoma was surprised that Fryda knew how to read them—most were in runes—but Fryda had always loved learning. Perhaps she had been a fool not to invite the novice into the catacombs sooner.

"Do you mind if I have a look around?" Fryda called from the entrance to a side-passage. She had taken a torch from one of the sconces. "Don't worry. I won't touch anything."

"Make sure you don't. I haven't seen any traps, but that doesn't mean there aren't any." Edoma smiled as Fryda disappeared down the passageway.

Wishing she could experience the catacombs with the same delight as Fryda, Edoma wandered down the hallway, lighting each torch until the hall was as bright as daylight. The hall ended at a grand door, etched in symbols and runes in a forgotten language and fashioned from godstone. Within the rune was a drawing of the First Priest. His white beard trailed to a belt cinched around gold-trimmed robes. A golden medallion hung from his neck. It was passed down through an unbroken succession of priests. Idmaer now wore it.

Not that he cared much for his office. Rumor was that he hadn't visited Tyme's Hill for months, possibly even years. Knowing that such thoughts would only cloud her mind, Edoma forced them away.

The door she now stood before had been the single greatest obstacle in discovering the catacombs' secrets. Behind it lay the sarcophagus of the First Priest. At least that was what she had gathered. Every door in the catacombs had been opened, except this one. She hadn't learned how to open it, and she wasn't sure she ever would. The greatest engineer in all the south had been unable to invent a mechanism capable of levering it open.

After that infuriating attempt, she had considered enlisting an alchemist, though she doubted even an explosive potion would scratch the door's surface. An explosion might also destroy the relics within the entrance hall, each with their own runes that Edoma hadn't completely deciphered. For all she knew, the key to opening the door was hidden in the riddles depicted on every surface, statue, and tomb. The First Priest apparently loved riddles.

What she had come down to see was the door. She thought maybe it would be opened, the giant having stolen the First Priest's grimoire from the tomb.

But that wasn't the case. The door was as closed as always, staring Edoma in the face like a token of her failure.

Fryda passed by with glee and was about to step into another room when Edoma called out to her.

"Come," she said, "we must return to the surface."

"But we've been here but a moment." Fryda's robes were filthy now, as though she had crawled through some of the passageways. "I want to explore. I've never seen anything like this."

"There will be more time for exploring," Edoma said, though she doubted there would be. The wraiths would be upon them soon. The same thing that happened to Mundos all those years ago would happen to Indham. She wouldn't be able to save them, just as she hadn't been able to save all those people in Mundos.

There was only one thing she could do—attempt to use magic again. She couldn't remember exactly how to draw the wards of protection, but she knew that they would require blood. A lot of blood.

8

FRYDA

FRYDA awoke to the sound of ringing bells. After a
long day with Edoma in the catacombs, she and Alfric
had drunk what felt like all the ale in Indham. He had
started training with the warriors two days ago, and he hadn't
stopped complaining the entire time about how sore he was.
She had tried to speak with him about the catacombs beneath
Enlil's Temple, but he hadn't been interested.

Propping herself up on one elbow, Fryda examined how
much damage the rain had done to her room. Dawn's light
filtered through a hole in the roof where water trickled into
a wooden bucket; Fryda's drunken attempt at stopping more
water from coming in. The bucket now overflowed as droplets
continued to fall into it.

Jaruman had adopted Fryda as his daughter, so the best
room in The Flaming Monkey had been hers. The best room
wasn't all that good, but in comparison to sleeping in Enlil's
Temple with the other novices, it was bliss.

Most of the Fatherless weren't given that kind of charity,
and Fryda didn't feel like she deserved it. Still, she was grateful.
Jaruman had done more than just give her a bed to sleep in
and food to fill her belly—he'd also taught her how to fight.

What he lacked in innkeeper skills, he made up for in fighting prowess. He had been a warrior from beyond the Scorched Lands. On the first day he brought her into his home, he'd taken her to the cellar, given her a short spear, and taught her how to use it. "Women are often smaller than men, but that doesn't mean they have to be victims," he had said. He'd given her other weapons to practice with, but she preferred spears.

Fryda picked herself off from the hay bedding and removed her nightclothes.

Her head rang again, this time louder. That wasn't her headache, but the town bells ringing.

Before she could dress, Alfric burst through the door.

"Fryda, you must come. The warriors are setting off on a quest." His scarred face was peeled back in a mischievous grin.

Fryda grabbed her bed sheets and held them to her chest.

Alfric's mouth dropped and his cheeks flushed. He turned around and said, "Quickly. Get dressed."

Fryda glanced at her yellow novice robes. Novice prayer would begin at Enlil's Temple soon. If one of the other Daughters saw her traipsing around the town, she would be given chores. Deciding that she was less likely to get caught wearing ordinary clothes, Fryda slipped on a blouse and then a dress over the top. She hiked up her skirts and waded through the murky sludge that had gathered in puddles.

Alfric tapped his foot impatiently, apparently forgetting the fact that he'd just seen her naked. "Hurry, or we're likely to miss them."

Fryda rolled her hair into a bun and slipped her hairpin through it. Jaruman had given the hairpin to her as an adoption present. "I don't have much money," he had said. "The inn makes sure of that. But the pin once belonged to my daughter back in Mundos. I want you to have it." So now Fryda never left without it. Her fiery curls were long and unruly besides.

Alfric pulled her out from her room before she could put her sandals on. She clutched them in her hand as they walked down the steps, wiping the sleep from her eyes and fixing wayward curls beneath the pin. "What's this about a quest?"

He whirled around, a dangerous gleam in his eye. "Remember how Idmaer told me Aern has grown weak and that's the reason for the storms?"

Fryda nodded as she slipped her feet into her sandals. "I don't know why you believe Idmaer. He lies all the time."

Alfric shrugged. "It makes sense. What else could be causing the storms?"

Fryda smiled politely. "You're being superstitious. There were far worse storms last winter."

Alfric raised an eyebrow. "It's summer."

He had a point. Storms like this weren't meant to happen during summer.

"And the quest?" she said, intertwining her fingers in his.

"You'll see soon enough," Alfric said, dragging her outside.

A small crowd gathered in the courtyard beneath Indham's gate. Fryda had seen the gates a thousand times, but she'd never grown accustomed to their immense height, crafted with what looked like metal, though they bore no signs of rust. Neither did they reflect the sunlight as metal ought to do. Instead, they seemed to swallow it.

Priests, Daughters of Enlil, warriors, peasants, and Fatherless all gathered in the courtyard. There were even acolytes—who so infrequently left the Basilica—leaning against the gatehouse, easily distinguished by their midnight blue robes with plum-colored tabards. The men of the warrior's watch monitored the sea of people from atop the walls.

Alfric dragged her through the masses. Fryda pulled away, refusing to be tugged along like a mule. She approached a cart outside the gatehouse stables and looked at it with interest. Climbing it would provide a better view.

Alfric smirked at Fryda. "How about you let me pick you

up, and you can sit on top of the cart?"

"A *lady* doesn't sit on carts," she joked. She'd never been a lady, but Alfric had always teased her about the other Daughters. Most of them were highborn sent from all over the continent to become consecrated virgins, and those who weren't pretended they were.

Alfric shrugged. "Suit yourself."

He always refused to play along. Rather than let him win, Fryda pressed through the crowd. She only got a few paces in before a hard shove and a mud-covered fall sent her back to Alfric.

"I'll sit on the bloody cart," she said to him.

He laughed as he surveyed her grubby dress. "Bloody? That's not the talk of a *lady*." He held out his hand. Fryda took it begrudgingly. Suddenly she was hoisted above his head and placed on the cart.

She had to admit, the view was perfect. She could see the entrance archway clearly. There was no sign of the warriors yet. The warriors were likely eager for the opportunity to go questing. After they'd stopped fighting the nomads and Indham had been in relative peace, there hadn't been much for them to do. Many of them had gone to fight in Beorhtel's army. Those who remained were mostly untrained or too old to fight in wars.

Hiroc, Alfric's brother, was standing outside The Flaming Monkey. Strange that they hadn't seen him earlier. He must have just arrived there. Even from this distance, there was clearly something wrong with him. He seemed to be lurking in the shadows, afraid someone might see him.

Intrigued, Fryda jumped down from the cart. Mud splashed at Alfric, but she didn't stop to apologize.

"Where are you going?" he called.

Fryda looked over her shoulder and winked. Some of the people glared at her and muttered curses. Without her Daughters robes, she was just a Fatherless. It was odd how many of them knew that, even in a town of six thousand. As usual, she ignored them.

She came upon Hiroc leaning against the front wall of The Flaming Monkey.

"Fryda," Hiroc said as if her presence had broken him from a trance. He cast a nervous look at the crowd. "What are you doing here?"

"I could ask you the same question. Any reason why you're hiding here when everyone else is there?" She nodded toward the crowd behind them.

Hiroc wore acolyte robes cinched tight around his waist and a belt knife. Beaded with sweat and popping with veins, his shaved head glistened in the sunlight. "I wanted to speak with Alfric. I thought maybe he might be in The Flaming Monkey."

Fryda tilted her head, unsure what Hiroc couldn't speak with the other acolytes about. Ever since he had joined the Holy Order, he hadn't spent much time with the other Fatherless. He had shaved his head to better fit in with the acolytes, but he still looked like someone from north of Babon's Pass, with his olive skin and green eyes.

Huffing, Alfric came alongside Fryda and smirked. "You're quicker than you look." He turned to Hiroc. "And you're looking in as high spirits as ever." He chuckled, but no one joined him.

Something was different about Hiroc. There was no sign of his usual confidence. It had vanished behind eyes ringed with dark shadows.

The muscles around Hiroc's cheeks grew taut. "Inside." He tilted his head toward the tavern's doors.

They retreated into The Flaming Monkey. There was no one else sitting at the tables. The only sound was dripping water from a leak in the roof.

Hiroc slumped onto a chair at the nearest table.

"This quest," he said, "it's all because of me. Well, not

really because of me. I was the one who saw what happened."

Fryda frowned. "Why are you speaking like this?"

Ignoring the question, Hiroc got up and walked over to the keg. He helped himself to a goblet of ale. He chugged the entire goblet in a few moments and sat down again.

"How do I know I can trust you?" he asked. "You're both terrible at keeping secrets. I've been sworn to secrecy by Idmaer. But it's too grave to keep to myself."

"I don't want to be here," Alfric said. "I'd much rather be outside waiting for the warriors."

Hiroc sighed and wrung his hands.

"Spit it out," Fryda said, though compassion tinged her words. She'd never seen Hiroc in a state like this. "Either you trust us or you don't."

"Aern is dead." He said the words quickly, as though they tasted like ash on his tongue. "I saw the shattered remains of his orb at the altar."

Fryda's eyes widened. It was a ridiculous concept, but so were the storms in summer. But Aern, dead? That was like the sun not rising in the morning. But Hiroc wouldn't lie. Nor would he state for a fact what was mere conjecture.

"Shattered?" Fryda said.

"It means broken," Alfric said.

Fryda sneered. "I know what the word means. I just don't understand how it's possible."

"It's not possible," Alfric said plainly. He shrugged his shoulders. "You must have been seeing things."

"You know me better than anyone. I am not susceptible to fanciful visions."

You think Aern talks with you, Fryda thought. *If that's not crazy, I don't know what is.*

"All right," said Alfric. "I believe you."

Hiroc studied Alfric's face. "Are you not concerned?"

"Of course. But I don't think fretting will do any good."

"You're a strange man," Hiroc said. "The Council was in

an uproar when they learned Aern was weakened. Even the pilgrims sense that something is amiss. You know the true extent of what's happened, and you simply nod your head?"

Alfric shrugged. Fryda knew he'd never been one to panic. He might as well have been a block of stone in stressful times.

"It was hard to believe that Aern had been weakened," Alfric said. "For some reason, hearing that he's been killed is easier to swallow."

"How did the murderers get past the guards?" Fryda asked.

"They were killed, too. I've never seen anything like it. With their own spears. I saw a giant at the top of the hill. I didn't see him shatter the orb, but it had to have been him. I think he was alone. I fought him, and he would have killed me. Saega came, and the giant ran away."

"Magic," Alfric whispered. "It must be magic."

"But all the mages are in Lamworth," Fryda said.

"Obviously not," Alfric said. "So this is what the Council was meeting about? What's the warriors' quest?"

"The Council is sending Cenred and Sigebert to Eosorheim. They are going to ask Hurn to take us in."

"The quest will surely fail if they send Cenred and Sigebert," Fryda said. She had never spoken to either of the warriors in person, but the rumor mill said they were more likely to solve conflict with their swords rather than their brains.

"They aren't the most diplomatic men," said Alfric.

"Who else ought to go?" Hiroc's tone indicated it was more a challenge than a question.

"Us," Alfric said with a smile.

9

EDOMA

WARD after ward covered the stone courtyard of Enlil's Temple. The overhanging rooftop prevented the rain from washing away Edoma's hard work.

The Daughters of Enlil had wanted to see the warriors off on their quest, and Edoma had agreed to let them go. They'd stepped over the wards like they were poisonous. It was likely that none of them had seen blood magic before.

Edoma was constructing the wards with the hopes of warding the warriors before they left for Eosorheim. It was unlikely they'd encounter any wraith clouds since they would be traveling northwest. But it wouldn't hurt to ward them.

The wraiths would come from the northeast through Babon's Pass. Winhurst would be the first place within Aernheim to be hit, and they would light their signal fires as soon as they were under attack.

Edoma stared at the machines Mildryd had retrieved from the dungeons of Idmaer's Spire. They were once used as torture devices to bleed out prisoners. Ropes hung a lamb in midair. A half-dozen iron arms reached up from the bottom of the device, cutting into the lamb's underside. Blood dripped along a narrow channel in the device's arms, trailing into a wine barrel at the bottom. Tonics made the lamb unconscious so it wouldn't feel any pain. It was important to keep it alive during the bloodletting process, but she didn't want it suffering.

While the thought of what the machines might have been used for many years ago was gruesome, they were perfect for extracting the required blood from the lambs.

After twisting a gear to begin extraction from another wound in the lamb's side, she wandered around the ward she'd just finished painting. It still wasn't right.

Only the most powerful magic required the use of wards. Inconsequential magic, like healing minor wounds, could be done without them. But wards were required to protect against powerful creatures like wraiths.

Squatting over the empty half-circle, she traced a number of runes. Every rune had to be drawn in blood because blood contained the lifesoul required to open the portal from this world to the realm of the gods. Edoma continued drawing wards in lamb blood, still unsatisfied. Each iteration was better than the last until finally she came upon a fair approximation of what she remembered.

Throughout Mundos, mages had drawn bloody wards on the ground and the sides of buildings. The rich and the powerful had their homes warded first. Edoma had asked her father why the mages hadn't simply painted wards around the walls of the city. Being a scholar, he had told her that a ward of that power required an incredible amount of lifesoul. Smaller wards work better, he had said. She was never quite sure whether he had explained things that way because he was rich and powerful with the benefit of a warded home.

Now, the ward beneath her feet was drawn in two half-circles, connected in the middle by the symbol of Mun—a spider. In most depictions, Mun was a praying woman. But her real form was that of a spider. That woman had come to Edoma in many nightmares, morphing into a spider, demanding the blood of her loved ones for sacrifice. She remembered the symbol well, which is why that particular part of the ward formation had come easily.

It was the half-circles that were causing her difficulty. They appeared identical except for one minor deviation. The left half-circle contained the rune of lifesoul while the other half-circle was empty. It should not have been, but she couldn't remember what went there. The unknown rune represented something else; its existence a secret known only to those mages who'd conquered the third trial.

Edoma had never conquered the third trial.

Frustrated, she kicked at the wards, smearing them until they were illegible.

"Did you find anything in the catacombs?" a voice croaked.

Startled, Edoma looked up to see Saega. The skin on his face was peeling, as though he'd been in the sun for days. His sickness must be getting worse.

"Nothing," Edoma said. She couldn't help making her frustrations known. "From the looks of it, Aern's murderer didn't use the grimoire from the catacombs. We're not going to know for sure unless we can open the damned godstone door."

"Another task for another day." He nodded at the wards. Nearly every stone had a ward upon it. "What's the meaning of all this?" Chuckling, he looked up at her. "You've drawn a hundred wards, and not one is correct. Having a bit of trouble?"

Edoma scowled. "More than a bit." She wanted to slap Saega's smile from his face. Instead, she slumped her shoulders and avoided his gaze. "I can't remember what goes in the second half-circle."

"I always thought the mages were taught well in Mundos." Saega was originally from the Isle of Sulith. He had only been in Mundos all those years ago because he had been lecturing students on the importance of collaboration between the various mage schools. Edoma had never told Saega that she was only an apprentice, but that secret would be out soon enough. It would be plain from her poorly constructed wards.

"We weren't allowed to learn protection runes until we passed all the trials," she said. "I'm only piecing together what I can remember, which isn't much."

"You've already done the rune for lifesoul. That one looks fine to me. It's just spiritsoul that's needed now."

Edoma's heart stopped. Could he be right? But there was just one problem. "I don't remember the rune for spiritsoul."

Saega's knees cracked as he knelt down. He rubbed out Edoma's poor attempt from the second half-circle of a rune. Dipping his finger in the bucket of blood, he then traced a crescent moon. The rune pulsed with a deep red light, brighter and brighter until it suddenly stopped.

Cursing, Edoma said, "I should have known. The rune for lifesoul is a sun. The rune for spiritsoul had to be the moon."

"Sometimes the simplest things are hidden to us," he said. "Now it's just going to take a mage to empower it. You do remember how to do that, don't you?" When Edoma grimaced, Saega barked a laugh. "I always thought that you were a greater mage than I. It's no wonder you made me swear the vow. You're not even a real mage!" Noticing Edoma's glare, he cleared his throat. "It requires spiritsoul."

Edoma's face reddened, and she tried to sink into herself so he wouldn't see that she didn't know how to use spiritsoul.

Saega sighed. "With one hand holding your runestone, stretch the other hand toward the rune circle and invoke Mun. Surely you've done this before?"

Edoma nodded. "With healing runes. I never knew what spiritsoul was. I just infused my will to the wards."

"Then you've already used spiritsoul."

"At what price?"

Saega shrugged. "You never got your chance to bargain

with her. She's not exactly a just god, so you might find yourself paying your debts a while after you're dead. But what choice do you have? I can't empower the runes for you."

He was right. Only she could empower these runes. Mun's magic provided protection. Healing. Wards against evil. That kind of thing.

Saega, however, was called by Sulith, the god of fortification. Sulith allowed him to use the lifesoul of another to make himself stronger. Although he looked like an old man, his magic could make him stronger than the greatest warrior in Indham. He had sworn off the magic, but now that Edoma was practicing again, she supposed he might return to it, too.

From the way he looked today, it seemed that she might have to use healing magic again. His sickness hadn't abated. His face was starting to break out in boils.

"I'll leave you to make the decision," Saega said, seeming nervous under her gaze. "We're already late. Idmaer will be annoyed."

"Better not keep him waiting," Edoma said, her tone cold.

"You should give him another chance," Saega said.

Edoma was startled by his advice. He had strongly recommended she separate from Idmaer. Saega had been among the people who thought Idmaer had framed the warrior Durwin for the crime that led to his execution. Edoma had thought otherwise, but she had separated from Idmaer all the same. She couldn't remain with a man who loved his spire more than his wife, whose every poor mood caused their home to rattle and shake.

"He only gave up the twins because he thought it was for the best," Saega continued.

"It wasn't," Edoma said with a certainty she didn't quite believe. The warrior Durwin had hated Idmaer because of what he had proposed—the dragon trade. Had Durwin found out that Idmaer fathered twins, they might have been harmed,

Edoma knew that. But Idmaer would never have had such a deadly enemy if he hadn't captured that first dragon. The twins would have been raised as theirs, and their marriage might have survived.

"I wanted to raise my children," she said to Saega.

"You did raise them."

"As my own. The way they've been treated . . ." She paused, unable to continue. How many times had she forced herself to do nothing while she saw her children chided and spat upon? There were at least three occasions she'd seen one of them walking through the town with a black eye. She didn't know whether it had been simply the result of some boyish fighting or because of prejudice.

"Well, they're faring well now, aren't they? Not another has been given what they have."

"They don't even know I'm their mother."

Saega shrugged. "Do as you wish. But I know how much you loved Idmaer. I lost Bodil, but I had no say in the matter. Your love isn't lost yet."

Edoma turned away, not wanting Saega to see the tears welling in her eyes.

"Come to the town gates when you're ready," he said. His sandals pattered on the stones until they went quiet.

10

FRYDA

HIROC narrowed his eyes. "A terrible idea."

Fryda was having trouble herself believing that it was anything other than the worst plan she'd ever heard. The warriors would never allow the three of them to go to Eosorheim. She was so surprised, she couldn't speak her objections aloud.

Alfric smoothed back his blond hair. "We both know how to fight should we come upon trouble, and you have a mouth that could convince a tortoise to leave its shell. All the Fatherless respect you. Any one of them would do whatever you ask. You could reason with Hurn better than Cenred and Sigebert."

Hiroc massaged his shaved scalp. "I don't know . . ."

"Think about it. Everyone hates the Fatherless, but if one of us were to return from the quest, then we would be respected."

"It might be dangerous," Fryda said. Alfric seemed to be avoiding her gaze. She suspected this plan of his didn't include her.

Annoyed, Fryda left the table and peered out the window. The warriors still hadn't arrived. The crowd had grown so much that people had even climbed onto the parapets above the walls.

"I could not sleep at all last night," Hiroc said from behind her. "The memory of the altar haunted me."

Fryda couldn't help thinking that a sleepless night would be good for Hiroc's humility.

Hiroc continued. "I thought of something the Council never mentioned during their meeting."

"What's that?"

"What if the giant who killed Aern has done the same to Eosor, the Guardian of Eosorheim? Even if the giant hasn't killed Eosor yet, he might be hiding someplace, waiting for the right moment to do it. What good would we be against someone who can kill a Guardian?"

Alfric smiled and removed the necklace from beneath his tunic. A dragon rune marked the pendant's jade surface. "We have this."

When he was ten years old, Alfric had been obsessed with playing warrior. One afternoon during the Summertide feasting, he had ventured outside the walls and grown lost in the Eastern Forest. Wolves had attacked him. From there, he said he didn't remember much. He awoke when Wulfnoth and his trackers found him unconscious on a bed of leaves. Surrounding Alfric were the charred remains of his lupine attackers. The pendant had been hanging around his neck, though he hadn't been wearing it when he ventured outside the walls.

Alfric always thought he had been saved by dragons, though the warriors refused to acknowledge it. Fryda wasn't sure what she thought of the story. Alfric had been young and taken with imaginings. Still, his face bore the scars of that day, so it couldn't have all been make-believe.

Now, Hiroc frowned and shook his head, as though the runestone were simply a rock. "Even if it is somehow magical, you don't know how to use it. You can barely remember that day."

"So how do we plan on convincing the warriors?" Fryda asked.

"*We* aren't going to be doing anything," Alfric said. "Hiroc and I will be going."

"I thought you were playing at something like that. I'm not going to stay behind."

"You're not a warrior," said Alfric.

"Neither is he," she said, nodding at Hiroc.

Hiroc grumbled too softly to understand.

It was clear from the determination in Alfric's face that he wasn't going to budge. Fryda decided she would leave it there, at least for now.

Jaruman walked down from the stairs and stifled a yawn. "What's all this noise about? There'd better be an execution in the courtyard, or I'm going to cause some trouble." He scanned the faces of Fryda, Alfric, and Hiroc, and then frowned. He was wearing his regular clothes and didn't appear to have been sleeping. "Enlil's scrotum, you lot look like you're about to burst into tears."

"Best not to talk about it," Hiroc said.

"The warriors are going on a quest," Fryda said, disregarding Hiroc. "Alfric and Hiroc are going to join them." She made sure to glare at Alfric. From the way he cowered, it had done the trick.

"Eosorheim is no place for a woman," Jaruman said. He must have noticed the meaning behind Fryda's words.

She rolled her eyes. "I am more than capable of handling myself."

He grunted. "The warriors wouldn't let you go with them anyway. Alfric's going to have a hard enough time convincing them to let him go, let alone Hiroc. Do you really think they'll allow a Daughter of Enlil to accompany them?"

"The answer is no," Hiroc said. He still looked out of

sorts, but the ales had enlivened him.

Fryda glared at him.

Jaruman crossed the room and removed the sword from above the fireplace. He ran his fingers over the lengthy scabbard. Jewels encrusted the pommel. It was probably worth more than three inns.

"I carried this sword with me across the Pass," he said. "I killed orcs, trolls, and worse with it." He turned to Alfric. "You can have it. I was meaning to hand it down to a son, but I doubt I'll ever remarry."

"I don't know what to say," Alfric said as he took the weapon, a look of awe on his face.

"'Thank you' would be good," Fryda jibed, trying not to appear jealous. The sword was far too large for her ever to wield, but to see Jaruman give away something that might have otherwise been hers was difficult. She planned on marrying Alfric, so she consoled herself with the fact that the sword would one day be hers anyway.

Alfric smiled sheepishly at Jaruman before fixing the sword to his belt. Even on Alfric, who was just about the tallest person in Indham, the sword looked massive.

"You need a weapon, too?" Jaruman nodded at Hiroc.

"No," Hiroc said. He tapped the blade at his waist. "I have my knife."

Jaruman scoffed but didn't say anything. He had treated Hiroc differently after he'd joined the acolytes. According to Jaruman, the Holy Order was a den of vipers. That remark had Hiroc leaping to defend them. If it weren't for the ale they'd consumed on that night, it might not have escalated. But it ended soon enough. Jaruman wasn't one to lose a fistfight, nor would he back down when challenged by a man much younger than himself.

"What if we run into trouble?" Alfric said to Hiroc. "That knife isn't meant for fighting."

Hiroc curtly shook his head.

"I have something else." Jaruman went into the back room and returned with a fur cloak. He buttoned it around Alfric's broad shoulders. "A pilgrim came in here wearing it and left it behind. Never seen something so thick, but I imagine it'll keep you warm. They say the road to Eosorheim can get mighty chilly." He looked at Hiroc and shrugged. "Sorry, I don't have another one."

Hiroc didn't seem perturbed in the slightest.

Jaruman peered through the window. "It looks like the Council is about to arrive. Enlil's blessings to the two of you." He had emphasized the word *two* while looking at Fryda.

Hiroc left without saying anything. Like all the other acolytes in the Holy Order, he despised the old god Enlil, so Jaruman's blessing had likely infuriated him. Alfric clasped Jaruman's hand and bid him farewell.

Still angry, Fryda went to walk outside, but Jaruman stopped her. "Don't go getting any fancy ideas."

"Like what?" she said with a forced smile.

"Those warriors catch you following them and there'll be trouble. You might be a novice with the Daughters, but you're also Fatherless. My word holds little weight. I'm just as much a foreigner as you. They might like me more because I give them ale, but they won't listen to my protests when they drag you back here to be flogged."

Fryda hadn't thought of following them. But Jaruman had given her a great idea.

"Or worse," he said as if reading her thoughts. "You could be stuck out there when the wraiths come."

Fryda wondered whether Jaruman had been upstairs listening when Hiroc recounted what had happened at Tyme's Hill. "It's not like you to eavesdrop."

"Didn't have to eavesdrop." He turned his nose up, as though he wouldn't deign to do such a thing. "I was in Mundos when our orb was shattered. There's a feeling about a place without an orb. I get that same feeling now. I close my eyes, and all I see are clouds of flame." He shook his head, as though rousing himself from a vision. "Take my advice. Stay here. Let the warriors do their business. I've taken you in as my own. You owe me that much."

"I won't get into trouble. I—"

"Promise me," Jaruman interrupted.

Fryda sighed, slumping her shoulders. "I promise."

It was a promise she couldn't keep, but she didn't have a choice but to tell him what he wanted to hear. Jaruman would be watching her more carefully if she didn't say it. She wasn't going to stay here in Indham while she could be out there helping. Even so, guilt weighed upon her as she stepped outside.

11

HIROC

THE rain had made people cover themselves more than they would have before the storms began. Even compared to them, Alfric looked like a long-haired winter beast. It didn't help that he was a head taller than the rest. The sight was almost comical. Hiroc might have laughed had he not been still consumed with the sight at Tyme's Hill.

For three days, while he remained inside his room at the Basilica, not going to prayer or training, all he thought of was the broken remnants of Aern's orb. When he wasn't thinking of them, he was fiddling with his ring. No matter which god he invoked, there was no lightning. He'd felt a slight breeze once and a strange smell, but no lightning.

It had been almost enough to make him think he had imagined the entire afternoon at Tyme's Hill. Perhaps the giant had been imaginary, the lightning bolt that had struck it a mere phantasm. If only that were the case, maybe Aern's orb would still be whole.

That morning, he had forced himself to go outside so he could speak with his brother. The last thing he had expected was for Alfric to decide that they would both be accompanying the warriors on their quest.

There was no chance of that. At least not both of them. Hiroc needed to learn more about the strange lightning and the blue fire. It would be impossible to do that if he was traipsing across the countryside with Alfric and the warriors.

The fresh air and the brewing excitement of the people as they waited for the warriors reminded Hiroc that Aern's death didn't mean it was the end of the world. Life would go on. Besides, who else could say that they had summoned fire from the heavens to fight off a giant?

The town crier announced the Council's arrival.

The crowd parted, allowing four members of the Council to pass through. High Priest Idmaer, Saega the augur, and the warriors, Sigebert and Cenred.

The last time he'd seen her had been at the Council meeting. Hiroc had stood before the Council and told them how Aern was too weak to speak with him at Tyme's Hill. Idmaer had congratulated him on a lie well told, but Hiroc wasn't so sure the other Council members had believed him. Some had laughed when he'd said he sometimes spoke with Aern, while others glared at him with eyes that bore into his soul. Edoma had scowled the whole time. She'd asked Hiroc whether Aern's orb had looked any different. When he said that it glimmered a little less brightly, she'd stormed out of the hall. Her absence today was unsurprising.

The Council members' presence quieted the crowd. The sense of foreboding was almost palpable. It was clear that the crowd, even though they didn't know the real reason for the quest, could gather that it was one of supreme importance.

Idmaer blessed the crowd by tracing a six-pointed star in the air. "Greetings, people of Indham. As many of you have already gathered, this weather is most unusual. Do not be afraid. Aern is weak, yes, but the Council will do what we must. Sigebert and Cenred will journey to Eosorheim to beseech Hurn in our time of need."

"What happened to Aern?" someone yelled from deep

within the crowd.

Idmaer smiled, an expression that seemed to pain him. "The Council wishes to keep your homes and shops from flooding, that is all. They will set out this afternoon."

The town crier blew his horn to conclude Idmaer's announcements. Everyone began talking among themselves about the real reason the warriors were going to Eosorheim. It appeared no one had believed Idmaer's lie. Despite the number of conversations Hiroc could overhear, none involved a theory that matched the truth.

"Ready?" Alfric said.

Fryda leaped down from the cart in a most unladylike fashion, splashing mud over the hem of Hiroc's robes. "I'll come with you."

"I don't think so," Hiroc said, brushing at the mud.

"Just stay here, okay?" Alfric said to her as he brushed her arm. "I'll tell you what they say afterward."

Alfric went to kiss her, but she pulled back. Hiroc stifled a snicker, and she glared at him. The rain had frizzled her hair, curls fighting free of her hairpin. Glowering, she looked like a petulant child who hadn't gotten her way.

Leaving Fryda behind, Hiroc and Alfric weaved their way to the front of the crowd where Idmaer was speaking to others from the Council.

Saega the augur was clad in a washed-out habit, a hood obscuring his face. He seemed to be hunching more than usual over his fox-head staff. It was hard to believe that this decrepit old man had fought off the giant with the same staff he now used to prop himself up.

The two warriors, Sigebert and Cenred, were wrapped in tattered fur cloaks, nothing like the fine garment Alfric was wearing.

"You're only taking two?" Saega said to Idmaer. "What if the road is dangerous? Surely more warriors would serve our purposes better."

"There'll be no danger," Idmaer replied. The medallion on his neck reflected what little light the sun offered. "There's been no sign of nomads for three years, and there haven't been bandits for twice as long as that. There are only villages and the like from here to Eosorheim."

"Besides," Cenred said gruffly, "we can handle ourselves."

"So be it," Saega said. "I hope you're happy placing our fate in the hands of these fools, Idmaer. I don't need to remind you what's at stake."

When Idmaer saw Alfric, his expression turned jubilant. "And what are you doing arrayed in such splendor? It looks like you've robbed my collection of exotic clothing before leaving my employ." He laughed while the warriors smirked. The way Saega had been looking at Idmaer was nothing compared to the glare he now gave Alfric.

"We have something to request of you," Alfric said boldly.

Cenred raised an eyebrow. He'd probably seen Alfric about, training with the other warriors, but it would be unusual for one of the trainees to address them in a public place like this.

"Wait here," Hiroc said to Alfric. "I'll speak with them first."

Alfric begrudgingly agreed.

Hiroc approached Idmaer and spoke softly so that Alfric wouldn't overhear. "Good morning, your grace. This Fatherless wishes to accompany the warriors on this quest."

Idmaer looked confused. "Is that so?"

Hiroc nodded. "I believe it will do much good for the Fatherless if one of them returns from Eosorheim having completed the quest. He's been admitted into the warriors, so it wouldn't be against tradition."

"I've seen him fight," Sigebert the warrior said. "He's decent with a sword. I'd wager Hurn might even listen to a Fatherless more than he'd listen to us. Let the lad come along."

Although Cenred didn't speak, his scowl suggested he

didn't agree.

"Sounds like a reasonable idea," said Saega.

"It would certainly improve public perception." Idmaer scratched his beard. "It will be done."

Hiroc returned to stand beside Alfric.

Idmaer raised two fingers into the air. The town crier sounded the horn again.

"Idmaer, High Priest of Aern," the crier announced.

"It seems it won't be two seeking out Hurn," Idmaer said, "but three. Alfric, warrior and Fatherless, will set out with Sigebert and Cenred."

There was a moment of silence before the crowd gave a half-hearted applause.

"Why didn't Idmaer say you were coming on the quest?" Alfric said to Hiroc once the noise had died down.

"Because I didn't tell him I was going."

"What?" Alfric's face contorted with confusion, his scars bunching up, giving him the appearance of a man three times his age.

"I'm staying in Indham," Hiroc said, staying firm despite Alfric's deepening scowl. "Idmaer might need me." It was a lie, and not a very good one at that. The truth was, Hiroc wanted to stay in Indham because he needed to know more about that strange lightning.

"What could be more important than getting Hurn's help? Indham needs you."

"Not anymore. It needs you, little brother." The words were hardly out of his mouth before Alfric stormed off.

12

EDOMA

TRYING not to think about what Mun might have her do after she died, Edoma tapped power into the ward. Magical energy raced along the bloodlines until both half-circles of the ward glowed crimson.

Despite not knowing how much spiritsoul empowering the wards had cost, Edoma was pleased. Finally, she had the means of protecting Indham—at least for a while. Mundos had had two years before the wraiths got through the wards. Those had been formed by mages much more powerful than her, with years of experience. Indham wouldn't have two years. But all they needed was sufficient time for the warriors to journey to Eosorheim and back.

The sound of a galloping horse drew Edoma's attention away from her wards. Outside the gates, Idmaer dismounted and walked through the entrance courtyard. His presence shocked Edoma—he hadn't been to the temple since their marriage had dissolved—until she realized that she had forgotten the time. She had spent the morning perfecting the wards. The warriors must be ready to leave for Eosorheim.

But why had Idmaer come and not Saega? The reason came to her suddenly. Saega had probably told Idmaer to retrieve her, especially after the conversation they'd had. It was just like Saega to meddle in the affairs of others.

"Have the warriors left?" Edoma asked, trying not to appear surprised at Idmaer's presence.

"Not yet," Idmaer replied. Oils darkened his graying beard and braided hair. His purple robes glistened like dew in the morning light. His eyes widened at the wards as if only noticing them. "You were once my wife, yet I know so little about you."

His expression was a history of their relationship exemplified in one hard look. He had always complained that she was too reserved, but she had every right to be. She had seen the destruction of her entire homeland and never wanted to speak of it again.

"Where did you learn to create them?" he asked.

"We were without a Guardian for two years in Mundos before we had to flee. We learned how to live during that time. These wards were responsible for those two years of safety." She had said it all before. But never this plainly. "I don't know for certain that they will work. I can only hope." Edoma didn't like to admit it, but it was true. Her memory of them had faded too much to recall their exact construction. The wards on the ground were still glowing, and they certainly seemed to hold their magic, but it still might not be enough. But it was all she had. She pointed at her best attempt. "I'll paint each of the warriors with this one."

Idmaer, like everyone except Mildryd and Saega, didn't know she was a mage. Surely he was suspicious at the moment with all the wards painted in the courtyard, but he knew so little about magic that it was doubtful.

"You seem to know a lot about wards," he said.

"Librarians tend to know things."

"An apprentice librarian," Idmaer corrected her.

"Even the period of apprenticeship involves much learning." Edoma didn't want to remain long on the subject.

Even though she had spun many tales about being an apprentice librarian in Mundos, they had all been false. She had been an apprentice mage. But she had kept that a secret from Idmaer all this time. During their marriage, she had come to trust Idmaer enough to tell him the truth, but there'd never seemed a proper time. She certainly wasn't going to tell him now. All territories allied with Wostreheim had their Talented taken by Beorhtel's inquisitors, and there was too great a risk that he might tell someone. If word reached the ears of a do-gooder, she would be carted off to Lamworth. It might mean safety from the wraiths, but she wasn't going to leave her adopted people behind, defenseless.

"I'm sure it does." His sly smile made her want to punch him.

"What are you doing here, Idmaer?"

"Saega said you were making wards, so I thought I'd see for myself. When you weren't at the gates, I wondered where you were. At the Council meeting, you seemed . . . distraught. Saega also told me you know the truth. About Aern," he added, as though she might be confused.

Edoma's stomach tightened. She had thought she wouldn't have to address the lies he had spoken at the Council meeting. But hearing him bring up the subject ignited her anger. "And no one else does," she said.

"I thought you would understand why . . . Saega told me what happened in Mundos."

She rolled her eyes. What *hadn't* Saega told him?

"There is one other thing," Idmaer said. His expression became sheepish, and Edoma clenched her jaw. Whatever he was about to say was something she wouldn't like. "Alfric is going with Sigebert and Cenred."

Edoma ground her teeth. "Why would you allow such a thing?"

"I doubt he'd be much safer here. Besides, it will be good for a Fatherless to help the town. People despise them almost as much as me."

"He's not a Fatherless," Edoma said, trying in earnest not to raise her voice. It wasn't that she didn't like the Fatherless. After all, she had seen them refused at the gates of Winhurst and then led them into Indham herself. The people had blamed Idmaer for allowing them in, and not her. The Fatherless were hated, despite how much she had tried to make the town see them as she saw them. They had been children without the care of a mother or father. She had tried to fill that void, but it had been difficult.

"I have saved Hiroc from the plight of the Fatherless," Idmaer said. "This would do the same for Alfric. He's a warrior now. Let him be one." Speaking with Idmaer alone for the first time in years had put Edoma off-guard. Past grievances suggested she should refuse. But Alfric wasn't hers to command, and he would do as he pleased. He was a man now.

"I will ward him," Edoma finally said. It was strange seeing Idmaer apparently care for Alfric now.

She went inside the temple and gathered her staff, bone necklace, and ram-horned cap. The staff was truly magical, endowed with wards of protection. The necklace and cap, however, were simply for appearances.

"I thought it would be nice for us to go to the gates together." Idmaer smiled and offered his hand. Edoma begrudgingly took it, feeling the warmth of his touch for the first time in years. He nodded at her cap and the staff in her other hand. "The wards require all of that?"

Edoma smirked. "Not at all. The process itself is rather mundane, but the people will be more assured with the pomp." Despite her levity, she couldn't help thinking that warding stone was much different from warding living people.

13

ALFRIC

ALFRIC waited in front of the blazing fire. Raindrops pelted the flames, yet the fire burned on. He felt out of place, squeezed between Cenred and Sigebert, two warriors who had defended Indham since before he was born. It didn't help that he was a head taller and half as wide as them both, wrapped in a cloak befitting a lord in a snow kingdom with a fancy sword at his hip. The people watching probably thought he looked like an overgrown child playing dress-up.

Countless pairs of eyes were enduring the pouring rain so that they could wish the warriors well on their quest. He scanned the crowd for Fryda but couldn't find her.

He watched Edoma pace around the clearing. She wore a cap with ram horns and a wolf pelt cloak. Her face was painted white and black, circles ringing her eyes. The heavy rain had made the paint run, soaking her robes enough to make her bow over from the weight. A collection of animal bones jingled around her neck as she started to skip around the circle with the grace of a woman half her age. More bones dangled from the skull-topped staff she was spinning through the air.

A choir of Daughters of Enlil, arrayed in deep blue robes, was chanting the Ode to Enlil. The solemn tune silenced the crowd.

One of the Daughters brought a lamb into the circle. Edoma drew a curved knife from her belt, the blade as long as her forearm, and slashed the lamb's gullet. With the other hand, she grabbed the lamb by the scruff of the neck and hung it over the flames. The fire spat and crackled as the blood fell upon it. The wind howled through the courtyard, making the tongues of flame dance across the air. Though the wind-touched flames tickled Edoma's arm, she did not waver until the Daughters had finished chanting the Ode.

Seeing the old woman made Alfric think of his mother, who would have been around the same age as Edoma had she lived. He couldn't remember a thing about her, but that was usual for the Fatherless. Despite his mother's fear of the dark things in the Scorched Lands, she had kept Alfric and Hiroc safe. She had fled to Indham so that they could both survive. She died soon after. Alfric tried his hardest to picture her in his head. A murky image came and went. It was like trying to capture a sugar crystal before it melted on his tongue.

Edoma approached him and smeared a blood-soaked palm over his face. Her fingers traced lines in the blood. When she held her runestone and whispered something under her breath, Alfric's face became hot, almost burning. When he reached to pull her hands away, she knocked him in the stomach with the knife's hilt.

"Don't," she said. "The magic won't work unless you endure the pain."

He grimaced until she took her hands away and the pain ceased. He bowed and offered a small prayer to Aern. It seemed appropriate, even if he was dead. He hoped the old gods would hear his prayers where Aern could not and grant them a safe return from Eosorheim.

Through the smoke rising from the sacrifice, Alfric caught

eyes with Hiroc for a moment, and looked away. He would forgive his brother's cowardice eventually, but not right now.

The ceremony concluded in a puff of smoke as the Daughters used long branches to fan the flames.

Sigebert and Cenred embraced their families before venturing outside Indham's gate. Alfric followed after them. He lingered a few paces back as a dozen or so other warriors, wearing no weapons or armor, wished Sigebert and Cenred well. None of them spoke to Alfric, though a few scoffed as they went back inside the walls.

Indham's gates lurched closed. Alfric shuffled over to the two warriors who were preparing their horses.

Sigebert clapped Alfric on the back and smiled broadly. He was the younger of the two warriors. His arms were thicker than most men's legs. Coarse hair grew on his shoulders. "It's good to have another warrior along for the journey."

Cenred sneered as he fixed a large battle-axe to his horse. Dozens of slash marks were engraved into his leather armor. "He's not a warrior. Not until he makes his first kill. Right now, he's barely a man."

"I know how to use a sword," Alfric said, deepening his voice an octave. He knew the way warriors acted. He'd spent a few evenings drinking in The Flaming Monkey with those who didn't mind the Fatherless. You acted as manly as possible, which, Alfric figured, included speaking like you'd swallowed a frog.

Most times Cenred didn't look happy, but today he looked positively furious. It didn't help that his gray hair had dreaded, giving him the look of an aged barbarian. "You might know how to dance around with a weapon so women fawn over you, but you've never spilled blood."

Sigebert chuckled. "I've seen him fight. He can do more than dance."

When Alfric had gone to the barracks for the first time after he'd won the tournament, Sigebert had greeted him with a few words of advice. "Become the best warrior, the best tracker, and the best swordsman, and no one will be able to refuse you, even if your father is Loric." Alfric intended to follow that advice, but it had only been training with the warriors, so he'd had little practice with bows and tracking. He was a long way from becoming the best at any of those things, let alone all three of them.

Cenred grunted. "This quest isn't a stroll through the forest. We're on important business." He spat on the ground and glared at Sigebert. "This is on you if things go badly. I don't want him complaining about a sore back and wanting to return home before we even get to Eosorheim."

Alfric was growing tired of them speaking as if he weren't there. "I won't get sore. And I can fire an arrow truer than most." His face went hot when he realized that he didn't have a bow.

From the disgust on Cenred's face, he didn't seem like he cared to put Alfric's claim to the test. "Perhaps you can twirl your pretty blond hair for Hurn. You any good at flirting, boy?" He laughed dryly.

"Leave him be," Sigebert said. "It'll do good for one of the Fatherless to succeed in something other than theft or drunkenness."

Cenred narrowed his eyes at Alfric. He was among those who thought the Fatherless a curse upon Indham. High Priest Idmaer did as much as he could to help by employing Fatherless in the spire, but there was only so much work.

The two warriors wandered ahead. Alfric had no trouble staying behind. Even though he had won the tournament, he was nothing like them. How many nomads had they slain in their lifetime? Alfric had never killed a living thing, let alone another human.

A small contingent of people had gathered along the parapets of the town's walls. They cheered and waved. Alfric waved back. Then he stopped, hand in midair. None of them knew the truth about Aern's orb. For how long could such a secret be kept in a town like Indham? Truth had a profound ability to reveal itself at the worst moment.

The gates clattered open again, and Fryda emerged with a pack clutched to her chest. She rushed over to Alfric. Before he could say anything, she planted a firm kiss on his cheek. "Good luck," she said, and thrust the pack into his arms.

Alfric rubbed his cheek ruefully. "Thanks," he said, feeling unsure. How had Fryda changed her mood so quickly? She'd seemed furious with him before. "You're not upset you can't come?"

"Of course not," Fryda said. "Why would I be upset? You're a warrior. I'm just a Daughter of Enlil, and a novice at that."

Before Alfric could respond, Fryda walked away. She swung her elbows in what could only be frustration.

Shaking his head, Alfric waited while a stable boy prepared a third horse. While he was waiting, he overheard people on the parapet speaking about him. They called him orphan and son of Loric, the god of cursed folk. Their chiding only made him more determined to prove them wrong, even if Hiroc wouldn't be there with him.

The stable boy finished fixing the saddle to the horse and adjusting it for Alfric's size. Alfric peered back at the parapet. Ignoring the dark looks the people gave him, he searched for Fryda. She wasn't anywhere to be seen. Nor was Hiroc. He was likely too ashamed for having let Alfric go on the quest alone.

Frustrated, Alfric quickly tied the pack to the horse's saddle. The horse looked to be in good condition, though his evaluation didn't come from experience. He mounted the horse and trotted to catch up with the other warriors. Sigebert smiled when Alfric got in line with them, but Cenred continued ignoring him.

14

ALFRIC

SIGEBERT woke Alfric gently. It was the first time in a while that Alfric hadn't been woken by his own screaming. They packed the small camp and continued along the well-trodden path, Cenred riding ahead.

When they'd been traveling an hour, Sigebert asked, "I heard you yelling while you slept. I think most the countryside did. What do you see in these dreams?"

"Mostly I'm running," Alfric said. He had no reason not to tell Sigebert. "There's a lot of screaming. At the end of every dream, I'm burned alive."

"Every time?"

Alfric nodded.

"Perhaps you can speak to Hurn about your dreams," Sigebert said.

"What does Hurn know about dreams?"

"Some mages can travel to the dream world. Maybe he'll know what ails you there."

Cenred glared at Alfric. "Warriors aren't scared of night terrors." They were the first words he had spoken to Alfric since they'd left Indham. Although it was to poke fun at him, Alfric was thankful he wasn't being ignored entirely. "If you're going to be a warrior, you have to be brave. Dreams cannot harm you. They are meaningless things of the imagination."

"Not all dreams," Sigebert said.

"Bah, you fill his head with mystical nonsense." Cenred drove his heels into his horse and trotted over the hill.

"He forgets that the aim of this quest is to seek out a mage," Sigebert said. "Would he accuse Hurn of mystical nonsense? I sincerely doubt that."

They passed over the hill. Below them was a patch of woodlands with wooden structures in its center. A strong wind blew, and Alfric retreated into the cloak.

"You might look like an idiot," Sigebert shouted above the wind, "but it was a damned good idea to wear that coat."

"What's that place?" Alfric pointed to the woodlands.

"Many years ago, that's where the dragons from Grimwald Forest migrated during the summer. Not anymore, though. It now houses the abandoned enclosure where we captured them."

Alfric's eyes shot open. He had heard how Indham had suddenly become rich after the warriors sold dragons to King Beorhtel. Surprisingly, he'd never seen a dragon up close. When he was younger, he had seen dark figures flying over the town, but that had been so long ago, it almost felt like a dream.

"When I was a boy," Alfric said, "I thought a dragon saved me from wolves."

"Aye, I remember that day. I was one of the folk Idmaer sent looking for you. You probably don't remember it was me, but I found you huddled under a tree. I don't know about it being a dragon that saved you, but there were three wolves burned to cinders beside you."

Alfric palmed the medallion. It was shaped like a dragon. He had never seen it before that day. When he'd recovered from the wolves' attack, it had been hanging around his neck. It all seemed so long ago.

"No one ever speaks of dragons anymore," Alfric said.

Sigebert's face flushed with shame. "We captured them from Grimwald Forest the season after we routed the nomads. We thought to use the dragons in case they ever returned, but they didn't. King Beorhtel approached us, and we sold the dragons for him to use in his campaigns. Without the dragon trade, we would have no money. There aren't many farms able to produce up here, and we have little of value to export. Even so, the dragons were a terrible idea."

They continued riding, not stopping to eat or rest. There were a few hamlets and towns along the way. Alfric waved to the people as he passed, but he couldn't help thinking about what Aern's death meant for them. Soon, they would need help. He hoped that Hurn might provide refuge for not only the people of Indham but all those in Aernheim.

As the sun began to set, they reached the top of a hill, revealing a small hamlet surrounded by farms that were more yellow than green. Cenred dismounted and began preparing the camp. Alfric began unsaddling his horse. He'd been thinking about the dragons most of the day, and he still had questions. With Cenred occupied, he turned to Sigebert.

"Didn't the dragons fight back?" he asked.

"We wouldn't have been able to capture them if they had," Sigebert said. His horse was already unsaddled. Without a word, he went over to Alfric and helped him. "We found suppression stones in the ruins of Babon's Pass. Whoever holds a stone in their palm can force the dragons to obey their every command. It's something to do with dragons being magical creatures. The stones don't work on ordinary folks like you and me."

Alfric had heard of places where people were enslaved, but this was far worse. "That's horrible."

"I told the Council the same, but Idmaer gave the final command. Few people wish to trade this far north, and King Beorhtel was more than happy to accommodate us. The warriors who were sent to Lamworth were experts in using the stones." Sigebert made a point of looking northwest toward Eosorheim. "Convincing Hurn would be a lot easier if we hadn't stolen his dragons."

Alfric could hardly believe his ears. They had taken Hurn's dragons, enslaved them, and then sold them to become weapons of war, and they were expecting Hurn to help them?

The allure of being on a quest with Indham's greatest warriors had vanished. Hurn might never give them the chance to even speak before he killed them.

15

FRYDA

FRYDA climbed out from the bushes and stepped back onto the road. The cart's wheels rattled into the distance, kicking up mud. She had considered requesting transport from the man driving the cart but thought better of it. It would be asking for trouble. Even though Aernheim was a peaceful region, women tended not to travel alone. To avoid the fate of those women foolish enough to do so, Fryda had changed into a tunic and breeches before leaving Indham. Anyone who saw her close up would know she was a woman, but she'd avoided anyone on the road.

Unfortunately, she'd been unable to wrestle a horse from the stable boy. The day she'd been gone from Indham had been slow traveling on foot. All the while, she maintained a good distance behind the warriors.

In some ways, it was a benefit that the warriors rode on horses where she did not, lest they discover someone was following them. They were seasoned warriors, after all. She didn't know what they would do if they learned of her, but Jaruman's warning wouldn't be far off. Their quest was too important for them to bring her back to Indham, but they'd likely find the nearest person traveling that way to take her there.

A map she had stolen from the temple guided her. She would have taken a short spear from Jaruman, but she didn't want to risk him discovering what she'd planned. Using the map, she discerned the warriors' movements easily. They were traveling the shortest distance to the bridge on the border of Eosorheim and Aernheim. Unfortunately, the map wasn't very detailed, so there was no telling when she would come to the next town with an inn.

After waking that morning from a fitful sleep provided by the hard ground beneath her, she had almost lost the warriors. They'd taken a different direction than she thought they would. The map, however, had gotten her back on track quickly enough.

Now, she continued on the road. To either side stood towering elms. Even though it was summer, their leaves had started to fall. Rumbling thunder sounded, soon followed by rain.

Fryda cursed the weather before sighting a small village in a clearing not far off the road. She hiked down the slope. Movement on the road behind her drew her attention. A speck danced across the road, so far away that she could barely make it out. Whatever it was, it had hidden among the trees.

Was someone following her?

It certainly seemed like they'd run to the trees to hide when she'd turned to look at them.

Thinking that it could be one of the villagers, Fryda decided to wait at the edge of the road. She was hidden from view by the overhanging ledge. Squinting, she tried in earnest to make out what it was that she had seen. After waiting for what she guessed was an hour, she circled through the elms until she was in front of where the speck had been.

It was a man. He had stopped to wait, leaning against a mound. A hood obscured his face, so she couldn't tell whether he had fallen asleep.

Not wanting to wait to find out, Fryda went back through the forest and came to the village. Wooden fences surrounded a half-dozen huts. Fryda made for the closest hut where a horse grazed in an adjacent paddock. Outside the hut, a middle-aged woman was throwing feed to chickens.

"Good day," Fryda called out to the woman. "I was wondering if there might be some place for a lone traveler to stay the night."

The woman produced a broad smile. "There's always a place to stay in Gillian's old hovel."

Gillian beckoned Fryda into the hut and fed her a warm meal of rabbit and turnips. It wasn't long before they started talking about rumors of what had happened at Indham. Gillian thought that the Holy Order had done something to anger Aern, and that he was punishing them with the storms.

Fryda simply nodded her head. She couldn't tell Gillian that Aern was actually dead.

A thought came to Fryda, and she dropped the rabbit leg from her hand, splashing juices over the table. *Even if Hurn was to grant the people of Indham refuge, what would happen to the rest of Aernheim?* Surely Hurn wouldn't allow an entire region to enter Eosorheim? Besides, Eosorheim was the smallest region of them all. Fryda had seen that clearly from her map.

She stared at the woman who, without hesitation, had welcomed a stranger into her home. Gillian bore a kindly face. She couldn't be more than forty. If cause called for it, she would be able to travel.

"Do you have family in one of the other regions?" Fryda asked Gillian.

Gillian nodded. "A second cousin in Lamworth. The poor old girl got herself married to a blacksmith there. Why do you ask?"

Jaruman's story about the wraiths made the hairs on Fryda's neck bristle. "The storms aren't the worst thing.

Something worse will come."

"I don't know how you know that, but even if it's true, I can't go to Lamworth. Shelny lives two huts down, and he reckons King Beorhtel said that no one can cross the border. Under pain of death, apparently." If Shelny was right, then Gillian and her village were doomed. "Can't go to Eosorheim, either. That terrible mage killed the last person I heard went there."

Not wanting to speak anymore, Fryda thanked Gillian for the lovely meal and asked where she was sleeping.

Gillian pulled out a blanket and laid it down before the fire. Above the fire hung a saddle and a sword. Gillian hadn't mentioned a husband or a son, but from the size of the sword, it wasn't likely they belonged to her.

"I don't expect you to tell me why you're so far from Indham, but I'd be doing you a disservice if I didn't tell you that it's not wise for a woman to travel alone. There are bandits about these parts. They never bothered me because I never had anything to steal. But a girl like you . . ."

"I don't plan on being alone for much longer," Fryda said. "I'm meeting some friends soon." It wasn't exactly a lie. If she took Gillian's horse, she would be in Eosorheim by the week's end. There was even a saddle she could use. She unpinned her hair and rested the pin beside the bedding.

"I take it you're not married," Gillian said as she watched her. "You should let your hair down more often. Show off your curls. I hear the young men these days love them."

Thinking of Alfric and how she desperately wanted to see him again, Fryda smiled and bid Gillian goodnight. The woman retreated into the only other room in the house and closed the door behind her.

The saddle above the fire beckoned to Fryda. She considered how she would take it down and fit the horse with it. She'd ridden horses before, and she remembered enough that fixing the saddle wouldn't be too difficult. The sword, however, was much too big. But a horse as large as the one outside would probably be able to outride most things she would want to hack with a sword anyway.

Most things except wraiths, that is.

Ignoring the terrible thought, Fryda cocked her ear, listening for any sign that Gillian might be asleep. The floorboards creaked, but from within the other room. A shuffling sound came from outside.

Gillian's door slowly opened. She stepped outside from it, a hatchet in one hand.

"Did you hear that?" Gillian whispered as she approached Fryda.

Fryda nodded.

Gillian's face hardened. "Then it wasn't just me. Go and hide in my room. It might be bandits."

Without another word, Fryda obeyed. She went into the other room and moved the door so that there was only a crack between it and the doorframe. Peering through the crack, Fryda realized she had cowered while an old woman searched out what might be bandits.

Fryda's gaze flitted over the room for a weapon. Despite the significant number of random things scattered over the dresser and the bed, she could only find a broken table leg. Without anything else, she gripped the table leg and stepped out from the room.

Gillian was outside the house, speaking with a hooded man. It was the same man Fryda thought had been following her. Gillian still held the hatchet in one hand, waving it frantically.

Fryda rushed outside, table leg raised over her shoulder, and slammed it down on the back of the man's neck. The man crumpled to the ground.

Gillian gasped. "What have you done?" She knelt down beside the man and lifted his head. A bloody gash where Fryda had struck him dripped blood onto his face. Onto

Jaruman's face.

The hooded man was Jaruman!

* * *

"I'll let you two speak," Gillian said before retreating into her room.

Jaruman's expression turned hard. "What are you doing here? You made me a promise."

"I only wanted to follow Alfric," Fryda replied. "As much as he might think otherwise, he needs me."

"You're not a warrior. You're a novice with the Daughters of Enlil. Your place is at the temple."

"He has nightmares, you know," Fryda said. She had never told Jaruman about Alfric's dreams. Jaruman could be a strict man, and if he thought Alfric were plagued with dark spirits that caused nightmares, he might withhold his blessing for their marriage. Jaruman wasn't truly Fryda's father, but that didn't mean she would marry without his blessing.

"What kind of nightmares?" Jaruman asked, looking intrigued.

"Terrible ones. Sometimes I wait by his bedside at the spire, stroking his hair while he whimpers. Who will be by his side while he has dreams of such terror? I don't think Cenred or Sigebert will comfort him."

Jaruman frowned. "I've heard some strange stories about folk they call dreamers. The reason why their dreams feel so real is because they are."

"That sounds foolish."

"Now, now, I wouldn't be so quick to reject something you don't understand. There's magic in this world, even if King Beorhtel's inquisitors do their best to scoop it up as soon as they find it."

"You think Alfric's dreams could be real?"

"Maybe. Maybe not. I wouldn't be surprised if the both of

you have some magic in you. All the Talented can trace their bloodline back to folk north of Babon's Pass."

"I don't want him to end up like Garmund," she said. Wulfnoth's son had been taken by the inquisitors because he was called by the gods and given their magic.

"Don't you worry," Jaruman said, lifting Fryda's chin with a stubby finger. "If they try and take him, they'll have me to answer to."

The way Jaruman spoke filled Fryda with warmth that stretched from her head to her toes. She didn't mind not having a father, not when she had a friend like Jaruman. But even Jaruman would be powerless against a cohort of mages.

"Besides," Jaruman said, "he has bigger things to worry about than inquisitors." His voice dropped to a whisper. "The wraiths could cross into Aernheim at any moment. But he's chosen this path. As for you and I, we'll be heading back to Indham in the morning."

"But I've come all this way. You can't make me go back now."

"We don't have the wards."

"Those things Edoma painted on their faces?"

Jaruman nodded. "I wore those same markings when I crossed the Scorched Lands and came to Babon's Pass. They stop the wraiths from entering your body. If the wraith clouds come and we don't have wards, we'll become skinwalkers."

"The wraith clouds come through Babon's Pass, don't they?"

"We don't know for sure, but that's the closest place to the Scorched Lands."

"We're traveling west, and Babon's Pass is east," Fryda said, speaking her thoughts aloud. "The cloud isn't likely to come to us before we get to Eosorheim."

"That's not a bet I'm willing to take. We're going home in the morning. Say no more about it. I'd ride tonight, but my horse won't take any more travel. And I need rest more than my horse."

Jaruman lay down on the rug beside the front door. Using the moonlight coming through the window, Fryda opened the map. She had barely begun to examine it when Jaruman rolled over. Startled, she hid the map beneath her pillow.

Soon after, he started snoring. Although he normally slept lightly, Fryda couldn't remember ever hearing Jaruman snore. He must have been exhausted, which was good for her.

Cautiously, she stepped over to the fireplace and grabbed the saddle from it. The buckles clinked, and she grimaced. Jaruman didn't stir. Neither did Gillian's door open. Thinking of Gillian made Fryda feel guilty, but it couldn't be helped. A horse needed a saddle, and if she was to go to Eosorheim, she needed to leave now.

She shifted the window shutter and climbed through it. Almost giddy, she raced over to the horse. Jaruman's horse was beside it, looking disheveled. He had been right—the horse had needed the rest. Gillian's horse, however, looked bright. It didn't take long to fix the saddle.

Goading the horse out from the paddock, she walked it to the road. When she was sure they were far enough from the house so they wouldn't be heard, she mounted it and galloped down the road.

16

ALFRIC

ALFRIC wasn't accustomed to riding horses—there was little opportunity to do so in Indham. Fryda had always told him how painful it could be, but he had always laughed at her. Now he knew the true pain of saddle sores.

The three warriors had slept the previous night in a cleft beneath a hill. After waking before sunrise, Alfric had sleepily saddled his horse. From the way the saddle moved about, he must have done it wrong. He couldn't ask the warriors to stop—Cenred would likely whack him over the head for being so stupid and then continue riding anyway.

Sigebert had ridden beside Alfric as they traveled west along the road, offering a few brief words of polite conversation. Cenred stayed ahead, neither speaking nor acknowledging Alfric's presence in any way. It had been too much to hope that Cenred's advice about bravery was the beginning of a more amiable relationship.

Alfric was starting to learn why Cenred was referred to as the Wolverine of Indham. Even the hail that fell from the sky didn't make him consider stopping for shelter. Had the shards of ice been a little larger, Alfric thought they would have risked a concussion, or worse—death. They all bore painful bruises from the falling ice stones—Alfric the least, thanks to the thickness of Jaruman's cloak.

They stopped that evening at an inn for a hot meal. It was a small town, much smaller than Indham. Alfric could hardly believe people lived in what was practically the wilderness. He would surely die of boredom. No sooner had they filled their stomachs, they were riding again.

The road gave way to grassy plains. There were no farms or buildings to be seen.

Cenred halted his horse at the edge of a precipice. He dismounted and stared out across the expanse. Alfric guided his steed until the ground dropped at a steep angle. Beyond was a valley with no clouds above it. Thousands of trees reached up from the valley, untouched by rain. The moon illuminated the river with tremendous light. The river divided the area where they were standing from the valley. There was no telling how deep the river was. A stone bridge, wide enough for ten men to ride abreast, was the only visible way of crossing.

"We're almost there," Cenred said without turning. "Those trees are Grimwald Forest. It sits on Eosorheim's border."

The division between regions was showcased in the sky, gray with clouds on one side, and dark blue spotted with stars on the other. It was like a divine cartographer had separated the two lands by their skies.

"You see that stone pillar beside the bridge!" Sigebert pointed to it. It was at least twice the size of the elms within the forest. Green wards glowed along its surface. "That's an obelisk. Wherever there's a border, there are obelisks. They extend a Guardian's power from the altar. Aernheim has them, too, but they're far from Indham. If you get two from different regions that are close together, strange things happen."

"Like what?" Alfric asked, intrigued.

"If you tip a bucket of water upside down, the water

doesn't fall to the ground; it goes up toward the sky. Roll a pair of dice, and you might roll two sixes. A hundred more rolls would bring those sixes again and again."

Alfric stared at the obelisk. He'd never heard of them before, but he supposed their existence made sense. How else was a Guardian's power meant to extend from the altar to a region's boundary?

They had reached Eosorheim without incident. But that was the easy part. Now, they had only to convince Hurn to help them.

Swallowing his fear, Alfric began to move down the hill but stopped when he saw a peculiar cloud. It seemed to intentionally avoid moving over Eosorheim, skirting around the border like sheep around a fence. Fire swirled within the clouds, illuminating it with a demonic light as it raced across the velvet sky.

"By Enlil's scrotum, what's taking you two so long?" Cenred had stopped in the middle of the hill. "Goodness . . ."

"There's nothing good about that thing," Sigebert said, peering up at the cloud that made his face glow red.

"Hurn doesn't want us here," Alfric said.

"That's not Hurn," said Sigebert. "That's the bloody wraiths."

Alfric's heart stopped. When he was a child, the Daughters said the wraiths would chew off his toes if he didn't sleep after lights-out. As he got older, he heard more stories of what they were actually capable of—possessing people and turning them into monsters.

The cloud pulsed, a flicker of light, except not like thunder. It was something else, as though the cloud were a living thing. It shifted, slowly descending as it moved toward them. The three horses screamed and stomped their hooves before bolting away.

"Looks like they've noticed us," Sigebert cried. "We need to cross the bridge."

Alfric was rooted to the spot. The flickering light of the cloud was impossible to turn away from. He could hear the two men yelling. He could feel strong hands tugging at him, fingers pressing into his flesh hard enough to bruise. But he didn't want to go. He wanted to stay there until the fire-colored cloud came.

Then pain shot through his arm, breaking him from the trance.

"Sorry, lad, but you weren't going to shake out of it unless I hurt you."

Alfric rubbed his stinging arm, and his hand came away sticky with blood.

"Let's go," Sigebert said as he cleaned his belt knife, sheathed it, and turned toward the precipice.

Alfric looked down the steep hill. The climb down required time and skill, neither of which he possessed. One ill-placed step or taking hold of a loose rock and he'd fall to the bottom. The drop wasn't high enough to kill him unless he landed on his head, but he'd break a few bones.

Cenred was already down the mountainside and halfway across the bridge. Sigebert called out for him to slow down lest he break a leg, but the man was plain ignoring him. He was meant to be the greatest warrior in Indham, retired only a season ago. He was either really a coward, or these wraiths were everything Alfric had heard they were and more.

Alfric steeled his courage and started descending. His boots struggled to find purchase on the scree, and he fell. The sky pin-wheeled as he tumbled. His necklace looped around a crag. He was jerked to a halt, suspended in midair for a moment before the necklace broke. There was more tumbling, and more pain, until he lurched to a halt. A dozen cuts and bruises made their presence known, and his leg pulsed with his heartbeat. He lay on his back, groaning. The dizziness faded, revealing Sigebert's bearded face.

"Steady on, lad," Sigebert said as he slipped under Alfric

and helped him stand. "I've got you."

"My necklace." Alfric turned to retrieve it, but Sigebert urged him forward.

"Forget about it. Better you lose your necklace and save your life."

Together they carefully navigated the rest of the hill until they came to the bridge. It was about two hundred paces wide, much longer than it had seemed from atop the hill. Cenred was already on the other side, sword in one hand as if it might be capable of stopping the wraiths should they cross. He yelled at them to hasten.

The entry to the forest was guarded by a grand statue of a man with an elk's head. If Alfric's heart weren't already beating at an alacritous speed, the statue with the cold eyes would have quickened it. Alfric's fall made putting any weight on his leg impossible, but Sigebert half-carried him along the bridge.

"Just a little farther," Sigebert said. Before he'd finished speaking, the mists crawled down the mountain like a twin-forked wave.

Alfric cried out in desperation and hauled himself forward. But something seized him.

Sigebert's face whitened with horror, and he stumbled backward.

A chill ran down Alfric's spine. Darkness engulfed him. A harsh, crackling sound like the locution of demons invaded his ears. Although he couldn't see, he knew that Sigebert was somewhere. Maybe lost within this darkness, or maybe he had crossed the boundary point where the mists couldn't get him.

A jolting pain penetrated Alfric's temple. Involuntarily, his hand grabbed his sword hilt and released the weapon from its sheath. Unable to do otherwise, he stepped forward, out from the mists and into new light.

Sigebert stood but a pace away, the mists unable to touch him.

The thing inside Alfric's mind wrestled for control. It winked in and out of existence—in his mind for a moment and gone the next.

Alfric knew he had scant moments to gain control or be lost forever. On instinct, he reached for the dragon pendant, but his hand came away empty. He tried to remember Fryda's face, hoping that the memory of her might tear him from whatever now controlled him. But all he saw was the terrifying image of a devil in a cloud of fire.

The demon chorus got louder. Every bark and scream made Alfric grow more desperate. Forcing every ounce of will into a single intention, he jumped across the bridge. He slammed into an invisible wall and was thrown to the ground. He scrambled upright and ran toward Sigebert again, but the same force hurled him backward.

The bridge was uncrossable.

"I'm sorry, lad." Sigebert stared at Alfric with a mournful frown before leaving the bridge and fading into the forest alongside Cenred.

The same guttural tongue Alfric had heard in the mists erupted from his throat in a deafening roar.

His body was not his own. Something had taken over it, and he could feel it smothering his mind. He fought against it, but the thing was too strong. It snuffed him out like a candle.

17

FRYDA

FRYDA realized too late that she hadn't brought the map. She must have left it behind in Gillian's hut. Without it, she didn't know where she was going. She had traveled along the road until it ended at a stream. For the life of her, she couldn't remember what direction the map had said to go. There had been many streams that flowed from one river or another.

"Enlil, guide me," she said before turning left. From there, it was just rolling hills filled with three-foot-high grass. Not a single building could be seen. Not wanting to give in to despair, she continued riding. The horse beneath her was a magnificent beast. It responded to the slightest tightening of her thighs. Where she was hesitant and fearful, it was confident.

But all confidence fled from the beast when the fiery cloud raced across the sky. The horse reared onto its hind legs, throwing Fryda from the saddle. Her shoulder hit the ground first, but the grass cushioned the fall. She stood and raised her hands, hushing the beast. When it finally stilled, the cloud was merely a crimson speck on the horizon.

She mounted the horse again and tried not to think

about the cloud. She had ridden only a little distance before something shifted through the grass. The horse snorted and stopped moving. The grass was far too high to see what exactly the horse was reacting to. Maybe an animal of some kind.

The horse breathed in and out loudly, its lips curling back to reveal its gums.

"It's all right," Fryda whispered, stroking the horse's mane.

Something snarled beneath them, and the horse reared again. This time, Fryda clenched her thighs and gripped the reins. She remained in the saddle as the horse bolted. Unable to control the direction, she could only pray. The horse finally stopped when they'd left the tall grass.

Fryda dismounted. At least the sun had now risen, making it easier to see. But there were no landmarks for her to tell which direction they had gone in.

The horse stomped and pawed at the ground.

Not again, Fryda thought. She eyed the grass steadily, unsure whether something was about to leap from it and attack them.

A series of barks came. The horse shifted about, but it didn't leave. There would be no mounting it now. It would surely throw Fryda from the saddle if she tried.

What burst out into the clearing was no dog.

It was Alfric.

Fryda thought of running to him but stopped herself. Something was wrong with him. His hands and feet were bloodied as if he had been running on them for hours. Strangely, the dragon pendant wasn't around his neck. He had never removed it since he'd received it. He still wore Jaruman's cloak. It was dirty and fraying, giving him the look of a wild beast.

Fryda moved toward him, cautious. As she got closer, his eyes flickered over her. He licked cracked lips, his tongue staining them red.

"Don't get any closer." Jaruman entered the clearing

astride his horse. He must have followed her. "That thing isn't Alfric. It's a skinwalker."

Alfric snarled, opening his mouth. His jaw continued extending, his mouth splitting along his cheeks until it reached his ears. He reached for her.

Fryda screamed and pushed him. He fell, only to land on his hands and feet, his back arched like a spider. He scuttled backward.

Sword in hand, Jaruman yelled and started to ride toward her. He was still so far away.

Alfric came for her again. Fryda couldn't move.

Gillian's horse rode in from nowhere. It stomped on Alfric, crushing him beneath its hooves. Fryda gasped, pausing only to see Alfric's soulless eyes before jumping onto the saddle.

"Ride!" Jaruman turned his horse toward the grass again.

She needed no convincing. She dug her heels into the horse's sides and left Alfric, her one true love, behind.

* * *

They didn't stop riding until the sun was at its peak. Fryda took the horses to a pond to drink while Jaruman prepared a meal. As Fryda removed the saddle from her horse, Jaruman handed her dried meat wrapped in thick bread. She sat on a rock and watched the horses drink while she chewed the food.

"Gillian wouldn't let me leave without taking something to eat," Jaruman said. "She's a good woman, that one. She said not to worry about the horse."

They both sank into silence. Rainwater trickled into the pond.

"I saw the cloud go west," Fryda said. "It was the wraiths, wasn't it?"

Jaruman tore a piece of bread with his teeth and nodded.

So Alfric was a skinwalker. She knew something bad had happened to him but hadn't gathered what it was until later when she considered what the cloud had been. The way he had moved was horrifying. And those eyes . . . whatever that thing was, it wasn't Alfric.

The last time she had seen him had been to give him the pack. But she had barely spoken to him then. In truth, anger had still filled her. But what good was that anger now? At the moment the wraith took Alfric, had he known that she loved him?

Suddenly, she began to cry. Jaruman pulled her upright and wrapped his arms around her. Resting her head against his chest, Fryda let the tears fall. Why did it have to be Alfric? She was going to marry him. Balling her hands into fists, she pounded against Jaruman's chest. He took her hands and kissed them.

"My daughter," he said, "I am sorry."

Sniffling, Fryda sat again. She wiped her face with her sleeves. Gillian's horse came to her, nuzzling her with its nose. Fryda leaned into the horse's ear. "Flight—that will be your name." Rain clouds parted, and sunlight warmed her face. She closed her eyes and took it in.

With the sun out now, what had happened earlier almost seemed like a dream. Where was the wraith cloud now? Fryda opened her eyes. "Does the cloud disappear in the morning?"

Jaruman nodded. "It goes someplace else. Somewhere not in this world. It vanishes when the sun rises and appears when it sets."

"But the sun had already risen, and Alfric was still that . . . thing."

"That's because he was a skinwalker."

Was. He had become a skinwalker and was now dead, crushed beneath Flight's hooves. Fryda had to force herself not to break down again.

"Skinwalkers are the way the wraiths remain while it's daytime," Jaruman said. "They're dangerous things. They might look like the person they were before, but they're not. That thing that attacked you wasn't Alfric. He died the moment the wraith took hold of him."

Fryda swallowed, but the lump in her throat wouldn't go away. Tightness in her chest prevented her from taking in anything more than a slight breath. She sat on the ground for a while, watching the sun play along the water.

"We'll need to get moving soon," Jaruman said as he saddled the horses. "The wraiths will come again tonight. There's no way we can dodge them without wards, but hopefully they'll be somewhere we're not. I don't want to risk a second night if we can help it."

"How many wraiths are there?"

He shrugged. "A lot. Fewer in the first wave, far as I know."

"The first wave?"

"These are just the scouts. More will come soon."

Fryda shook her head, unable to believe the doom that had come to Aernheim.

"Why was the cloud so far east?"

"I guess the wraiths found out what the warriors intended to do. If Alfric and the others reached Eosorheim, that might have meant less hosts. I doubt Sigebert and Cenred made it."

Fryda had so many questions, all of them threatening to overwhelm her once more. The more she thought about things, the more difficult it was to breathe.

Jaruman continued, "We need to get back to Indham to warn the others. They might not be able to do much with the knowledge, but it'll be better than being surprised."

Fryda recalled the markings on Alfric's face. "You said that the wards Edoma had painted on Alfric and the others would stop the wraiths."

"Another reason we need to get back to Indham quickly," he said. "When we get back to Indham, don't tell Edoma about Alfric. She won't take well to her son becoming a skinwalker."

"Her son?"

Jaruman looked away, but not before Fryda caught the

shock on his face. "Edoma thought of Alfric like a son."

"That's not what you meant." Fryda's eyes widened as she realized the meaning behind his words. "Hiroc and Alfric are Edoma's sons?"

"I didn't say that."

"You didn't have to. They could have been raised in luxury. Instead, they are Fatherless."

Jaruman sighed, shaking his head. "It wasn't Edoma's doing. Idmaer convinced her of it."

Fryda scowled. She was quickly coming to hate Idmaer and his lies.

"Don't say anything," Jaruman said. "I won't ask you to promise me." He paused, as though he knew any promise Fryda made might be broken. "But do it for Edoma. She loved that lad, even if she never claimed him as her own."

I loved him, too, Fryda thought. *And now he's gone.*

18

HIROC

THE howling winds and pelting rain drove Hiroc to the Basilica. He had been halfway to The Flaming Monkey when the storm broke. Though he was now an acolyte, and had been for a year, he still visited the old tavern in secret to drink and banter with his old friends. Now that rumors had spread about what had happened to Aern, it was becoming increasingly difficult to do so. People were suspicious.

Hiroc clutched the ring. Try with all his might, he couldn't manage to make the lightning come again. The gods had responded to him on Tyme's Hill, of that he was sure.

Frustrated, he went inside. The acolyte's eating hall was empty. He sat on the stool beside the fireplace. Staring into the fire, he couldn't help but think about Alfric and what danger he might now face. At the thought, Hiroc felt his heartbeat quicken. Had he been a coward to send his brother away?

No, not a coward. A god had responded to his cries. He needed to learn which god had shown their benevolence to him. As he considered it, the fire seemed to dance before his eyes. Deep within its center, at the hottest part, he swore he saw a flicker of blue flame.

Grabbing his ring, he concentrated on where the speck of blue had been. "Aern, hear my prayer," he whispered, afraid someone might hear him.

Nothing happened. The flames continued to pop and crackle as they did in a regular fireplace.

Hiroc slammed his fist on the table. A splinter as large as a toothpick lodged into the side of his palm. He yelped and plucked it out. Blood trickled from the tiny wound onto his robes.

He was a fool. A stupid accident had stained his robes with blood.

An *accident.*

Was there a god he might have invoked by accident when the fire had come? Hiroc considered the gods he knew. He counted two dozen. Most were Guardians—the gods contained within the carcaern orbs. He knew few old gods. The old gods were said to roam free throughout the world, not relegated to the confines of an orb. Some said that these were mere stories told by folks who were stuck in the old ways. Mother Edoma would have argued strongly against such people.

Thinking of Mother Edoma, Hiroc wondered if he'd called upon Enlil at Tyme's Hill. It was possible. He'd never been devoted to Enlil, though, so it was unlikely. Nevertheless, he invoked Enlil's name.

Was it just his mind or had the fire followed his gaze?

Emboldened by the appearance of progress, Hiroc grabbed the ring. "Enlil, hear my prayer," he called, much louder than he'd intended.

Like ink in water, the orange flames turned bright blue. The flames swirled from the fireplace, extending themselves like fingers stretching toward him. Surely this was Enlil's power Hiroc was seeing before him. But why Enlil? He, like the others in the Holy Order, had disdained Enlil every chance he got. He had no orb to house him, so he was a false god.

Without thinking, Hiroc reached out to touch the blue

fire. His whole hand was amid the dancing flames, but he felt no pain. His skin was unharmed. This wasn't the power of a false god. As he turned his hand, the ring seemed to glow beneath the flames. The rust around the ring's insignia disintegrated. Clearly now, he could see the insignia as the eternal flame of Enlil.

Someone gasped behind him, and he quickly pulled his hand back. The fire flashed and was orange again. It retreated within the fireplace, as though it had never been anywhere else.

Kipp was standing in the doorway. "What was that?" he said, eyes wide.

"Nothing," Hiroc said. He stood, gathered his things, and started to walk past him.

Kipp grabbed his arm so he couldn't leave. "It wasn't nothing. You had your hand in the blue fire, but it didn't burn. That's magic." He had always been a good friend of Hiroc's, but finding out that someone was Talented tested even the best of friendships. Hiroc had heard about children whose parents had given them over to the inquisitors after they'd been called by a god.

"Not magic," Hiroc said. "Just a trick. A harmless trick."

"A *Talented* trick." Kipp's face seemed to darken, and his mouth moved, as though he were whispering a prayer.

Hiroc glanced back at the fireplace. He might have doubted what he had seen had Kipp not seen it too. He wanted to try it again, but he feared who else might walk in.

But he had done it. Finally, that sensation lurking within him had shown itself. He now knew for certain that he was Talented.

Hiroc stared at the ring. The flame insignia was glowing.

* * *

Later that evening, Hiroc returned to sit beside the

fireplace. He was hoping that it was late enough in the evening that he wouldn't be disturbed. That hope, however, was dashed when Ealstan entered the room and sat across the table from Hiroc.

"So," Ealstan started, his voice customarily high-pitched, "what happened at the altar when you went there four nights ago?" He spoke as if it were a question about some menial event. His calculating gaze suggested he knew otherwise.

Hiroc kept his hands beneath the table so Ealstan couldn't see the ring. "What do you think happened? There was a little rain and a flash of lightning or two, but that was the only thing out of the ordinary." He recalled the dead bodies of the guards. He was surprised not to have thought of them until now. Their deaths seemed inconsequential compared to what had happened to Aern.

"Did you speak with Aern?" Ealstan leaned back in the chair so his knife was exposed at his belt. His fingers tickled the knife's pommel. He had a habit of doing that. At the pommel's tip, carved out of bone, was a figurine of Aern in the form of a winged imp.

"I offered a litany, and then we spoke a little." Hiroc was the only acolyte who spoke with Aern. At first, he thought his conversations with the Guardian made him special among the acolytes, but he soon learned that they all thought he was either lying or crazy. Hiroc had started to think himself insane, but the response he'd had at Tyme's Hill made him think otherwise. But why would Ealstan have suddenly changed his mind about Hiroc being crazy for hearing voices? There was only one explanation.

Remembering that Ealstan might be trying to find out what had really happened to Aern, Hiroc added, "Aern was too weak to talk at length." He breathed, a sound more like a growl than a sigh, and stood. "I've had enough of this. I don't answer to you."

"No," Ealstan said, "you don't. At least not yet. But when

the others discover what you really are, then you will be taken, and I shall be finally rid of you."

Hiroc clenched the table's edge, bridling his wrath lest he reach over the table and strangle Ealstan. "Is that a threat?"

"You may interpret it as you wish," Ealstan said with a flutter of his hand. "But Kipp saw you whisper to the fire. I know that you are Talented."

A chill rushed down Hiroc's spine. The fire still roared from the hearth, but the room had become deathly cold.

19

IDMAER

I DMAER traced a finger along an incision running down the middle of the godstone altar, feeling the clean slice of some weapon of otherworldly origin. Whatever it was that had struck the surface, it was something that shouldn't exist. Godstone was supposed to be impenetrable. By the same token, though, Guardians were meant to be immortal and invulnerable. Much that Idmaer had once believed was dissipating at a pace too swift to preserve.

Torchlight flickered off the golden hands. They were empty. The stone pillars lay on their sides, symbols of defeat. The wards no longer shone with ethereal light. Blood stained the altar that the rain couldn't wash away.

"All I found were these." Wulfnoth reached into his coat pocket with shaky hands and withdrew a rectangular box. He opened it and held it out for Idmaer to inspect. Inside were crystal shards—the remains of Aern's orb. Moonlight piercing through the clouds made them spark with life, though the orb no longer contained the essence of a Guardian.

Over the years, Idmaer had ventured to the altar countless times. As an acolyte, he had been terrified. The terror soon dissipated, and with it, his faith. The truth was, Aern was nothing more than a spark within the carcaern orb. He wasn't a god. Hiroc had been right—gods were immortal. But whatever was inside the orb was gone. Snuffed out by someone who hadn't left a trace.

Idmaer turned to Wulfnoth. "Still no sign of whoever did this?"

"Except for the blood, the storms washed everything away." He glared at the altar for a moment before turning away. "I can keep looking, but I won't find anything. Thing is, I reckon it had to have been a Talented."

"You think Beorhtel sent one of his inquisitors to shatter the orb?" Idmaer had never thought of that. Beorhtel still hadn't responded to their second letter calling for aid. He had to have received it by now. But what reason would he have to doom Indham?

"Maybe Beorhtel," Wulfnoth said. "Maybe someone else." He sighed like he thought the world was coming to an end. Once, he had been a man of optimism, with nothing that could bring him down.

Things had changed.

Too many things were changing of late, and not for the better. Aern's end was merely the capstone for what had amounted to the worst decade of Idmaer's life. He had fallen away from Edoma, the Council was turning against him, and the populace hated him most of all. Maybe life had always been bad. Maybe the truth of life's vapidity had been shrouded in the ignorance of youth.

In the distance, he spotted his spire. It called out to him, urging him to return. Taking the medallion in hand, he ran his fingers over the number eight fashioned into the gold. An energy coursed through him as he did so. He had been gone too long from his old friend.

"How do you reckon they did it?" Wulfnoth asked. "Saega never said what happened in Mundos."

"I'm not sure he knows. As far as I'm aware, it was the

same as here. A mysterious person with no apparent motive."

"Except death and destruction."

Unable to help himself, Idmaer chuckled. Did Wulfnoth really believe there were people who simply wanted to see others suffer? No, the world was not so black and white. "Regardless, the people are without protection. I fear they will learn the truth soon. And what then? I doubt even my spire would be able to stop them from bringing me to account."

"It would be terrible to learn that their god is dead. I find myself lying awake at night wondering how it could be."

"Aern was no god. He was merely a force locked within a crystal cage."

"The Guardians aren't gods?"

Idmaer shrugged. "Maybe they were once. Maybe they were never gods. All I know is that they don't deserve our worship. In truth, I think them energies. Like fire or lightning."

"Elements, then?"

"You could call them that."

"Never thought I'd see the day High Priest Idmaer lost the faith."

Idmaer wanted to say he'd never thought he'd see Wulfnoth turn into a drunkard, but he left it unsaid. He removed the false orb from his pocket and placed it within the golden hands. It looked much like Aern's orb, but that wouldn't matter. The dulled wards and the broken pillars would be enough to tell anyone that Aern was no longer present. Guards would need to be stationed at the bottom of the steps as they had been before.

"Still don't see why someone would do it," Wulfnoth said as he kicked a pebble over the precipice.

"Knowing why will not bring another Guardian to take his place." Still, the question was an intriguing one. What could they gain? Idmaer stepped away from the altar and into the outer circle. "You haven't spoken to anyone about what happened here?"

Wulfnoth shook his head. "This is far beyond me. I doubt anyone would believe me even if I spoke of it."

"Don't go testing that theory," Idmaer said. "Only scant few know what really happened. It must remain that way."

"The warriors we sent to Eosorheim don't know, either. What happens if that same killer has already been through there?"

"Then their quest will fail." Though he doubted Hurn would allow Eosor to be killed. He was a mage of legend with unspeakable power. Then again, whoever had killed Aern would also be powerful beyond measure.

"I've known you for a while now," Wulfnoth said, "but I'm only just starting to think you don't know what you're doing."

A smile touched Idmaer's lips. *You wouldn't be the only one to think that.* He had been playing along for much of his life, feeling like an impostor.

"I saw something else to the north when I was tracking the giant," Wulfnoth said. "A group of people were traveling south. About fifty of them. They've caravans and things. Not bandits, by the looks of it, mostly women and children." There had been no crows to arrive in Indham to state that there was a large group of travelers. "I thought maybe they were a traveling circus, but there were no beasts among them besides horses. Think maybe they're escaping from something, like those from the North did eighteen years ago?"

Idmaer turned to look out over Indham. He remembered when the barefooted wanderers came. Their faces had been painted in what Idmaer now realized were dulled wards. Their bodies were still alive, their hearts still beating, but their eyes were vacant. Soulless bodies doomed to wander the world with their tongues falling from their mouths. They'd lasted a month before Idmaer decided it was a mercy to kill them. Their children had been spared, and had then come to be called the Fatherless.

"What if they knock on our doors," Wulfnoth asked, "demanding asylum?"

"The Council won't let them through the gates. Not after I convinced them to let the Fatherless in last time."

It had only been through his and Edoma's combined efforts that the Fatherless hadn't been cast out from the town. Much of the gold in the spire's storeroom had been used to employ them, gold that was required for trading goods since Indham had no farmlands. Because of that, the rest of the Council still harbored ill will toward Idmaer. The Fatherless's propensity for crime had only made the feeling fester over time until the others eventually showed open hatred toward him.

"By all that is holy, what is that?" Wulfnoth pointed at a cloud moving across the sky. It gave off light, as if fire writhed within it. The entire town below it was bathed in a crimson glow.

"The wraiths," Idmaer cried.

He rushed down the hill's steps and mounted his horse. The mist hovered above the town while Idmaer and Wulfnoth spurred their steeds onward.

A few hours later, they entered the town gates. The crimson cloud remained above them as if a storm were waiting to break. The air was thick with fog and smelled like sulfur.

"Get inside your homes," Idmaer yelled as he galloped through the cobblestone streets to his spire.

A figure was veiled in the spire's shadow. It was Edoma, waiting in the garden with her horse. She wore a heavy cloak, though her nightclothes were still visible beneath it.

"You saw them, too?" Idmaer asked as he reined in his horse.

"They'll be upon us in a few hours, maybe less." Painted wards, deep red and glowing with arcane power, slashed across her face.

This was it. The wraiths had finally come to Indham.

"We are doomed," Wulfnoth said from behind him.

A wail split the air, followed by shouting from a few streets away. The crimson mist was descending. The shouting increased in volume and then subsided into an eerie silence.

"It seems the wraiths have already arrived," Edoma said. "There is hope yet. I can construct wards around Enlil's Temple to keep the wraiths out. We should be able to fit everyone inside. At least for tonight. But we must be quick. Already the wraiths are taking hosts."

Another cry sounded.

"We need to go to Merefin's barn and get lambs," Idmaer said, his hands shaking as he clenched the horse's reins. "How many will we need?"

"Lamb blood won't hold them off. We'll need something with a stronger essence."

Idmaer's stomach clenched. "What kind of blood?"

"Human. There are dead folk's bodies for the funeral pyres. We can use them."

"That's sacrilege," Wulfnoth whispered.

Edoma ignored Wulfnoth's accusation and mounted her horse. "Sacrilege might save our people this night."

20

HIROC

EALSTAN'S expression wavered, as though he, too, had felt the ethereal chill. His hand stopped playing with the knife's pommel. His fingers gripped it until they became as white as the bone it was carved from. "What was that?" he whispered, his voice flickering.

Shouting filtered from outside. Hiroc grunted at Ealstan. He had also felt the chill, but he wasn't about to show his fear to the other man. He stood and walked outside, following the shouting.

Three men were gathered in the alleyway, arguing with each other. Even through the fog, Hiroc recognized Oswin, the shortest of the three men. The other pair of men was middle-aged and covered in grime, one with a drooping belly peeking out from the bottom of his filthy tunic, and the other a muscular man whose face was hidden beneath wild hair.

Hiroc turned to Ealstan, who was trying to peer over his shoulder and into the alleyway.

"I'll deal with this," Hiroc said, squaring his shoulders to further obstruct Ealstan's view.

Ealstan pouted, his thin mustache like a little worm above pursed lips. He grunted before leaving the hall.

Hiroc shut the back door and returned his gaze to the alleyway. Big Belly was still yelling, prodding Oswin's chest with a grimy finger. As soon as Hiroc stepped out from the eatery, he was struck by the scent of sulfur. He couldn't place where the smell was coming from, so he ignored it.

"What's going on here?" he asked. He was careful to keep his tone level. It would be unwise to reveal his relationship with Oswin.

Oswin nodded at Big Belly and Wild Hair. "These two accused me of lurking around the Basilica."

Hiroc reared back at the stench of ale on his breath. Not only was his friend trespassing, but he was also drunk.

"So I punched him," Oswin said, as though that were the only reasonable reaction.

Hiroc rolled his eyes. It was typical of Oswin to go around punching people who disagreed with him.

"Then you are all guilty of trespassing," Hiroc said to them all. He let his gaze linger on Oswin for a moment. He wanted Oswin to know how foolish it was to enter the Basilica District. "Do you know the punishment for being in holy areas?"

Big Belly stepped forward and pointed an accusatory finger at Oswin. "This pretty-boy is the one who's trespassing. Not us. We were fixing the roof from the flooding. High Priest Idmaer ordered us to do it." He removed a parchment from his pocket and handed it to Hiroc. It was a cleaning notice, signed by Idmaer.

Hiroc peered at the alley. Tools were scattered along the ground, and a ladder leaned against the fence. Wild Hair was lurking in the background. He seemed to have grown uninterested in the fight; either that or he was acting guilty about something. Regardless, the laborers had a better reason for being here than Oswin.

Hiroc turned to his friend, making pains to hide their relationship behind a gruff tone. "You need to leave now before I call the guards. These two have a legitimate reason for being here. You do not."

"I needed to speak with you," Oswin whispered. The next few sentences were a mess of garbled syllables as he seemed to lose control of his tongue. ". . . rumors you saw something at the altar. Figured better to speak with you than someone else. You weren't at The Flaming Monkey, so I decided to come 'ere. Thought something happened to you. I wasn't planning on making this public, but these two saw me." Oswin nodded at the laborers obscured behind the growing fog.

"Quit your whispering," a deep voice said, coming from behind the fog. "This Fatherless owes us an apology."

A muscle-laden arm shot out from the fog and grabbed Hiroc by the shoulder. A fist slugged him across the chin. His vision sparked before clearing to another meaty fist. He ducked and drove his own fist into the mist. He felt it plunge into something soft and fleshy, followed by a cry of pain.

Hiroc spun around. Wild Hair's face materialized from within the mist. Oswin grabbed Wild Hair's shoulders, while Hiroc uppercut his jaw. Wild Hair dropped to the ground, unconscious and twitching. There was no sign of Big Belly. He had probably turned tail when things had become violent.

"Well, I reckon we've had our fun tonight." Oswin wiped his hands. "How about we go to The Flaming Monkey now? I think I'm starting to grow sober."

Hiroc rubbed his jaw where the man had struck him. "I'll meet you there. I have to deal with these two first." He couldn't be seen fighting, especially on the backend of Ealstan's threats. He needed to get Oswin out of there quickly and then have someone send the laborers outside the Basilica District.

Something let out a deep growl behind Oswin. Wild Hair appeared, hands raised. His fingernails were so long, they looked like talons. He growled again, revealing canines sharp enough to belong to a wolf.

"Now I know I'm not sober," Oswin said, shaking his head.

Wild Hair slashed at Oswin with his clawed hands. Jumping back, Oswin dodged the attack. Hiroc touched his ring as Oswin grabbed Wild Hair's wrist and spun him around.

"Help me," Oswin yelled.

Hiroc let go of his ring. Together, Oswin and Hiroc managed to pin Wild Hair against the ground. He thrashed against their grips. Hiroc looked down at the man's hands. The blade-like nails were covered in blood. Human nails lay on the ground, along with two dozen fragments of human teeth. In a matter of minutes, Wild Hair had changed into this vicious man-beast.

"Where'd the other one go?" Oswin said through clenched teeth. Before Hiroc could answer, the mists swayed in the wind, revealing Big Belly face down in a pool of blood. Deep cuts slashed across his stomach.

Wild Hair struggled. His skin rippled and grew transparent. Veins pressed against the surface of his face. His blood glowed like hot coals.

"What's wrong with him?" Oswin asked, clearly terrified.

Wild Hair screamed a series of guttural words in a language Hiroc had never heard. He spat and frothed at the mouth. Even with the two of them using all of their strength, they were having trouble keeping him down. A crack sounded when the man's shoulder bent the wrong way. He didn't cry out. He continued to struggle despite the injury, oblivious to what must have been excruciating pain.

"Hiroc!" a female voice called from behind.

Hiroc looked over his shoulder. Carrying a staff, Mother Superior Edoma stepped from the acolyte's eating hall and into the alley. Her dress was covered in blood. Runes drawn in harsh lines on her face shone crimson in the low light—two half-circles with a spider in the center. Those same runes marked the tip of her staff, making it flare like a torch.

"Get to the temple," Edoma shouted. She seemed oblivious to the man they were holding down. "If you see anyone else along the way, tell them to—"

Wild Hair's eyes shot open, and he wailed like a banshee.

Hiroc touched his ring and whispered, "Enlil, deity of the sacred flame, hear me—"

Edoma pushed him back before he could finish the incantation. "That man's not human anymore." She swung the staff onto Wild Hair's neck. With a crack, his neck snapped. Twitching, he seemed to be completely paralyzed. Edoma grabbed a wineskin from her belt and emptied its contents around Wild Hair. Mouth agape, Hiroc could only watch as she quickly drew a ward onto the ground and dragged a convulsing Wild Hair onto it. A final crack with the staff and Wild Hair's skull caved in. A crimson mist trailed from his corpse before vanishing. It left behind a strong smell of sulfur.

"A great evil has descended upon Indham," Edoma said as she leaned on the staff. Her breathing was ragged. "It possessed this man. The wards destroyed it."

"You killed him," Hiroc said.

"That man was dead as soon as the spirit took him."

Was she avoiding calling that thing a wraith? That's surely what it had been.

Four Daughters of Enlil filtered out into the alleyway. They were also wearing bloodstained clothing and bore the same wards on their faces.

Edoma nodded at Big Belly's corpse and said to the Daughters, "Take the clean man to the temple. His blood will be useful there."

Hiroc stepped in front of the Daughters. "What do you mean to do with him? Human blood should not be used in sacrifices."

"We aren't sacrificing him," Edoma said. "Go to Enlil's Temple. If Idmaer thinks it necessary, you will learn more there."

21

EDOMA

EDOMA guided Indham's people through the temple gates. Outside the gates was a rune circle she had painted. It glowed whenever someone possessed by a wraith tried to pass. They were then bound and imprisoned inside the temple's stables by warded warriors, to be dealt with later.

"Take anyone who makes the wards glow out back," Bertram, captain of the warrior's watch, said to a group of fresh warriors. Those they'd come to relieve were wide-eyed and trembling. They'd been forced to kill many they'd called friends who had turned. Some had even hewn down family members.

Feeling herself growing faint, Edoma started walking to the temple for water. She watched as a warrior took a woman by the chains that shackled her wrists and ankles. The woman snarled like a rabid wolf and wrenched against her bonds.

"You cannot take my wife," a frail pilgrim cried out, slamming his fists against the warrior's back. His wife's hands clawed at the ground. Edoma gasped when she saw the woman's nails pull away from her fingers, embedded in the stone.

"Mother Edoma," the old pilgrim called out, "you must

stop them from taking my dear Elena."

"I cannot," Edoma said. "She is taken by plague." It wasn't the first time that night she had told someone that a loved one had been stricken by plague. This one was far along and was difficult to hold down. She spotted a warrior who couldn't decide where to start. "Help him." Edoma pointed to the warrior struggling with the crazed woman.

"She's a noble," the other warrior replied. He was a young man, probably not much older than the age of admittance.

But he was right. While the woman was wearing the plain garb that all pilgrims wore, she bore the look of a noble from Winhurst. It didn't matter. There was no such thing as highborn or lowborn now. Clean or unclean. Human or skinwalker. That's all that mattered now.

"Do it," Edoma said to him.

This time, he obeyed. He ran after the chained woman and helped his comrade drag her out of sight. Edoma knew the people would be safe even though the skinwalkers were within the temple. When they were executed, the wraiths would vanish because the temple's boundaries were warded.

Taking the old pilgrim's hand, Edoma took him to the crypt. She gave him words of comfort that didn't seem to touch his ears. He shifted through the mass of other pilgrims busy bickering over blame for the night's calamity.

In the next room were the Council members. Edoma was glad none of them had become skinwalkers. Executing a Council member would have surely sent the town into civil war. Some demanded to know what Edoma was thinking with imprisoning folk and forcing everyone else to sleep in the temple that night. Such objections were quickly silenced after a handful of terrifying accounts about those who had become skinwalkers. In the morning, they would learn that the warriors weren't just imprisoning people.

The warriors and priests had been sent to the rear rooms where the Daughters of Enlil normally slept. When

Edoma visited them, they were on the verge of a fight, so she commanded the priests to take the northern commons, and the warriors the southern.

"A good choice, separating them," Saega said. Each heavy breath was dry and raspy. "It seems the lamb's blood didn't work. I'm afraid I only ever used the blood of cattle for my magic. It was always sufficient. I suppose protection magic requires something stronger."

"I know that now," she said. "I'm afraid I don't know how strong human blood is. There's not an endless supply of it." She thought about what she'd seen in Mundos and shuddered.

"Human blood will provide protection for a night. I wouldn't risk anything longer than that. You'll have to ward the buildings every day. You don't have anything stronger available? Dragon blood, perhaps? That would last at least a week."

Edoma considered Saega's words. She did have something.

Leaving Saega behind, Edoma went to her personal chambers. A chest was at her bed's foot. All her most precious belongings lay inside it. She unlatched the lock and heaved open the lid. Avoiding the shiny allure of the scrying crystal, she removed a small vial. A dark liquid sloshed within it—onyx dragon blood. There was only a tiny amount, but it would be enough should she absolutely need it. At most, a few people could be warded with it. It was the strongest blood she had available. Or, at least, the strongest blood she was willing to use.

Edoma came to the nave and was immediately relieved. There was a quietness there. No one was bickering. Unlike the others, they knew something dreadful had come, and the only thing that might stop it was prayer. They were kneeling before icons of Enlil's Flame. Families huddled together, their hands linked, while they petitioned for mercy.

The sight brought a tear to Edoma's eye.

The quest was interrupted as Idmaer stepped forward to speak. "It's too dangerous to be in your homes this evening. A terrible plague has come upon us that makes the sane lose their minds. Edoma and her Daughters, along with the warriors, have ensured that anyone who bore the signs has been imprisoned." Idmaer paused, adjusting the First Priest's medallion at his neck. "My condolences for those you have lost to the plague already. These were unavoidable casualties. If we learn that the plague cannot be cured, then the worst may happen."

Why did he always have to be so cold and unemotional?

A man Edoma recognized from the docks stood. "What will you do if we leave the temple? Will you have the warriors imprison us like they did our kin?"

A chorus of agreement broke out. People started to argue until it became so loud that Edoma could barely think.

Edoma put two fingers in her mouth and whistled. There was silence. "Leaving the temple tonight is out of the question," she said. "Without the wards you see on my face and the faces of others helping me, you will catch the plague."

Even so, a group of fishermen stood. The tugging hands of their wives and daughters were ignored. Their departure earned a few envious glances, but no one followed them.

Edoma shuffled through the people and stood next to Idmaer. The wards on his face still burned crimson, producing their own light.

He turned toward her. "Do you know of any other ways that we might determine who has become a skinwalker? The wards light up, but that is . . . insufficient."

Edoma glanced at the children at her feet. This wasn't the kind of thing to speak about where children could overhear. She took Idmaer to the kitchens since it was the only place not filled with people.

"There are scrying crystals that can detect wraiths within people," she said. "It takes the soul to another place—a world between worlds. But I cannot use it. There is a darkness inside it, a desire to consume completely. I fear if I was to enter that realm, I might not return." Why was she telling him this? It was more information that might lead to him learning that she was a mage.

"A librarian's apprentice shouldn't know all this," Idmaer said, confirming her fears. "You know of scrying crystals that take you to a world beyond our own. And the wards. Deep magic runs through these. What were you really when you were in Mundos?"

Edoma turned away. From the moment she'd first met him all those years ago, every time Idmaer had asked her a question about her past, she had evaded it. She had only ever given him snippets, and they were mostly inconsequential tidbits. Lies had been mostly avoided, but some had been necessary.

"You still have no knowledge of who shattered the orb?" Edoma asked, wanting to bring the conversation elsewhere. She doubted he would know any more than she did, but finding out who had done it was still important, although less so now that the wraiths had arrived.

"None at all." He appraised her with his gaze as if he had known her intention for asking the question. "Wulfnoth found no evidence at the altar, only the broken remnants of Aern's orb. When he was tracking the giant, he saw a caravan of about fifty people traveling along the southwestern road. He thought them from Winhurst. If true, I can't understand why the city's signal fires weren't lit."

"The wraiths must have come in large numbers. I was perfecting the wards so that when the beacons were lit, I could ward all the major buildings in Indham. Winhurst's beacons might have saved those who became skinwalkers tonight."

"You mean their possession is final?"

Edoma nodded mournfully. "I know of no cure. What they once were, the wraiths have snuffed out. We can execute those we've captured in warded zones. Either that or we can wait until morning. The wraiths disintegrate when within warded zones. As creatures of the night, they also cannot remain in this world during the day."

"They die?"

Edoma sniffed. "That would be too easy. No, they just go elsewhere."

"Where?"

Edoma shrugged. She had told him most of what she knew about the wraiths. They used the skinwalkers as hosts to walk in the mortal world in places they could not otherwise go. It was only carcaern orbs that kept both wraiths and skinwalkers out. And those didn't exactly grow on trees. She'd never heard of an orb being replaced. Even though it had been twenty years, Mundos was likely as desolate as the Scorched Lands. Probably overrun with creatures of the dark and other foul things that the wraiths didn't care to torment.

"Let's hope that the warriors made it to Eosorheim before the wraiths came," Idmaer said.

Feeling her hands grow sticky, Edoma rubbed them on her robes. "I fear the wards I painted on Alfric and the others were insufficient."

"What do you mean insufficient?" Idmaer's jaw clenched, and he clutched his medallion.

She struggled with the words that would suitably admit her oversight. How could she have known? Saega had told her that lamb's blood would suffice. It would be more appropriate to blame him than her.

"You used lamb's blood, but human blood is required," Idmaer said, answering his own question. "That's why they were insufficient." Anger boiled behind his eyes.

"It has been three days now—maybe they've already arrived in Eosorheim," Edoma said. Her answer had seemed to placate Idmaer's anger. "There is nothing at all we can do now to assist the warriors in their quest. We can only hope and continue to do our best to help those here."

"How long before we can have the other buildings warded?"

"It's too dangerous to be out there now. We'll have to wait until morning. The wards are only a temporary measure. They'll last the night. Tomorrow I will make more. Unless we decide to sacrifice a number of our own for protection, we're going to run out of blood. There aren't enough dead to last longer than a month."

"I'll have your spire warded," she said. Despite how much she didn't want to seem like she was giving him preference, the spire was the largest building in the town. Idmaer wouldn't like it, but if she were warding the spire, then he would have to fill the rooms with people. But she would tell him that tomorrow. She realized then that maybe the skinwalkers wouldn't need to be executed. They could be kept within the spire's dungeons. At least that would ensure those wraiths couldn't possess more people. It would also keep the populace from thinking their loved ones had been put to death.

Idmaer raised an eyebrow. "And here I was thinking you no longer cared for me."

Edoma bowed her head to hide her scowl. "You are the High Priest of Aern. I think it necessary that you receive protection," she said sarcastically.

"And a great lot of good Aern does for us now." He hadn't seemed to notice her mockery.

"These skinwalkers will need to be contained. We can't go killing them—the people will riot. Can you have them in your dungeons?"

Idmaer shuddered. "Those things are monsters. I'm not sure I'll ever have an unbroken night's sleep again." He stroked his beard. "If human blood can be used in the warding, can't we simply use bloodletting? Leeches?"

"Leeches would taint the blood. It's the same reason skinwalker blood cannot be used. They are parasites." At least that much she remembered from her schooling.

"Surely one of the mechanisms within the spire's dungeons is capable of bleeding someone out without killing them?"

"And who would volunteer for such a thing? Will you be the first?"

"We don't need volunteers," he said.

Edoma shuddered. "Never again," she whispered, refusing to think about what she had seen in Mundos all those years ago. The people had been lied to then, too. It had been a disaster. When they had found out, there was a riot unlike anything she'd ever seen. It was almost worse than the wraiths. Humans were capable of terrible evils even without demons possessing them.

22

FRYDA

THE sunset bathed Indham's walls in golden light. Fryda thanked Enlil that she and Jaruman had made it back safely.

"Halt!" a voice cried out from the parapets.

Jaruman cursed and kept riding. "I'm not stopping for anyone until I get inside my tavern. Rowena has probably run the place into the ground."

"Don't you think we should listen to them?" Fryda said, searching for whoever had made the call from above.

"I've been here twenty years. I know every one of them warriors on the walls. I won't allow them to play their games with me."

Many times Fryda had experienced Jaruman's grumpiness when he didn't get sleep. She could understand how tired he was—she felt much the same. But he was going to get them into trouble if he wasn't careful.

As they drew closer to the entrance gates, Fryda spotted a circle of wards outside. They were so large that anyone going through the gates would have to step onto them. The iron doors were closed. The last time she'd seen them like that was when the bandits had attacked the town.

"Halt!" the voice called again.

Before they could get any closer, an arrow thudded into the dirt in front of them.

Fryda stopped her horse, but Jaruman kept riding.

"I know they're better marksman than that," he said over his shoulder to Fryda. "If they wanted to hit me, they would have." He looked up at the walls. "Which one of you decided it was a good idea to fire an arrow at me?"

Faces marked with wards peered down from the parapets. There were close to twenty warriors up there, all wearing their customary green hoods. Half of them had arrows nocked, ready to fire. There were more warriors than Fryda had ever seen guarding the entrance to Indham.

The gates lurched open. Out stepped Bertram, captain of the warrior's watch. It was often said that Bertram was given the job because he was the only warrior who couldn't hunt. Fryda wasn't sure whether that was true, but she'd seen him around enough to know that even if he could hunt, he was allured by Indham's dark side.

During the day, pilgrimages were made to either Tyme's Hill or Enlil's Temple. The real fun, it was said, happened at night. Fryda had never been wherever "real fun" was meant to happen, but she knew people who had. Their stories never sounded like much fun at all. Drunken fights, sex with strangers, and other things she didn't want to think about. It was all part of living in a town where people came to seek forgiveness from the gods and do penance. Sometimes, people fell. Hard.

"You getting deaf in your old age?" Bertram said to Jaruman as he walked out, a longbow in one hand. He stopped behind the rune circle so that it was between them. He was grinning, the wards on his face making him look like a blue-headed fool. "I told you to halt, old man. I'll let you off this time. Idmaer's given me—" He stopped and stared at Fryda. The way his eyes meandered about her body made her skin crawl. "So you went off to fetch yourself a young bride while the rest of us are fighting..." He paused, as though wondering whether to tell Jaruman what manner of foe troubled Indham.

"We've been doing our own share of fighting," Jaruman said. As soon as he urged the horse forward, Bertram's hand shot over his shoulder and drew an arrow from his quiver. The bowstring grew taut as Bertram pointed the drawn arrow at Jaruman's head. From that short a distance, it wouldn't matter if Bertram was the worst shot in the world, the arrow would find a mark.

"Not a step farther," he said.

Unconcerned, Jaruman's gaze crept down to the rune circle. "So the wraiths have come to Indham, have they?"

"How do you know about that?" Bertram said, his arrow still pointed at Jaruman. "We told folks about a plague. Seems you know a little too much. You have anything to do with Aern becoming weak? You weren't born here, so you're not one of us. In all the years you've been running that tavern, I never seen you visit the hill either."

"You're not one for devotion yourself," Jaruman responded. He looked like he was willing to risk an arrow if it meant getting his hands on Bertram. "I've seen you crawling around the alley."

Bertram's arm trembled, as though he were getting tired of keeping his arrow nocked. He wasn't grinning anymore.

Sweat trickled down Fryda's spine. She didn't like the way the two men were staring at each other. Nor did she like the warriors gathered on the walls. Their expressions were grim. If the wraiths had come, then Indham's people would be on edge. This could get bloody very quickly.

"You're mighty lucky not to have become one of them skinwalkers," Bertram said, eying them suspiciously as if he didn't quite believe they weren't skinwalkers. "Now, get down from your horses. The both of you."

While Fryda and Jaruman dismounted, Bertram called

out to the warriors on the walls. A minute later, they filtered out through the gates. Like Bertram, they remained on the other side of the ward circle. They held arrows to their bows, eyes watching. Every one of them appeared rattled. Fryda didn't blame them. They'd seen skinwalkers. The memory of Alfric, moving like a spider, came to her. She forced it back. Dealing with it now was out of the question.

"I'm reminding you both that Indham is under attack," Bertram said. "Neither of you are of any importance. Should you try and avoid the conditions of entry, you will be shot. My men here need the target practice anyway." His smile had returned. None of the other warriors joined him in smiling. It made Bertram all the more unsettling.

Leaning his bow against the iron gate, Bertram walked across the ward circle to Fryda. Her eyes narrowed as he stopped only a pace away from her. The scent of ale drifted from his breath. He was close enough that she could see the cancer sores cracking on his nose.

"You are a pretty little thing," he whispered.

From the corner of her eye, Fryda saw Jaruman bristle. She hoped he wouldn't be foolish enough to try something with the warriors' bows trained on them. "I am sworn to Enlil," she said. It wasn't actually true since novices hadn't made final vows, but she wanted Bertram to back down and get the "conditions of entry" over with.

"Don't even try it, Bertram," said Jaruman.

"High Priest Idmaer has given my full reign over who comes and goes through these gates. These are perilous times we're living in."

"They'll be much more perilous for you if you lay a finger on her."

Bertram smiled and reached toward Fryda. His hand came within a few inches of Fryda's breasts, but she slapped it away. A rushing sound passed her head. Jaruman's horse screamed, an arrow quivering in its side.

In a blur, Jaruman grabbed Bertram in an arm-lock. One hand kept Bertram in place and the other pressed a knife to his throat.

"You're going to let us pass," Jaruman said. "We're not skinwalkers."

"Now you've gone and assaulted the captain of the warrior's watch. You're not leaving here alive."

Fryda had to admire his conviction. A knife to the throat and he wasn't trying to weasel his way out.

The injured horse, lying on its side now as blood seeped from the wound, scraped its front hooves against the ground. It screamed again, the sound putting Fryda's teeth on edge.

"Would one of you deal with that thing?" Bertram said.

A warrior's arrow pierced the horse through the eye, and it died with a flutter of its tail.

"If we're not getting out of this alive, then neither are you," Jaruman said, gritting his teeth. But there was no conviction in his voice. He glanced at Fryda, concern filling his brown eyes.

"Let him go," Fryda said to Jaruman. "He's a despicable rat, but Idmaer's put him in charge of guarding the walls."

One of the warriors put down his bow and called out, "The woman is a novice with the Daughters. If Mother Edoma finds out . . ."

Bertram seemed to grow uncomfortable. Jaruman's knife still at his throat, he said, "I won't have the men kill you."

"On your word," said Jaruman.

"Aye, on my word."

Jaruman dropped the knife. With a shove, Bertram went tumbling. He stood and brushed down his tunic and breeches. Narrowing his eyes, he grabbed a throwing ax from the belt of a nearby warrior and pointed it at Jaruman. "Step on the wards. You first, and then the bitch."

Jaruman's face reddened with rage, but he obeyed. The wards remained the same as he stood on them.

"Looks like you're clean," Bertram said. The ax blade turned upon Fryda. "Your turn now."

Fryda shifted over to the ward circle. As soon as both feet were within it, a warmth rushed through her. The wards burst with light. They dulled again almost immediately.

"Don't move," Bertram said to her. A nod over his shoulder sent the warriors fixing arrows to their bows. Jaruman protested but was cut off. "Don't test me, old man. You said you did your share of fighting. You see any wraith clouds while you were out there?"

"We saw one," Jaruman said. He swallowed loudly. He seemed to have realized just how dire their situation was. "But none of them came for us."

Fryda's eyes were fixed on a warrior's arrow a half-dozen feet from her. There were at least a dozen other arrows, but that one was the closest. It would likely be the first to kill her.

"Fryda!" Robes clutched in both hands, Edoma ran through the gates. "What's the meaning of this?"

"These two were trying to get through the gates without the necessary processes," Bertram said.

Edoma looked from Jaruman to Fryda. "I didn't even know you were gone . . ." Her face paled as the wards buzzed again beneath Fryda's feet. She stared at them as if trying to discern something. Her shoulders dropped, and she exhaled. "You're unharmed. It must have been a powerful skinwalker to leave such a strong trace that the ward circle would pick it up."

"We dealt with it," Jaruman said. He gave Fryda a meaningful look that reiterated the promise she had made not to tell Edoma about Alfric. "Actually, Fryda's horse dealt with it."

Edoma looked at the horse with an arrow through its head and another through its side.

"Not that one," Jaruman said. "That was the fine work of these warriors. It was the other one."

Fryda turned and beckoned Flight. She had been watching while the events played out, but now she clopped over to Fryda.

"A beautiful animal," Edoma said.

"If it's all the same to you lot, we've got things to do." Bertram turned up his nose.

"Thank you for your diligence," Edoma said. "You'll have your men deal with the remains of the horse they butchered?"

Bertram grunted and left, the warriors following behind him.

Edoma turned to Fryda, her face hardened by anger. "What were you doing outside the walls? You could have been killed, or worse—been taken by a wraith." Jaruman went to speak, but Edoma snapped at him. "And you went with her? I never took you for a fool. You've seen what the wraiths can do."

Surprised by Edoma's sudden wrath, Fryda stepped back.

"You're not to leave the temple until all this is sorted," Edoma said to her. "You're not a free spirit. You've given yourself to Enlil. The temple is where you belong."

"I'm still a novice."

"And you'll be one forever if you continue."

"I may be a Daughter," Fryda said, clenching her fists, "but I'm not *your* daughter."

Edoma's eyes bubbled with tears, but none fell. She sniffed and stormed through the gates.

The anger drained from Fryda. Now that she was thinking clearly, she thanked Enlil she hadn't said anything about Alfric.

Jaruman glared at the men atop the parapets. "Had you not been here, I might have wet my blade with their blood."

"Then I'm glad I was here." She sighed. "Edoma seemed so angry."

"I suppose that means you won't be coming back to the tavern for a drink."

Fryda shook her head. "I doubt I'll be able to go back there for a while. Maybe not ever."

"Remember what I said. Not a word of Alfric to Edoma."

Fryda didn't see how it would be possible to keep the promise. Eventually, Edoma would ask what she and Jaruman had been doing outside the gates. Then she would have to tell her more about the skinwalker that had touched her. Fryda doubted she would be able to contain her emotions if it came to speaking about that particular skinwalker.

23

HIROC

THE domes of Enlil's Temple greeted Hiroc as he walked through the gates. He kept his eyes forward while maneuvering around the Daughters and their machines. It was a task made all the more difficult by the sound of crunching bones and the trickling of blood. By the time he reached the temple itself, sweat had glued his robes to his skin. He glanced back and immediately regretted it.

A Daughter pushed her weight against a crank, and gears squeaked as they turned. Hanging from the top of the barbaric mechanism was a fresh corpse—a woman, not much older than twenty. The machine had consumed everything from the waist down. As the Daughter turned the crank, the corpse descended. The corpse's eyes were open, and her tongue drooped over her mouth. The puncture wounds in her neck made it clear how she had died. Another victim of the skinwalkers.

The pupils moved. Hiroc's heart stopped until he realized that the black circles had been collections of flies eating at the soft matter.

Wiping her forehead, the Daughter met Hiroc's eyes. The corner of her mouth turned up into a smile. Had seeing his disgust pleased her?

Struggling to hold his breakfast in, Hiroc entered the temple. He hadn't visited it since he became an acolyte of the Holy Order. Not because he didn't like Edoma or the Daughters—they'd been good to him all his life—rather, visiting Enlil's Temple was improper for someone consecrated to Aern.

Sometimes Hiroc wondered whether he had made a mistake in choosing to become an acolyte of Aern. Ever since he was a child, he had a burning desire to please the gods, and it wasn't like he could have become a Daughter. The equipment between his legs forbade that.

But Enlil had been the one to respond to his call, not Aern. The fire from the heavens had come at Enlil's name. The fire inside the Basilica commons had only reached out to him after calling upon Enlil. Invoking Aern had done nothing.

Hiroc found the nearest Daughter. She was cleaning a statue of Enlil—a figure bathed in azure flames. The depiction was often called "the burning man." She looked at Hiroc's robes with surprise. This Daughter had none of the confidence as the one outside.

"I'm not here to cause trouble," he said. Tensions between the Holy Order and the Daughters had grown lately. Those pilgrims who had been in Indham to pay homage to Aern had been forbidden from going to Tyme's Hill. Many had decided to offer their alms to Enlil instead. Things had only gotten worse after the wraiths had come two nights ago and Edoma had offered everyone refuge inside the temple. "Where is Mother Edoma?"

The Daughter seemed relieved. "She's in the library."

Walking the hallowed halls, marked with ancient paintings of the burning man, reminded Hiroc of being a child. Smiling, he remembered racing through the temple with Alfric, stolen cakes from the kitchen sitting at the bottom of their bellies, while the Daughters tried to catch them. But the brothers were too fast.

Even though it had been four days ago, Hiroc's betrayal at the gates still made him feel ill. Where was Alfric now? Had he made it Eosorheim? Or had the wraiths gotten to him like they had so many others? The dungeons of Idmaer's Spire held at least a dozen skinwalkers now. But Hiroc didn't allow himself to think anything except good things about Alfric's quest. Anything other than thoughts of success wouldn't do.

The library was at the top level of the temple, a gangway stretching from one corner to the other until it ended in a grand entrance arch. Along the archway were the words: *Seek Knowledge and Prosper.* Hiroc entered through the archway, hoping it wouldn't take too long to find Edoma.

Luckily, he soon found her tucked away in one of the many inlets. She was bent over a number of books that were lying face open on a table. She didn't look up as he stepped toward her.

Hiroc cleared his throat, and she glanced up, startled. When her deep brown eyes recognized him, she smiled. "Hiroc, how are you faring?" She always smiled at him with a mother's care. It was an expression she gave all the Fatherless.

"Well—considering the circumstances. The acolytes have you to thank for warding the Basilica." He didn't know how Edoma knew that the wards would stop the wraith clouds or where she got the knowledge of the wards in the first place. Maybe from one of those books. Or maybe she had always known how to make the wards. She was a very mysterious woman, after all. Regardless, every single person in Indham— at least those who hadn't become skinwalkers or been killed by one—had prospered from her knowledge. It was this knowledge that had brought Hiroc to the temple.

"I did what I could," she said. "I'm researching more about wards now." She peered back down at the books with a frown. "I cannot seem to find what I'm after."

"There *are* a lot of books here." The library was the largest Hall in all of Indham. Shelves filled the room, and every one of them was overflowing with books. It was in this very room that Edoma had taught Hiroc to read. He still wasn't very good, and he could only read in the common tongue.

"How very astute of you." Taking a book in hand, she peeled it open and started flipping through the pages. After a few agonizing moments with Hiroc trying to think how to phrase his question, Edoma lifted an eyebrow and gave him a wry smile. "I don't expect you came just to watch me read."

Hiroc paused for a moment, thinking how best to say it. "I want to know more about the Talented."

The book slipped from Edoma's hand, falling to the table with a thud. A hand pressed against her mouth. "You are . . ."

Right then, he knew he had made a mistake. Of course she would have thought he was Talented after he'd asked that question. He had reasoned with himself for many hours before deciding that Edoma would be the best person to speak with about such a matter. She was probably the only one he could trust not to send a raven to Lamworth. It was still a risk he shouldn't have taken. He should have been more tactful. Instead of lacing his words with honey, he had told Edoma outright.

Hiroc's mind filled with the image of King Beorhtel's inquisitors, clad in golden robes and astride white horses, coming to collect him. There would be no point fighting.

Before he could think up a lie, Edoma reached out and touched his arm. Heat burst from her fingertips, even through his robes. But it bore no pain. It was the warmth that followed the swallow of strong firewine.

She pulled her hand back and nodded. "You are Talented." Sighing, she muttered to herself, "I suppose one of them had to be Talented."

"One of what?"

"Never mind," she said, shaking her head. "I doubt King

Beorhtel's inquisitors will be willing to cross into Aernheim to retrieve you. At least not until we deal with the problem of the wraiths."

Hiroc sighed in relief. It felt like a weight had been removed from his shoulders, but another quickly took its place. "What will I do now?" he asked. Ealstan already had his suspicions. Kipp had seen him put his hand in the blue fire. Hiroc could be careful, but what if he accidentally called out to Enlil in his sleep and the entire Basilica was consumed by blue fire?

"Nothing," she said. "Keep it to yourself. The last Talented burned down the bakery in Alchemist's Alley because he couldn't control his magic. Those in the alley aren't exactly the kind of folk to make enemies of. They find out you're Talented and you'll be in a world of trouble." She palmed the end of her braid and twisted it between her fingers.

Was Edoma angry with him? Hiroc couldn't understand why she would be. Sure, she had been more like a mother to him than any other woman, but she'd paid him almost no heed since he'd become an acolyte.

She narrowed her eyes. "How did you find out?"

"On Tyme's Hill. I summoned blue fire from the heavens when the giant attacked me."

Edoma's eyes widened. She glanced behind her at the eternal flame of Enlil that marked the stone wall. "So Enlil has chosen you for his own."

"Invoking his name only seems to work when I touch the ring."

"May I see it?" Edoma reached out, and Hiroc gave her his hand. She studied the ring for a moment. "It's a runic device. It provides a pathway for you to reach Enlil. A runic device is infused with the faith of the one who forged it. The greater the faith and the greater deeds done in homage to the god, the more powerful the runic device. But it won't work forever. Each has a limited use."

Hiroc had found the ring in this very temple. As a child,

he'd hidden from Alfric in one of the storerooms. He'd tripped over a floorboard and almost broken his neck. When he'd finally stopped cursing, he realized the floorboard had been intentionally pulled upward. Inside the hidden cavity beneath the floor was this ring. There was nothing else to identify who had hidden it there, so Hiroc had taken the ring. Alfric had always said that he'd stolen it, but if anyone had ever said it was theirs, Hiroc would have given it back. But they hadn't. So he still wore the ring. Still, it was strange to hear from Edoma that it was magical. It looked like an ordinary trinket. The jewel wasn't even real. The metal was bronze, not gold.

Hiroc thought of the warmth that Edoma's touch had produced. "Are you Talented, too?"

"Mun claimed me." He was expecting a story of some kind, but her lips were pursed, as though she refused to say any more about who Mun was. "I'm sure this is all very confusing for you. Myself, I know little about magic. What I do know is pieced together from memories of my homeland, combined with what I've been able to glean from these books in the last week since Aern's orb was . . ."

Hiroc wanted to finish her sentence, but he found himself equally unable to say the word aloud. *Shattered.* Two days ago, it would have been easy, but now the reality of Aern's death had come to them with the wraiths.

"Now that you have little duties with the Holy Order," she continued, "I think you can help me here. Fryda is coming along later. I need you both to look through the books."

Hiroc picked up one of the books and flicked through its pages. It was written in a language he couldn't understand. "I can't read this."

"You don't have to. I need you to find any depictions of this ward." She unfurled a scroll and pointed to a ward comprised of two half-circles, each with a rune in its center. One rune looked like a sun. The other looked like a crescent moon. He recognized them as the same wards she painted to protect against the wraiths. But there was no symbol of the spider. "You might find some other books worth reading on magic. Put them aside, and once you've found the book I seek, you may read them. But don't let Fryda see you. Best to keep your Talent between us. May I leave you to it now?"

Hiroc nodded, and Edoma left him. He stared at the vast array of books. Behind him. In front of him. All around him. In truth, he wanted only to look for those books about the Talented and magic. A few days ago he would have cast aside Edoma's desires and fulfilled his own. But he had seen the terror of skinwalkers. Sighing, he forced himself to look again upon the scroll and began the search for a book with a matching drawing.

24

FRYDA

ONCE she passed through the iron gates, Fryda hailed the Daughter busy preparing the bloodletting mechanism. The Daughter stepped away from the mess of gears and iron piping and scowled at Fryda. "Where have you been?"

Fryda was about to defend herself when Edoma appeared.

"Fryda," she said, "come inside where we can speak." She was being short, which meant she was still angry with Fryda about what she'd said.

The Daughter frowned, obviously wondering why the Mother wanted to meet with a novice. Fryda smirked at the woman and followed Edoma into the oratory.

Fryda sat while Edoma made tea over the fireplace. Fryda had fond memories of this chapel where Edoma had often consoled her. Most times it had been after one of the other novices had mistreated her. Many of the rooms in the temple were chapels of some kind. Most no longer functioned as places of prayer. This one included.

Fryda took a cup of tea from Edoma. It was too hot to drink, so she placed it on the table separating them.

"I'm sorry for the things I said," Fryda began. "You might

not be my mother, but you've been as good as any mother could have been."

"There's no need to apologize." There certainly had been a need, since Edoma's angry expression seemed to melt at hearing the apology. "The novices have many tasks now that the wraiths have come. We haven't made any official statement to the people, but most have gathered that Aern's weakening allows them to enter the town." Edoma seemed to notice Fryda's awkwardness. "Do you have something to tell me?"

Fryda had started chewing her lip when Edoma had said Aern was weakened. If she couldn't help showing what lay within her mind because of nervous ticks, then Edoma would soon find out about Alfric.

"What are you keeping back from me?" Her voice was strained.

"I know that Aern is dead." It was the first thing that came to her mind that wasn't about Alfric.

Edoma sat back in her seat. Beneath the surprise was a look of admiration. "How do you know this?"

"Hiroc told Alfric and me."

"That explains why Alfric went on the quest. He always considers himself a hero. Perhaps he will be."

Heart aching, Fryda forced the conversation elsewhere. "Jaruman told me what happened in Mundos."

"Then you know how imperative it is that Hurn allows us to enter Eosorheim. Tell me, where did you go when you left the town? I was thinking about it, and you had to have been gone at least since the warriors left."

"I intended on following them, but I got lost. Jaruman retrieved me."

"And the skinwalker you fought?"

Fryda looked away. She couldn't bear to lie to Edoma while looking her in the eye. "Some man. I don't know who he was."

"We have had many like that. They become so different that they're more monsters than human. Unfortunately, there's no coming back once a wraith takes you."

No coming back? Fryda stifled a sob. Jaruman had said the same thing, but to hear it from another person was heartbreaking. Even if Alfric had survived Flight running him down, he wouldn't be anything more than a skinwalker. The Alfric she had loved was gone.

Edoma walked over to Fryda and placed a hand on her back. "Enlil will protect us," she said as she rubbed comforting small circles.

Fryda sniffled. "What do you want me to do?" She imagined Edoma would have her punished for leaving the town.

"I was going to have you look through the library with Hiroc...You don't like him?" Edoma looked at Fryda. She must have noticed the way she scrunched her face when Hiroc was mentioned.

Fryda shrugged. The way he had betrayed Alfric still annoyed her.

"Then you'll be pleased to know I've decided upon something else," Edoma said. "I think we should go to the catacombs again."

Fryda tried not to smile, but it was impossible. This was no punishment! She had loved going into the catacombs. She hadn't had much time to think about them since she'd last been beneath the temple, but now that the opportunity had come again, she was ecstatic. It was the perfect thing to alleviate her mind of thoughts of Alfric.

"When can we go?"

"We'll prepare right away. I'll need some tools. You can help me make sense of that statue you noted. Hiroc is looking for a book that might contain information on how to make stronger wards. One of the library's books *might* contain such information, but I know for sure there's one within the First Priest's tomb."

"That's the tomb you've been trying to open since forever." Fryda couldn't help but think this was a futile quest. Years with no results wouldn't suddenly change.

"I have you now. While Hiroc is looking through the shelves, we can work together in the catacombs."

Fryda didn't like having that large of a responsibility. Did Edoma really think they'd be able to find this book?

As Edoma bent down to take Fryda's cup, a vial hanging from her neck slipped out from beneath her collar. It was filled with a thick liquid, but the color of the glass made it impossible to tell what color it might be.

"What's that?" Fryda knew that Edoma was unlikely to tell her, but her curiosity didn't allow the question to remain unasked.

Edoma surprised her by answering. "Dragon's blood." She held out the vial for Fryda to see. "Specifically, the blood from an onyx dragon." On closer look, the blood sparkled within the vial. It was as if magic were visible within it.

Thinking of the machines outside the temple, Fryda said, "You're going to use them for wards?"

"Possibly. The blood of an onyx dragon is much more powerful than human blood. Wards written with it should last at least a week. There's not much here, but it might save a few people."

A few people? There were far more than a few people in Indham.

25

HIROC

HIROC tossed what had to have been the hundredth book he'd sifted through onto the table. The table was now overflowing with books, and he had only emptied two shelves. His fingers were dry and covered with tiny cuts from scouring the pages. His back ached from leaning over the table.

Edoma had given him an impossible quest. Not a single drawing looked like the pair of half-circles with runes of the sun and the moon inside them.

There was also no sign of Fryda. She had likely had enough sense not to come to the library.

Laughter came from the shelf behind Hiroc. A steady clopping sound followed it until Mildryd, the librarian, came, donned in the robes of a Daughter of Enlil. Each of her steps was punctuated by the clap of her walking stick upon the marble tiles.

"She's got you looking for the wards, too, has she?" She squinted at the books in teetering piles on the table and laughed again. "I told her it would be impossible to find what she was looking for. Impossible unless you know where to look." The woman wriggled her eyebrows at Hiroc and then removed a book from within her robes. She opened the book and handed it to him. On the left-hand page was a drawing of the wards he was looking for.

"Looks like your job here is done," Mildryd said. "I might even let you take the credit for it."

Hiroc had always thought the woman old, but she seemed to have aged so much since the last he'd seen her. People talked about the librarian's vast knowledge, but he had never been interested in any of that. As a child, he'd only ever wanted to play within the temple's halls, not spend his days hunched over a dusty book like Alfric had. Strange considering where they both were now. Alfric had become a warrior where Hiroc had become an acolyte.

"Never thought I'd live to see the day that you grew into a man." Mildryd looked at him with fondness. "I remember you as a babe. Barely a few days from your mother's womb and you couldn't stop crying. To think that such a loud baby would become an acolyte."

"You must have me confused with someone else. I am a Fatherless." It was impossible for Mildryd to have known him as an infant. He had been six months old when he'd entered Indham with his twin brother, Alfric.

"Nonsense. I watched your mother birth you."

It was as everyone said—the woman had become crazy in her old age.

But she seemed to be taken with him. And she was a librarian. Those two factors could be useful.

"Do you know much about runic devices?" Hiroc asked offhandedly.

"That's an interesting question."

Hiroc slumped his shoulders. She wasn't going to talk about it.

But she proved him wrong. She repeated what Edoma had said about runic devices allowing the Talented to use a god's power.

Glad that Mildryd had opened up to him, he decided to ask another question. "Do you know where I might find one of these runic devices?"

"Another interesting question. This one is more difficult to answer. Not because I don't know the answer, but because the answer might lead me into trouble."

"I won't tell anyone what you tell me."

Mildryd smiled from the corner of her mouth. "I don't suppose you would. Wulfnoth owns a glove. It is a runic device. He keeps it in the stables. It won't do you much good— not unless you're Talented." She smirked.

He tried to ignore the way she looked at him. "What is Wulfnoth doing with a runic device?" Hiroc said more to himself than to the woman.

"His son, Garmund, used the glove to control his power. He was a Talented. Wulfnoth tried to hide him, but eventually the inquisitors came as they always do. Talented cannot control their magic, and something terrible always happens to them when they don't."

"How can someone be imprisoned for something they have no control over?" Hiroc thought about himself and how he might be taken away even though he had done nothing except be who he was.

Mildryd shook her head. "They're not imprisoned. The university is a good place for those cursed with the call of the gods. The inquisitors take Talented to save them from themselves." The last sentence was infused with meaning, as though Hiroc ought not avoid being taken.

"Now, this is the last place I expected to find you."

Hiroc cringed and slowly turned around. Ealstan was leaning against one of the shelves, arms folded across his chest. He wore his customary smirk. His robes were pulled back, and the dagger bearing Aern's likeness seemed to glow.

"I best leave you now," Mildryd said, avoiding looking at Ealstan as she hobbled off. She had probably heard about how spiteful Ealstan could be toward the Daughters. Perhaps she had even been victim to his taunts before.

"What do you want?" Hiroc said, trying to keep the anger from his voice.

"I want to apologize." While Hiroc was recovering from shock, Ealstan walked over and held out his hand. He suddenly appeared genuine. "Really. It doesn't matter that you are Talented. Not now. The wraiths have come, and we all have to do our best to get along."

Hiroc had never heard Ealstan apologize before. Not to him. Not to anyone. Sighing, Hiroc took Ealstan's hand and shook it. It seemed that even the worst people could be good during bad times.

"Can I buy you an ale?" Ealstan asked.

He was the last person Hiroc wanted to drink with, but it had been a long day, and he had finally found Edoma's book. So he agreed.

He scrawled a note to Edoma on a piece of parchment and placed it atop the book the old Daughter had given him. He didn't take credit for finding the book. Instead, he wrote that the librarian had found it. He didn't hesitate to add, however, that Fryda had not come to the library that day.

Hiroc followed Ealstan out from the temple. Like when he had come in, Hiroc avoided looking at the Daughters as they worked the machines. Ealstan stopped a number of times to look with appreciation on the machines. Hiroc kept walking.

When Ealstan finally got out from the temple, he led Hiroc to the Basilica. Rather than walk into the tavern where all the acolytes drank ale, though, he kept walking.

"Where are you going?" Hiroc said.

"I have a surprise for you," Ealstan said, not slowing down.

They eventually stopped on the far side of the Basilica where there was a small vineyard. A handful of other acolytes were huddled in a circle, Kipp among them. He smiled at Hiroc. "Look what we found."

As Hiroc got closer, he saw that the group had gathered around a deep pit, laughing. He stepped over to the ledge and peered into the pit. At the bottom, scratching at the dirt walls, was a skinwalker.

"It turns out that the wards only keep out the wraiths," Ealstan said smugly. "The skinwalkers are unaffected."

Kipp hurled a fruit at the skinwalker, splattering a rotten mess onto its deformed face.

Clenching his fists, Hiroc spun to face the group. "Blood and bones, what are you lot doing? Don't you know how dangerous skinwalkers are? I've seen what they can do. This one needs to be killed. Now."

The others looked at him with skeptical expressions.

"We know exactly what we're doing," Ealstan said. "We're having a little fun. And it's about to get a whole lot more exciting."

Ealstan reached and grabbed Hiroc's knife from his belt. He unsheathed the knife and then shoved Hiroc with his other hand. Hiroc waved his arms as if they might somehow cause him to stay upright. But all they found was empty air as he went over the edge. The breath was knocked out of him as his back slammed into the dirt floor of the pit.

"Now, who wants to place a bet?" Ealstan called from above. "The Talented or the skinwalker?"

Hiroc groggily stood. The skinwalker snarled at him. It barely looked human anymore. This one had been a host for a long time. It was probably one of the first. A massive mound arched from its neck to the middle of its back. Two appendages stuck out from the mound, as though it were halfway to sprouting wings.

Again it snarled.

Cheers erupted from above.

Hiroc had eaten with many of those acolytes above him. He might've even called some of them friends. Seeing them above him, placing bets on who would win, made him realize just how much the Talented were hated. It was more than any Fatherless. And he was both.

There was no point holding back. Those spectating what might be his death already knew he was Talented.

The skinwalker looked up to the people on the edge above and then to Hiroc. It cocked its head and grinned, as though it knew Hiroc had been betrayed. One moment it was looking at him, and another it was in midair, coming toward him. Twisting, Hiroc tried to avoid its attack. He cried as talons raked across his back. Still turning, he rolled along the ground. He scrambled to his feet, breathless. The wounds stung, but they must have only grazed him. Even so, he could feel a stickiness grabbing at his robes.

Hiroc eyed the skinwalker as it licked the blood from its talons. He squeezed his ring. "Enlil, hear my prayer!"

My child, a voice spoke in his head. It was the same voice that had spoken to him every time he visited Tyme's Hill. Something stirred inside Hiroc. With certainty, he realized now that it wasn't Aern's voice he had heard at Tyme's Hill. It couldn't have been. It must have been Enlil's.

He allowed the warm feeling to run through his body. He didn't fight it. It coursed through his limbs, electrifying him with energy. It finished at his fingertips, and small tongues of blue flame came from each of them. Ten ribbons of blue flame shot toward the skinwalker. The skinwalker darted to the other side of the pit. The fire ribbons found nothing except dirt wall, and disintegrated.

Knowing that death was imminent, Hiroc grabbed his ring again. "Again I request your help, Enlil of the Eternal Flame."

But there was nothing. Only a void. Where power had once been was now emptiness. Had the runic device run out as Edoma and Mildryd said it would?

Before Hiroc could consider his next move, the skinwalker rushed him. It landed on top of him as he was driven to the ground. Its long talons punctured the flesh below his shoulders, pinning him. He struggled as the skinwalker opened its mouth. Hot saliva dripped onto his face.

Hiroc put a hand to either side of him and scrounged for something, anything, that might stop the skinwalker from tearing open his neck and drinking his blood. His left hand found a rock. The rock in hand, he slammed it against the side of the skinwalker's head. The first blow struck the skinwalker stupid. The second cracked open its skull. Brain matter exploded with the third. Again and again, Hiroc drove the rock into the skinwalker until his arm ached and he couldn't lift it anymore.

Everything was quiet except for Hiroc's labored breathing. Applause and whistling sounded above him.

A red cloud drifted from the mangled remains of the skinwalker's head. It burst into tiny flecks of crimson.

Hiroc couldn't get up. Although the skinwalker was dead, its taloned hands were still pinning him down. His vision blurred from blood loss, but he could see shapes moving in the pit around him. The skinwalker was removed from where it had died on top of him. Someone came alongside him and helped him to his feet.

"You did well," Ealstan said. "I can see why Beorhtel wants Talented in his army. A couple of you Talented and we might not even need wards to stop the wraiths. It was close, though. I almost thought he had you at one point."

Gasping, Hiroc wavered on his feet as if he were drunk. Managing to stay upright, he grabbed his ring and whispered Enlil's name. Again he was confronted by the void. Perhaps it was a good thing, because, right now, he could've torched Ealstan to a cinder and not felt a sliver of regret.

"What?" Ealstan asked, his voice nasally. "You're going to burn me? I doubt very much you have the balls for that."

But it wasn't balls that Hiroc didn't have—it was a working runic device.

Ealstan's grin wavered. He must not have been sure whether Hiroc was, in fact, going to use the ring. Even though Hiroc felt like he was about to die, he couldn't help being amused at Ealstan's ignorance. Still, it seemed the other man knew that the runic ring had lost its power. How would he know that?

Pain silenced the question. Hiroc could barely breathe, but he mustered up enough energy to say, "Are you done playing games now?"

"King Beorhtel's inquisitors won't be coming for you anytime soon." Ealstan's voice was sinister. "I'm only getting started."

With all the energy he could muster, Hiroc punched Ealstan in the nose. There was a satisfying crunch beneath his fist. Ealstan clutched his nose as blood escaped through his fingers.

Hiroc laughed dryly and coughed, blood bubbling out from his mouth. The ground shifted beneath his feet, and he felt weightless as he crashed in a heap.

26

EDOMA

EDOMA ran her fingers over the rune that was causing her difficulty. It looked like the number eight. She withdrew a tome from her satchel and tore a page from it. The book wasn't particularly interesting, mostly a taxonomy of plant life in the Southern Isles written by a seer. And that was part of its secret. Supposedly, the seer, rumored to be the same man who had enlisted the builders to fashion this godstone door, hid a code within the book. When the page was placed over runes the seer had written, special ink on the pages would translate the runes into the language of the person holding it. Mildryd had given it to her in the hopes that it might finally open the godstone door.

Her hand shook as she pressed the paper against the eight on the door. She closed her eyes, hoping for the words to spring to her mind's eye. The only thing she could see was the afterimage of the torch. She concentrated harder, searching for some semblance of meaning in the runes.

Nothing.

Yelling, she threw the tome against the wall. It fell to the ground with a meaningless thud as her cry echoed through the hall. But her fury wasn't yet quenched. Storming across the corridor, she stomped on the tome until her feet were shooting with pain.

Another dead end. Another day wasted. How could she possibly have thought a piece of paper would be capable of translating ancient runes? It was foolish beyond belief. The younger Edoma would have laughed until her sides hurt. Instead, the old and weary woman slumped against a statue.

She looked up at the statue's indifferent gaze, and cursed the day she had begun this futile endeavor. Her time could have been devoted to more important things. Her sons, for one. But that wasn't her lot. Life had become an endless path of frustration after frustration.

Fryda appeared in front of Edoma. Dust caked her robes. She had obviously been enjoying this trip to the catacombs. "Is everything okay?" she asked.

Edoma sighed, and her gaze settled on the statue of a woman clothed in fine robes, her left sleeve drawn down over her shoulder so that a single breast was exposed. The statues within the room were all people who the First Priest believed worthy of veneration. Edoma supposed this woman had been his mother, and the exposed breast symbolized her weaning him. The statue's eyes were open, fixated on the leftmost corner of the room.

Edoma stood, a possible discovery on the edge of her mind.

"You haven't gone crazy, have you?" Fryda said. "I heard shouting and—"

Edoma hushed Fryda with a hand as she followed the gaze of each statue. One led to another until they ended with a small boy clad in ill-fitting armor and a claymore twice his height. A single hand was outstretched in supplication. She had gathered him to be the boy-warrior Gunnar who had banished the sea demons from the Edin River. Unlike the rest of the statues, whose gazes led to another statue, his eyes were closed.

The First Empire never constructed something haphazardly. There was always meaning behind their handiwork. Why were the boy's eyes shut?

Edoma turned to Fryda, who had been quietly watching. "Help me onto the plinth."

Pouting, Fryda got underneath Edoma so that she was able to climb onto the statue.

"The torch," Edoma said, holding out her hand. Fryda retrieved the torch from the sconce and handed it to Edoma. The torchlight illumined the surface of the statue. There wasn't a hint of a secret lever or magical ward. Nothing about it was out of the ordinary except for the closed eyes.

Edoma leaped down from the statue and winced as pain shot up through her ankles. She was too old to be doing this.

She crouched down and read the inscription on the statue's plinth.

The gift I gave was not my own
I gave it for my friends alone
The gods granted me this boon
I did not take it to the tomb
Return it to me and you will find
Your soul at the gates declined

"Anything?" Fryda asked.

"I thought maybe there was something to this statue. But there's just this riddle. It's nothing new to me. I've read it and all the others inside the catacombs many times. And like the others, it makes little sense."

"There's definitely something different about this statue. His eyes are closed, for one." Fryda spoke matter-of-factly, as if it were plain.

Edoma almost choked. "You noticed that? I've been searching for years and today is the first time I've noticed his eyes were shut."

Fryda shrugged. "Sometimes you need fresh eyes on an old problem."

"Is there anything else you've noticed?"

"Just one thing." She jumped onto the statue's plinth in a single bound. Holding out her arms like an acrobat, she bowed.

"Get on with it," Edoma said. It was hard to be thankful when Fryda rubbed it in.

"This here"—she pointed below the boy statue's neck—"is an imprint of a medallion."

Edoma's eyes widened. How had she not seen that? To her, the imprint had looked like an embroidered sigil on the boy's oversized armor. But now that Fryda had pointed it out, she could see exactly what medallion would fit within the strangely shaped imprint. "Thank you, Fryda. You've been helpful beyond measure."

"You don't want more of my help?" Fryda asked.

"There are some books I can consult about the medallion," Edoma lied. It wasn't that she didn't want Fryda's assistance, just that she wouldn't be able to help further. The imprint of the medallion, she now realized, was the mirror image of the medallion Idmaer now wore around his neck.

"Since I helped you," Fryda said, "I was wondering if you could help me."

Edoma could have told Fryda that helping the Mother Superior was part of a Daughter's duty. Instead, she decided to hear what Fryda had to say. "Yes?" she asked.

"Can you tell me what happened to Jaruman's family?" She removed her hairpin and stared at it. "I know they died in Mundos. But I want to know how."

"Both he and I lost people to the wraiths there, but I was unmarried and had only my father." Edoma remembered how she had been forced to drive a dagger through her father's heart. That day would never leave her memory. At least she'd made peace with it. "Jaruman, however, had a wife and a newborn. The wraiths took them for hosts."

Fryda gasped. "The baby, too? I always assumed his

daughter was older."

"Jaruman had been mute when I first met him. He found his voice while we were in the Scorched Lands. He told us all about how he'd been forced to kill them."

"Are the wraiths demons? Surely only demons could be capable of such evil."

"They are spirits the gods did not allow to pass through the Eternal Tollhouses. Instead, they became trapped within a realm of darkness."

"How did they get out? I mean, if the gods trapped them, shouldn't they still be there?"

"That is a good question. One I do not know the answer to. Such wonderings are for philosophers. We must deal with the here and now—finding the grimoire while we wait for the warriors to return."

At the mention of the warriors, Fryda started brushing down her robes. Sure, there was dust on them, but she never seemed to care about their dirtiness. Not unless she needed something to do with her hands so she didn't chew on her fingernails.

"Tell me what you know of the warriors," Edoma said, tilting her head. "You saw something of them when you were outside the walls with Jaruman, didn't you?"

Fryda continued playing with her robes, as though she hadn't heard Edoma. But she didn't need to answer. The truth was evident from her unwillingness to meet Edoma's eyes.

Edoma folded both arms across her chest. "You will answer me, novice."

Fryda swallowed and nodded. "I saw him. Well, not exactly him. He was a skinwalker." She broke into tears.

Edoma's bottom lip trembled. Fryda could only have been speaking about Alfric.

Swallowing the desire to cry, Edoma said, "I . . . I must go."

Without another word, Edoma went to the shaft and

thrashed the crank until her arms lost all feeling, and then thrashed it some more. She swung violently from the speed before coming to the top.

Unclipping the harness, Edoma rushed to her private chambers, not stopping to answer the Daughters asking what was wrong. She closed the door behind her and swung the lock shut. She fumbled for the key on her belt and unlocked the chest. Taking the scrying crystal in her palm, she rested it on the floor and knelt in front of it. She had refused to use the crystal when Saega had asked her to, because of the other-realm's allure. But she was going to face it now.

"Enlil, keep me safe," she whispered.

Calming her mind, she drew her belt dagger and sliced open her palm. Blood dripped as she raised it above the scrying crystal. Droplets hit the surface and power surged through her.

Instead of using her will to send the power out, she turned it in on herself, rolling it like a baker does dough. Her consciousness compressed until it was a speck of white light. Moments before she would have winked out of existence, she burst, a sun of pure light. The light faded.

The world was the same, except gray. Gray, and more grays, every shade of gray. There were no senses except for those the mind produced. Something like sight, except not sight. Something like smell, but not quite smell. Each sense produced a feeling like drunkenness, except without sickness. Giving oneself over to the feeling was always a temptation, but one that would turn deadly if she didn't temper it.

She had used such a crystal as an apprentice mage in Mundos, so she was accustomed to the disembodied feeling. The euphoria washed over her. The kind of pleasure an evil deed begets. Before long, it would become more an assault than a caress.

Pushing the feeling aside, she shifted through the temple. She kept shifting until she was among the stars, staring at the entire continent from a vantage point few human eyes had seen. So many non-sights, non-scents, non-sounds, non-tastes, and non-touches threatened to overwhelm her. She screamed without sound, cried without tears, until everything faded.

She focused now on the warriors who had been sent out from Indham's gates.

The mental images of two men appeared in front of her: Sigebert and Cenred. The two older warriors were devoid of color, like a drawing etched in charcoal. They walked among the great trees of Grimwald Forest. But there was no Alfric.

Rejecting the thought that Fryda had been right, Edoma concentrated on Alfric's form.

The world blurred around her, and suddenly she was in front of him.

He was scratching at the ground. Strangely, a crimson light pulsed within his chest. As if sensing her presence, he turned his head all the way around. His eyes met Edoma's, and she almost released herself to the otherworld then and there.

Terror struck her. Then guilt.

Why had she allowed Idmaer to send Alfric away?

Alfric grinned at her. Horns protruded from the sides of his head. Behind him were many other skinwalkers, busy devouring the corpses of a waylaid caravan. They were plain gray, without a light in their chest like Alfric's.

Looking again at Alfric, Edoma pondered what that light might be. He continued looking her way but didn't move toward her. Instead, he took the arm he had torn from a corpse and chewed it contemplatively.

Edoma furrowed her brow and concentrated. Communicating in the other-realm required an effort she wasn't sure she could manage, but she tried anyway. All her strength sapped out from her as she spoke, "Alfric."

The crimson light within the skinwalker flickered. "Help . . . me . . ."

That was Alfric's voice. Somehow, his soul had not left

his body. He was still alive, somewhere inside that monstrous form.

A great happiness washed over Edoma. She would stay here with him.

No. That wasn't her thinking, but the euphoria. She had to leave. Now.

Edoma screamed as she emptied herself of power. Her spirit form was ripped into the air. Below her, she saw the warpath of the wraiths and their skinwalkers. Towns were laid waste and holy places defiled.

In the moment before she would be lost to the other-realm, Edoma pulled away from the sickness of pleasure. She took repossession of her physical form, and scrubbed every ounce of blood from the scrying crystal. It cast a wicked reflection at her, begging her to feed it more of herself.

With a grimace, she placed the crystal back into the chest. She wanted to heed its call but knew it was the euphoria speaking again. Despite her knowledge, she couldn't stop herself from reaching for the crystal. The call had never been this strong before. She must have lingered too long in the otherworld.

She bent over and vomited.

Peering down, she saw that the vial of onyx dragon blood around her neck was glowing. It tugged away from her, floating in midair, as though it were trying to reach the scrying crystal. Or the crystal was drawing it.

Clenching her teeth, Edoma wrapped her hand around the vial and tore the necklace. A great force pulled her arm even as she tossed the vial to the opposite side of the room. It clattered to the ground, unbroken.

With an exerted effort, she slammed the chest shut and locked it with trembling fingers.

27

FRYDA

FRYDA drank from the goblet, her hands quivering. No matter how hard she tried, she couldn't stop shaking. The firewine did little to calm her. She had already known that Alfric was a skinwalker, but Edoma had just told her that he was still alive.

Putting the goblet onto the table in front of her, Fryda met Edoma's eyes. "My horse, Flight, trampled him under her hooves. I thought she killed him."

"It takes much more than that to slay a skinwalker," Edoma said through clenched teeth.

Hope blossomed inside Fryda. "If he's still alive and he's different from the other skinwalkers, then we need to go after him. Maybe something can be done to save him."

"As far as I'm aware, there's nothing that can bring someone back after a wraith has taken them."

"But you said his soul was still inside his body—"

"Enough, Fryda." Edoma rubbed the bridge of her nose. "I've had enough. Indham is more important than one man. Please don't make me regret telling you."

"How can you let him go so easily? He's your son." As soon as the words were out of her mouth, Fryda wished she could take them back.

Edoma's face contorted with grief. "You know?"

"Jaruman told me."

Edoma stood and walked over to the window. She gazed through it as if she were watching the birds fly through the clouds on a sunny afternoon.

Something glimmered beneath the chair Edoma had been sitting on. Fryda scooted forward on the chair to see it better. It was the vial of onyx dragon blood.

"It wasn't easy giving Alfric and Hiroc up," Edoma said, still looking through the window. "I never would have done it were it not for Idmaer. He convinced me Durwin would use the children in their petty games."

"The more I hear of Idmaer, the more I think him a terrible man," Fryda said. The vial kept her attention. Why was Edoma no longer wearing it? Ever since she'd started drawing the wards, it had been around her neck.

"He wasn't always that way. Once, he was a great leader. Even a great husband." Edoma rubbed her hands down her dress and turned to face Fryda. "Nevertheless, as much as it pains me, we cannot go after Alfric."

The sudden revelation that Alfric was still alive had stirred Fryda. Now she was being forbidden from going after him? With the wraiths roaming Aernheim, she couldn't possibly hope to find Alfric. Not without onyx dragon blood.

Fryda didn't know how to empower the wards, but there had to be a way. Edoma certainly wasn't going to do it. At least not for the purposes of following Alfric.

"You saw Cenred and Sigebert through the orb?" Fryda asked.

"They are in Grimwald Forest. Hurn's magic prevented me from seeing anything except a glimmer, but they are there."

"Their quest is taking a long time," Fryda said. "Should we not send others?"

"What good would sending others do? They have the

best chance of convincing Hurn to help us." Edoma paused and studied Fryda for a moment. "You want to be sent into Eosorheim?"

Fryda nodded, hoping her true intentions remained hidden. "Hurn and I have something in common. I am a Fatherless. I have been mistreated by the people of Indham." Hoping this argument would convince Edoma, Fryda held her breath.

"No," Edoma said with finality. "I doubt you'll go to Eosorheim. More likely that you'll try and find Alfric. Even were I to send a dozen warriors along, you would find a way to escape them. I'm telling you, Fryda, there's nothing you can do. Despite what I saw, Alfric is lost."

"You cannot believe that. You said he was different from the others."

"Do not venture out from Indham. Enlil protected you from the wraiths before. He will not spare you the consequences of foolishness a second time."

"Where was Enlil when the wraiths came?"

"You walk a blasphemous path."

Fryda sighed. Arguing would do no good. "I'm sorry."

Edoma nodded. "I'm going to see Hiroc about his job. Don't do anything foolish." Edoma gave Fryda a stern glare before leaving.

When she was sure Edoma wouldn't return, Fryda bent and picked up the vial. She removed the cap. The blood inside looked almost black, but the magical specks dazzled her with their light.

There was no reason for her to take it. She couldn't empower wards without Edoma. Even so, she slipped the vial into her pocket.

28
EDOMA

EDOMA scanned the note in her hands. The writing was so poor, it was barely intelligible.

"He found your book," Mildryd said.

"It says here that *you* found it," Edoma said, pointing to a scribbled line.

Mildryd peered over Edoma's shoulder. "That it does. Although he misspelled *librarian*."

If he'd been sent to one of the schools in Winhurst, his writing wouldn't be scrawled etchings that strain the eyes. But that would have required money. And Fatherless had no money. Sure, she could have sponsored him, but it would have been foolish while Durwin had still been alive. Still, Saega had been right when he'd said that Hiroc had fared better than any other Fatherless. He was an acolyte now.

Edoma considered telling Mildryd what she'd seen within the scrying crystal. Fryda had only made Edoma feel worse. If Mildryd suggested that they send people to go after Alfric as Fryda had done, Edoma might just crumble.

"I spoke with Hiroc while he was here," Mildryd said. "I might have alluded to him that I was present at his birth."

"*What?*"

158

"It was an accident. I'm getting on in years, and it's hard to remember who knows what and who doesn't. There are too many secrets here. I can't be expected to keep them all." She folded her arms and pouted.

"No matter," Edoma said with effort. She wanted to chastise Mildryd, but it didn't seem right to correct a woman who was at least thirty years older. Besides that, Mildryd was an undeserved friend. She had encouraged Edoma to repair the dilapidated temple and institute the priesthood of Enlil. Enlil had been one of the gods who had been worshiped in the south long ago. He wasn't trapped within an orb as so many of the new gods were. Despite being a northerner, Edoma's mother had spoken of Enlil. She had said that he was one of the few gods whose spiritsoul bargains were a blessing rather than a curse. The presence of his temple within Indham had been fortuitous. It felt right to continue spreading devotion to Enlil as her mother had done. The keepers of the ancient library, an order of women who had taken vows to pursue and maintain knowledge, were perfectly suited to become Daughters of Enlil. So Edoma had taken them as the first initiates, and Mildryd had been the first.

"He also asked about the Talented."

"I suppose you told him all about that?"

"Not everything."

Edoma threw up her arms. "My words mustn't have been enough to placate him. I also had words with him about the Talented. Something along the lines of not to speak with anyone about it. It seems he's quite disobedient." *Like his father.*

"You think he's inherited your . . . *gift?*"

Even though Mildryd knew that Edoma had once been a mage, she still treated the subject with caution. It was to be expected with the way King Beorhtel had spread his lies about the Talented.

"I know he has," Edoma said. "Thankfully, it appears it's

not the god of my homeland who's called him."

"Aern?"

Edoma shook her head. "Enlil, I believe."

"Gracious," Mildryd said, clutching the prayer beads around her neck and glancing at the eternal flame on the wall behind her. "King Beorhtel's going to be eager to get his hands on him. I suppose he'll have to wait, though. Not likely he'll send his inquisitors into Aernheim with the wraiths upon us."

"I'm counting on that," Edoma said. She could barely wait to open the book. First, she had to clear something up. "Have you ever seen Idmaer venture into the catacombs?" Mildryd's room was adjacent to the stairwell that led there, so it seemed a logical question.

"Not that I remember."

"I believe the First Priest's medallion can be used to open a door to a secret chamber."

"Fine fortune getting him to give it to you."

Edoma grunted at that. She was thinking the same thing. He was more likely to burn the spire down than lend her the medallion. But maybe he would come with her to the tomb.

With the book Mildryd had found in her hands, Edoma started from the beginning and scanned its pages. Most of it was written in a language she couldn't understand, but it wasn't the words she was after. Halfway through, she came upon the diagrams of wards. On the left-hand page was the ward for protection against the wraiths—two half-circles, one encompassing a crescent moon and the other a sun.

Below the wards were pictures of various creatures. There was a number below each picture. The spot behind her ear itched as she thought of how much frustration could have been avoided had she possessed this book. She might have warded the warriors with something other than lamb's blood. Alfric might never have become a skinwalker.

"Is something the matter?" Mildryd asked.

"The tutors in Mundos used these same diagrams. I'm surprised their methods hadn't changed. This book has to be at least a few hundred years old."

"What do the numbers indicate?" Mildryd asked.

"The strength of certain blood types. The blood of humans is the strongest we have available."

Mildryd held out her hand. "Do you mind?"

Edoma passed her the book.

Brow furrowed, Mildryd flicked the pages forward and then back again. "You said that human blood is the strongest, but what's this?" She pointed to a page depicting various dragons.

"I only have a small vial. It would ward one building. If it comes to that, I don't know which I would choose. Or who I would keep out."

"It doesn't have to come to that. There is somewhere we can get more dragon blood."

"We can't go there now," Edoma said. "The enclosure was shut down. Wild dragons lurk there. We have no more suppression stones. It would be suicide."

"Maybe. At least you have another choice," Mildryd said. "There is another page."

Edoma swallowed and turned the page. There it was. The reason why she had sworn off using blood magic.

Etched in deep lines was a drawing of a child and its parents. The number "one" rested below the child. The same number was above the parents. The love between parent and child. The love between two joined in marital union. Both were the most powerful bonds, and to give them up in sacrifice would create the most powerful magic. The most evil magic. Few gods would accept such sacrifices, but Mun was certainly one. Edoma always thought it strange that Mun, a god who could grant healing, would also receive such terrible sacrifices.

"Never again," Edoma whispered.

"This happened in Mundos?"

Edoma nodded. "Not at first. We have no dragons in the North, but the mages tried everything else. The old. The sick. Great mountain beasts. The noble cats of the jungle. Eventually, the children were taken." There was no holding back the tears. Edoma hadn't spoken of it to anyone since she'd walked into Mun's temple on that dreadful day. "When I warded Alfric and the others, I never connected that human blood was required for the wards. I should have known. I used...lamb's blood. How could I have been so foolish?"

Mildryd rubbed Edoma's back until the tears stopped. "You must prepare a party for the dragon enclosures. From the look of this," she said as she pointed at the page, "human blood won't last long enough. The enclosures are a day's ride. Killing a dragon will take longer than that. Maybe much longer."

Edoma reached for the dragon vial around her neck. It wasn't there. She remembered tearing it away when she'd gazed into the scrying crystal.

A slamming noise echoed through the library. It was soon followed by someone yelling for help.

Two other acolytes were carrying an unconscious Hiroc. From deep wounds on his shoulders, blood dripped onto the stone below. A crimson puddle quickly gathered.

Edoma's mind raced as she knelt beside the puddle. "Put him down," she said to the acolytes. "Gently."

They obeyed with wide eyes, and she gripped Hiroc's robes from the collar and pulled outward. The cloth tore open down to his waist. The wounds were swollen and flaring. When she pressed her hand to stem the blood flow, a terrible feeling washed over her. There was a taint to the wound.

"A skinwalker did this," Edoma whispered.

"No," one of the acolytes said, "he fell into the pit outside the Basilica."

Edoma narrowed her eyes. "Lying will not save Hiroc."
Only magic will do that.

162

Edoma thanked Enlil that she already had the blood she needed. Using her finger, she traced the ward of healing over his chest. When she invoked Mun, the wards glowed crimson before winking out.

The wounds had closed, sealed shut by brown scabs. They weren't fully healed, but at least he wouldn't die from blood loss or infection.

Mildryd entered the library with a group of other Daughters, carrying a stretcher.

"Take him to the infirmary," Edoma said, wiping her bloodied hands on her robes. "Dress his wounds. If he wakes, give him water."

The Daughters nodded and carried him out.

"Now," Edoma said, turning to the other acolytes, "what are your names?"

"Ealstan," the one with the thin mustache said.

"Kipp," said the short one.

"You said he fell into the pit," Edoma said, addressing Ealstan.

"Yes," he said, "*Mother Superior.*"

She narrowed her eyes, not missing the scornful way he had spoken her honorific. "You are lying."

"The Holy Order abhors lying. It is most strange to be accused of lying by a false priestess who serves a false god."

"How dare you? You stand within the Temple of Enlil."

Kipp seemed to cower behind Ealstan, but Ealstan only grew more confident. "Tell me, why is it that Enlil was suddenly worshiped here again? Where does he live? Certainly not in this world as Aern does. In the imaginations of his followers?"

Edoma clenched her jaw. If only this fool knew the truth, he wouldn't be acting so smugly.

"These wards you paint around the town," he continued, "the way you healed Hiroc . . . You're Talented. When all this is over, you will be taken by Beorhtel's inquisitors, along with Hiroc. The Daughters will return to caring for old books, and

Aern will be the only god worshiped in Indham. As it should always have been."

"This is far from over. It could very well get worse." Edoma's gaze crept down to the knife at his belt. She'd seen it before, but she couldn't recall exactly where. The pommel was intricately carved, with the winged imp of Aern, and runes were imprinted on the sheath. Hadn't Saega once owned a knife like that? No, it was probably a family heirloom. Acolytes were meant to give up all personal belongings when they entered the Holy Order, but she suspected this particular acolyte wasn't the kind to obey rules.

Ealstan turned up his nose. "Come, Kipp, we have a real god to serve."

Kipp remained, even after Ealstan insisted a third time before storming out.

"Sorry, Mother Edoma, I didn't know Hiroc would get hurt so badly. I thought he was Talented, so he would . . . you know." He twirled his hands in a mock-attempt at something magical.

"Tell me what happened," Edoma said with a sigh.

By the time Kipp had finished his story, Edoma was ready to wring his neck. A fun game, he had called it. It had been anything but.

"You could be thrown before the Council for this," she said.

"It was Ealstan's idea. He doesn't like Hiroc a bit."

That much was obvious. Edoma waved Kipp out with a final warning.

29

HIROC

"IDMAER demands to know whether you've found anything about the shatterer," Hiroc said to Wulfnoth. Idmaer had said no such thing, but he needed an excuse to speak with Wulfnoth.

"Demands? Idmaer doesn't demand. He asks nicely. Like you ought to."

Hiroc reeled back at the stench of strong drink. Jaruman's ale was the best in all the town, but it smelled better when it was fresh from a keg, rather than the aftermath of Wulfnoth's poor digestion. The smell reminded Hiroc of the strong drink the Daughters had given him to help with the pain.

His arms still ached from where the skinwalker had punctured his flesh. He could barely lift them above his shoulders, but that was still a marvel. The wounds on his back had healed completely. All thanks to Edoma's magic. When he'd awoken that morning, he hadn't told her what Ealstan and the others had done to him. He feared that if she learned that others knew he was Talented, she might hide him away. She had a bad habit of treating him like a son.

Hiroc tried not to breathe through his nostrils, tempered the disdain in his tone, and asked Wulfnoth, "Any luck tracking the giant?"

Wulfnoth sighed, ejecting more detestable aromas. "Nothing. It's like he disappeared. Never seen someone who can be somewhere without leaving a trace. You sure this giant isn't a ghost?"

"I saw him. He's as real as you and me." He couldn't think of a convenient way to bring up Wulfnoth's son. That was, after all, the real reason why he was in Wulfnoth's home.

It wasn't much of a home. Empty wineskins lay on the floor. Hiroc lifted his boot. Dog shit, too. Wulfnoth had always been a drunk, but it seemed he had gotten worse just in the last week.

Why does Idmaer still employ this drunkard? He probably had his reasons. Idmaer wasn't the terrible man everyone made him out to be. And if there was one man whom Idmaer considered a friend, it was Wulfnoth. Hiroc didn't see things the same way.

"Or maybe the giant is a mage?" Wulfnoth said. "I know folk don't like to talk about it, but men can do strange things with magic. This one fella I caught once, he . . ." He grabbed Hiroc's arm. "You got any coin on you? I've run out of ale, and Jaruman won't let me back in the tavern until I pay my dues."

Hiroc frowned at Wulfnoth's dirty fingers. "Idmaer provides you with a stipend. It's your own fault if you piss it away." Realizing he had an opportunity, he removed Wulfnoth's hand as politely as he could manage. "Tell me what you know about the Talented, and I'll give you enough coin for a mug of ale."

"I don't know nothing about—"

"Two mugs. That's the most I'll give you. I already know your son was Talented."

Wulfnoth suddenly appeared sober. "He was. I'm surprised you called him *my* son. Most people thought he was Saega's. Truthfully, I was with Bodil from the moment she and Saega married. That boy, Garmund, he was mine. I think

Saega knew it, which is why he always treated him so poorly. As soon as Bodil came to live with me, I treated the kid right."

Hiroc wasn't so sure about that. He'd heard about the kind of father Wulfnoth could be after a long night at the tavern. From the little he'd spoken to Garmund, neither Saega nor Wulfnoth had been good fathers to him.

"Then they took him. Garmund never did anything terrible on purpose. Sometimes he needed a clip over the ears, but nothing serious. Only reason the bakery burned down was because he was antagonized. People don't like the Talented, so I told him not to even so much as whisper a god's name. But he was never any good at obeying me. I went to Saega to ask for help, but he said no one was meant to help a Talented evade the inquisitors. Idmaer forbade it, he said. I always felt sorry for Saega, me taking his wife and all, but it infuriated me. I spent an hour arguing with him. By the time I went to find Garmund, the bakery was just a pile of smoking rubble, and the inquisitors had Garmund in the back of their wagon." Wulfnoth sniffled and wiped his nose with a sleeve.

Hiroc had never heard the story like that. He couldn't help feeling sorry for Wulfnoth. "Do you know which god called Garmund?"

"Enlil. Never heard of Enlil calling anyone before my son. It's always been Aern who called in these parts." He studied Hiroc, as though he were capable of reading thoughts. He smiled. "If for some reason you think someone you might know is called by Enlil, then I've got something special for you."

Hiroc held his breath as Wulfnoth knelt next to a cabinet and brushed aside straw from the ground. He pulled open a small trap door and removed something bundled in rags.

"This is a runic object," he said as he unwrapped the rags. "Only a devotee of Enlil or someone called by him can use it."

Once the bundles were removed, a tattered glove was revealed. It must have been the one Mildryd had talked about.

"Where did you get it?" Hiroc asked.

"Belonged to my wife. The second one, that is. Wasn't long after Bodil passed that Saega came looking for anything she might have taken after their separation, but I managed to keep hold of it."

Hiroc turned the glove over. It looked a little large. He desperately wanted to slip it on now, but doing so would give away his motives immediately.

"Runes along the palm lit up like a lamp whenever Garmund wore it. Care to try it on? It shouldn't light up. Not with an acolyte in the Holy Order of Aern. Unless Enlil's called you for his Talented." Wulfnoth raised an eyebrow.

Hiroc searched for a defense but came up empty. He shook his head, determined not to allow Wulfnoth to bait him. "I'll buy the glove."

Wulfnoth snatched it from Hiroc's hands and hugged it to his chest. "It's a family heirloom. The last memory of Garmund and Bodil."

"Enough coin to buy a dozen ales."

"Sold."

With the glove in hand, Hiroc stepped outside and went down the steps. He hid among the shadows along the side of Wulfnoth's house. He glanced around to make sure no one would see him and slipped on the glove. He was wrong about it being too big. It seemed to fit perfectly. An invocation to Enlil was on his lips as shouting came from the gates. It sounded like fighting.

The window creaked open above him. Wulfnoth popped his head out. "What's all that about?"

Hiroc quickly removed the glove and stuffed it into his robe pocket. He didn't know, but he intended to find out.

* * *

Four warriors surrounded a man in a gray cloak outside

168

the gates. The only warrior Hiroc recognized was Bertram. He was pointing his sword at the cloaked man, a snarl on his face that suggested he might use it.

Hiroc's heart stopped. The last time he'd seen such a cloaked figure had been at Tyme's Hill. But this man was too short to be the giant.

At their feet were the ward circles. There were half a dozen ward circles inside the gates now. Edoma must have become more cautious. The ones the cloaked man was standing on were blindingly bright. But the man didn't look like a skinwalker. Those Hiroc had seen weren't shaped like humans, and this man was normal enough to be forgettable. He simply stood within the glowing ward circle, hands clasped together in a prayerful posture, oblivious to the armed men encircling him.

"Kneel," Bertram demanded.

The man stayed still. Bertram darted forward, his sword pommel slamming onto the man's head. The man dropped. The other warriors swarmed, binding the man's wrists. Another warrior ground the man's face into the cobblestone with his boot. The man wasn't struggling. Were it not for his open eyes, he would have appeared unconscious.

Those eyes locked onto Hiroc.

"He sure doesn't look like a skinwalker," one of the warriors said as he stepped away from the man, "but the wards burned brighter than I ever seen 'em burn."

Hiroc drew closer. Others had gathered to watch the event. All the while, the man's gaze remained, drilling into Hiroc like a hot iron.

As the cloaked man was thrust to his feet, the sleeves of his garment lifted. Wards like those that marked the ground beneath him covered his skin from the wrist up.

A guard tore the cowl from the man's head. Blood trailed from his forehead where the warrior had struck him. His scalp was bald. But for this, he appeared normal, until the sun reflected off his pale dome.

Flowing wards circled the man's head and neck, shimmering in and out of existence as the sun caught their edges. For a moment, they were a shade of plum, only to transmute themselves into a deep sapphire, before vanishing again.

Kipp pushed his way past Hiroc. He must have been hiding among the crates in front of the guardhouse, watching the scene play out.

He grinned as the guard handed him a small coin purse. He pocketed the purse. "He says he's from north of Babon's Pass. No way that's true. No one's come from there since the Fatherless. I told him to meet me outside the gates, and he came sure enough." It was just like Kipp to sell someone out for some coin. Hiroc was starting to wonder how he'd ever called the man a friend.

"It is true," the man spoke, a strange accent punctuating his vowels. The accent was similar to the way Edoma spoke. "I am from the North, and I know what really happened at your altar."

Hiroc's eyes shot open. There were too many people listening. Too many who would learn the truth if this man happened to know it.

"That's enough out of you." Bertram punched the man in the face. His neck snapped back and his chin drooped. Hiroc breathed a sigh of relief as they bound the unconscious man.

"I'll take him to Idmaer's dungeons with the rest of the skinwalkers," Bertram said. "He hasn't changed yet, but it's only a matter of time."

The warriors dragged the man to a carriage.

"I see you've recovered," Kipp said as he came alongside Hiroc. He wore a smile, as though there was no bad blood between them. "I wouldn't have let Ealstan keep the skinwalker in the pit if I'd known he was intending on throwing you in there with it."

"You were cheering along with the others." Hiroc glowered.

"No need to be like that. We were just having a bit of fun."

"Get out of my way," Hiroc said, shoving Kipp aside. He started walking toward Idmaer's Spire.

There wasn't a chance the tattooed man was a skinwalker. The wards had illuminated beneath his feet, but it must have meant something else. He had said that he knew what happened at the altar. He'd said that while looking at Hiroc. Had he been referring to the shattered orb or the blue fire Hiroc had summoned?

Hiroc intended to find out.

30

FRYDA

F RYDA stared at the strange man as the warriors threw him into the back of a carriage.

Did he really know what had happened at Aern's altar?

He couldn't know. Not unless he was the giant. But he was no bigger than a normal man.

Then who was he?

The warriors cast wary glances at the man behind the carriage bars. She overheard whispers about the peculiar wards tattooed on his face. Without the cowl to hide them, they shimmered in a whirl of colors. They were similar to the wards Edoma painted. If the wards protected against wraiths, then the man couldn't possibly be possessed. Why then did the wards outside the gates activate when he had stepped on them?

Bertram glared at Fryda. Heart racing, she stepped back inside The Flaming Monkey. The vial of dragon blood rattled beneath her robes. Without Edoma to draw wards and empower them, she hadn't been able to use the blood. There would be no going after Alfric without wards powerful enough to sustain the journey.

This man with the tattooed wards might be able to tell

her how to make the wards for herself. She wouldn't need Edoma's help then. It was a slim chance, but it was all she had.

She waited for the carriage to begin its ascent up the hill toward the spire. Hiking up her skirts, she ran for Alchemist's Alley. There were a few genuinely disreputable types in Indham, and they tended to congregate at either side of the misshapen alley. Even in a Daughter's robes, Fryda was vulnerable. Ignoring the catcalls, she kept her head down. Folk tended to leave you alone if you looked like you had somewhere to be.

Fryda passed the charred remains of the bakery. Because of people's opinion of the Talented and their cursed nature, no one had rebuilt it. She'd never known Garmund that well, but he'd been nicer than most to the Fatherless. She tried not to think too much about what terrible things the inquisitors might be doing to him now.

A brisk walk and a few swift turns later, she came to the archway that opened to the spire's rear. The carriage stopped outside the spire's garden. The plants were usually voluminous with flowers, but the wind had stripped all foliage from the branches. It afforded Fryda a perfect view as Bertram removed the prisoner from the back of the carriage. None of the other warriors helped. Bertram was yelling at them. Still, they refused.

Fryda didn't know how she would speak with the prisoner, but she had to try. She caught eyes with Bertram and spun behind the alley wall. The vial slipped from her pocket and clattered to the ground. Reaching out, she snatched it away. The crystal was untarnished. The blood seemed to ebb and flow as if it were alive.

"You looking for something?"

Fryda glanced up at Bertram. His gaze floated down to the vial in her hands.

"That's Mother Edoma's vial," he said. "What are you

doing with it?" He placed a gloved hand on his sword hilt. "Give it to me."

Fryda only now noticed how quiet this particular part of Alchemist's Alley was. No one was around who might see this man cut her down and take the vial. The desire in Bertram's eyes suggested he would do almost anything to get it.

"Why do you want it?" she said. "It's worthless to you."

"I know dragon blood when I see it. That much would provide passage for me into Lamworth."

"You can't leave Indham without wards."

"Edoma wards us of the warrior's watch every night to guard the walls," he said with a smile. "I could simply slip out one night." Fryda thought to tell him that he wouldn't last more than a night with wards made from human blood, but decided not to. "The word is that Indham won't last much longer. Better to try and escape than stay here. Now, give it to me." He lifted his arm, and a section of the sword's blade gleamed out from the scabbard.

Fryda swallowed and handed over the vial. "Mother Edoma will hear of this."

"And you're going to tell her? You'd have to admit to stealing it. Jaruman isn't here to help you. You're lucky I don't have the time to deal with you like I want to. Go on back to where you came from, Fatherless." He nodded down Alchemist's Alley. Bertram marched back to the spire, pocketing the vial.

There was no real reason to follow Bertram now. Fryda had no dragon blood, nothing to use for wards so that she could find Alfric. She was struck by the utter hopelessness of her quest.

"Is it true what he said?" A man stumbled out from the shadows. His tunic was torn and spotted with stains. "Indham's not going to last?"

"I don't know," Fryda said, eying the strange gleam in the man's eye. She removed her hair pin, and her curls sprang free. She held the pin in a clenched fist.

"You *are* a beauty," he said. He continued forward, not seeming to care that she had the pin. "You're one of them Daughters. I bet you know all about what's going on here. We don't know a lick of it. But I reckon what that warrior said is true. If this place is going down, I intend to have some fun." The man licked his lips and made to grab her. Before he could, Fryda slammed the pin into the man's eye socket. It sank into his eye with ease. He screamed and clutched his face.

She paused, thinking to grab the pin. Instead, she ran as fast as she could to The Flaming Monkey.

31

HIROC

HIROC watched the warrior Bertram emerge from the entrance to the spire's dungeons. The man was walking with such purpose that he didn't notice Hiroc until they brushed past each other. Bertram jumped with a start.

"What in Aern's name are you doing sneaking around?" His eyes were wide as they darted about the hall.

Hiroc raised an eyebrow. "I wasn't sneaking."

"You almost scared me to death." Bertram smoothed down his tunic with a shaky hand and muttered, "Bloody acolytes."

Hiroc looked over Bertram's shoulder, expecting to see the other warriors, but they weren't there. For some reason, Bertram had imprisoned the tattooed man alone. A foul stench drifted from his clothes.

"Has the prisoner been taken to a cell?" Hiroc asked, trying to ignore the rank odor.

"Any other reason why I'd be in this godforsaken place? It was terrifying to begin with, and now it's entertaining demons." Bertram closed his eyes and swallowed. After that, he seemed to have gained control of his fear. It was strange seeing Bertram afraid. He was normally well-composed to the point of arrogance. "There's a Fatherless waiting down there. Says Idmaer gave him the job of guarding the cells. I don't know why Idmaer employs them."

Hiroc narrowed his eyes. Bertram obviously wasn't aware of Hiroc's origins. With the runic glove inside his belt pouch, Hiroc could easily burn the man alive. It was a wicked thought, but one that brought a smile to Hiroc's face. Satisfied with his imaginary retribution, he stepped aside and held out his arm. "I should let you leave."

"Keep your eyes straight down there," Bertram said with a stern gaze. "You won't sleep for weeks otherwise. I got places to be. You know where that merchant lives now? The one who used to sell the good stuff, you know?"

Hiroc knew exactly the man Bertram was after. He'd sold potions, the kind that made you live in a dream for a time. There were folk addicted to the stuff in Alchemist's Alley. Thankfully, the potions maker had been thrown out of the town. "He's not in Indham anymore," he said.

"Just my luck." Bertram scowled. "There has to be someone else who wants to buy what I got."

Hiroc didn't want to know what Bertram was selling, so he said goodbye and entered the dungeons.

Oswin was waiting at the bottom of the staircase, dueling with an invisible opponent. He had taken Alfric's position as porter of the spire after the tournament.

He leaned on his sword and grinned as Hiroc approached. "You see the captain of the warrior's watch? He was scared half to death. It took the poor fella nearly an hour to find the dungeons."

Normally Hiroc would have found it hilarious that the magical spire had once again managed to confuse someone, especially Bertram, but the words the tattooed man had spoken still rang in his mind.

"Have you spoken with the man Bertram brought in?" Hiroc asked.

"I'm not an idiot. I made myself a rule not to talk with the skinwalkers. Although the newest one looks like they might have made a mistake. He seems fine."

"Where is he?"

"He's in the last cell down the corridor."

Hiroc turned toward the staircase.

"Can I come?" Oswin asked.

Hiroc thrust his hand into the other man's chest. "Stay here and keep watch."

Oswin nodded like keeping watch was the most important job in the world, and sat back down.

Keeping watch wasn't really important. The skinwalkers within the dungeon's cells kept people away. But Hiroc didn't want Oswin to overhear his conversation with the prisoner. He had a feeling that whatever the man might say would be better kept for his ears alone.

Hiroc lit a torch and drudged down the steps. He could handle heights; burrowing into the earth like a mole was a different matter.

"Watch out for the other prisoners down there," Oswin's voice echoed from above. Laughter came after.

Hiroc hadn't forgotten the other prisoners—he just didn't want to think about them. If they were anything like the other skinwalkers he had seen, they would be nightmarish.

The ragged stone surrounding him was like fingers grasping down from above. He ignored the thought and continued onward. He was eager to speak with the prisoner. The wards that had shimmered in the sunlight were similar to those the Daughters wore. It was possible that he wielded the same magic that Edoma used to construct the wards.

Hiroc paused and flipped open his belt pouch. He took out the glove and fitted it to his hand. Feeling better now that he had a weapon, should he need it, he continued down the stairs.

The bottom of the staircase led to an open space, the only objects a strange iron chair and a rack. He held his breath and kept his eyes focused on the corridor at the end of the room. Thoughts of what terrible things had once occurred in the chamber came unbidden, bolstered by the backdrop of the crazed ramblings of the skinwalkers that drifted out from the corridor and into the open space.

Keeping his gaze fixed on the back wall as he walked, he battled the stench of feces and urine from filling his nose. Soon, the smell became almost unbearable as the skinwalkers cursed in a garbled form of unknown and known words.

He risked a sideward glance at one of the cells. A figure was shrouded in shadows. Intrigued, Hiroc held out the torch. A skinwalker with burned flesh hugged its knees to its chest. A scarred head looked up and grinned. It had no eyelids, so its eyes looked like sunbleached eggs.

Hiroc now realized he had stopped walking. He could do nothing except stare at the skinwalker. Its pupils were black as pits and seemed to swallow light.

"Don't you remember me, Hiroc? It's Merefin. The wraiths have told me all about your little secret. What will happen when Beorhtel's inquisitors come for you?"

Hiroc's breath caught in his throat. Could that really be Merefin? The monster inside the cell looked nothing like the fat farmer who had provided the acolytes with their sacrificial lambs. This was the first time Hiroc had heard a skinwalker speak in anything except those demonic growls.

In a blink, the skinwalker was at the cell's bars. It reached through and grabbed Hiroc by the throat. Hiroc thrust the torch into the skinwalker's face. The monster knocked the flaming beacon aside, and it clattered to the ground. Still burning, it made the skinwalker all the more terrifying, casting long shadows over teeth like daggers.

Hiroc tried to call out to Enlil, but the hand around his throat prevented anything save for a garble from coming out. As he struggled, he felt the wounds on his shoulders pull open. Pain seared through his body as he scrambled for his belt knife. Drawing it from its sheath, he hacked at the skinwalker's wrist. It reared backward into the cell.

Holding out his hand toward the skinwalker, Hiroc yelled, "Enlil, hear my prayer!" Blue fire shot forth from his arm and enveloped the skinwalker. It screamed, the black eyes glowing red as if hot coals sat behind them. It crumbled into cinders. The red mist floated from the smoky pile of ash and vanished. With the wards surrounding the spire, a wraith could not exist outside of its skinwalker host.

Hiroc's chest heaved with exhaustion. Rubbing his neck, he realized he had almost died. And not for the first time that week. He touched his chest and winced. He would need to dress the wounds again, but he couldn't leave now. Not when he was so close.

Without any desire to gaze into the other cells, he picked up the torch and moved as fast as he could to the end of the corridor. Bertram had been rightfully terrified, but Oswin had been jovial as ever. Perhaps Oswin was so aloof that the sight of the possessed hadn't caused every bone in his body to rattle. Hiroc's bones were certainly rattling.

He steeled his courage and peered into the prisoner's cell, afraid of what might be waiting there.

The prisoner sat with his legs crossed and his eyes closed as if he were enjoying a respite. Without looking at Hiroc, he smirked from the side of his mouth. "I see I've got myself a visitor. Were you the one responsible for all that noise a moment ago?"

Hiroc gaped at the man. He seemed unperturbed by his present state. Save for a swelling wound, his shaved head looked normal. Without sunlight, the wards looked like ordinary tattoos. Few people had markings on their skin in

Indham, but Hiroc had seen some pilgrims from Jagged Peaks with them.

The man looked around the cell. "I like this place. It's a little cold and dark, but I could see myself staying here a while. The company isn't the best, but I've had worse. That dreaded dripping noise, however, is very close to driving me insane."

Hiroc could hear it now. The steady plop of water falling into a puddle. It was soft, barely loud enough to hear. If he were stuck in the cell, it would grow infuriating.

"What's your name?" Hiroc said.

The man jumped to his feet. "Peoh, devotee of the Guardian Mun." He bowed from the hip. "What's yours?"

Hiroc supposed that meant he was a mage. And Mun was the same god who had called Edoma. Did that mean they might have known each other? Hiroc decided against mentioning her, just in case it led to this man becoming tightlipped.

"There's no point in questions unless we are friends," Peoh said. "And I cannot be your friend until I know your name."

Hiroc sighed. "My name is Hiroc."

"Ah, that is a strong name."

"You said you knew what happened at the altar."

"Aye, Aern no longer resides there. I can feel the ebb and flow of a Guardian's protection—or lack thereof, in Aernheim's case. I feel also a god's power residing within you. You are called, aren't you? Which god has named you as his own?"

"Enlil." Hiroc wasn't sure why he had answered so quickly. He guessed that speaking with someone who might know more about magic had loosened his tongue.

"A good god. Was your father or mother Talented? It sometimes skips a generation, but it's mostly passed from parent to child."

"I don't remember my mother. She fled from the Scorched Lands eighteen years ago. She brought me and my brother here. Like all the adults who came from the Scorched Lands, she was insane. The Council deemed it better to have them die a peaceful death than live out their days with the burden of insanity."

"How very good of them to take that choice upon themselves," Peoh said, his face hardening. "I'm not surprised the adults were driven insane. Seeing such horrors can do that to a person. You must have been too young to remember coming south?"

Hiroc nodded. "My twin brother and I were barely a few months old."

"Thank the gods for that. You said she came here eighteen years ago. I was in the Scorched Lands at that time. I helped a group of people go south. I must say, you do remind me of someone. Perhaps your mother was from that same group?" Peoh's hard demeanor softened. "I'm sorry for your loss. Wraiths killed my entire family."

Hiroc didn't have any family to lose to the wraiths. None except Alfric. And he would be in Eosorheim by now. Still, he offered the man a few words of condolences.

"That was a long time ago," Peoh said. "But now I am here. I have never been south of Babon's Pass. It is a beautiful land you live in. Enlil's Temple is a magnificent structure. I suppose he called you since you go there to pray most days?"

Hiroc shook his head. "Not really." In truth, he'd almost never prayed to Enlil. The only times had been as a child when the Daughters had forced him to kneel in a chapel for punishment.

"You have called upon him, yes?" Peoh asked.

"A few times now."

"And which of his gifts did he grant you?"

"Blue fire."

Peoh's eyes widened. "A formidable gift. You did this

182

without a runic object?"

"No. I had a ring. And a glove." Hiroc held out the glove Wulfnoth had given him. Rather than inspect it, Peoh frowned and looked away. Embarrassed, Hiroc put the glove in his pocket. "You seem disappointed?"

"I thought perhaps you might be one of those special Talented who doesn't need runic devices."

"Are you one of those?"

Shaking his head, Peoh held out his arm and turned it over. "This tattoo was my first. I used it as a runic device." He held out his other arm. "This one was gouged into my flesh once the first no longer worked."

"So you have to get a new tattoo whenever the last one runs out of power?" The man was covered in tattoos. Hiroc couldn't imagine how painful it must have been to endure them all.

He nodded. "It's a good reminder that magic always comes with a price. I've since learned it's better to have more than one ready to use at any moment. They bleed a little to provide the lifesoul, and then the spiritsoul is traded."

Hiroc had never heard of lifesoul or spiritsoul. "Does all magic require blood?" He thought he might be able to impress Peoh, since he hadn't used blood to call the blue fire.

"That's the temporal price. Everyone must pay it if they're to use magic."

"I never used blood." Hiroc fought back a smile. If Peoh wasn't impressed by him using a runic device, then he would certainly be impressed by this.

"Impossible," Peoh said. "The first time you called blue fire, did you have an open wound?"

Hiroc furrowed his brow, wanting to prove the man wrong. There hadn't been blood when he'd fought the giant, had there? But as he recalled that moment at Tyme's Hill, he remembered otherwise. "I cut my hand on my ring just as I was calling out to Enlil."

"And the second time?"

"I cut my hand," he said, remembering the splinter that had embedded itself in his hand when he'd struck the table in the acolyte commons.

"The third?"

"A skinwalker attacked me." Hiroc sighed. He was no more special than any other Talented. "And the fourth time," he said before Peoh could. He pulled down his collar and removed the cloth dressing. The scabs had split. Blood now trickled from the wounds.

Peoh's posture tightened at seeing the wounds. "I see the skinwalker you killed earlier wasn't the first. You might find yourself a warrior-mage one day!" He grinned and clicked his fingers. "There you have it. Blood is always required."

Why hadn't Edoma told him this? Was she intentionally withholding information so that he wouldn't practice magic? "But what about spiritsoul?" Hiroc asked. "Whatever that is, I didn't trade it."

"You did. You made an unspoken bargain with Enlil when you called upon him. Thankfully, he is a just god, so he will not charge too much. One day you will visit the Bargaining Plaza to barter for your magic, as all mages do. I would advise against invoking Enlil until then. An eternity is a very long time to pay back your debts."

It was all so much to take in. Peoh was telling him more than Edoma had. But he still had so many questions. "How can I use magic without runes? I thought all magic required them."

Peoh shook his head. "They're not required to perform simple magic. Runes also prevent the runic devices from running out too quickly. The reason your ring only worked for a short while was because the devotion stored within it depleted quickly. Had you used rune circles to call the fire, it would have lasted for many invocations."

Unsure whether he was taking this all in, Hiroc rubbed his head.

With a laugh, Peoh said, "You need only remember three things. Only those Devoted or Talented can use magic. All magic requires the use of runic devices. And there is always a cost—lifesoul, and most times, spiritsoul."

The term "devoted" was foreign to Hiroc. He was about to ask Peoh what it meant, when the mage clapped his hands together, as though he were concluding a lecture.

"Now that I've given you a lesson in magic," he said, "it's time I requested something from you. Indham's Council must know about my presence if Aernheim is to be saved. There are some costs too great to pay for salvation, and I fear someone might pay them."

"What costs?"

"Best not to speak of them," Peoh said, shaking his head. "Tell your Council that I wait within these dungeons." He sat in the middle of the cell, crossed his legs, and closed his eyes. He hummed a whimsical tune while his nostrils flared with breathing.

Hiroc shook his head. Did this man truly think he could save Indham? He *did* know a lot about magic, but he also seemed aloof, maybe even crazy.

When Hiroc got to the top of the stairs, Oswin was no longer there. It was strange for him to abandon his post. The sound of feet dragging filtered in from outside. Hiroc put the torch back in the sconce and went to look.

Ealstan and Kipp were dragging an unconscious Oswin out from the spire. Hiroc ran after them, fumbling to fit the glove over his hand.

Laughing, Ealstan and Kipp threw Oswin onto the back of a cart and leaped onto it.

Hiroc realized he'd been fitting the glove to the wrong hand, but by the time he had it on his left hand, they were already halfway down the street.

185

He held out his hand, pointing at them like an archer aimed an arrow. If he called fire, it could hit the cart. What would happen then? It would go up in flames, Oswin along with Ealstan and Kipp.

Groaning, Hiroc dropped his hand and removed the glove.

Where were they taking Oswin? And why? The only reason he could think of was that they were trying to use Oswin to get to Hiroc. It was strange since Hiroc wasn't exactly close with Oswin. Sure, he'd drunk with him a couple of times at The Flaming Monkey, but little more than that. But that was the only explanation.

Hiroc glanced back at the spire. He had been given a mission. It would mean foregoing that to help Oswin. No, not foregoing, just postponing. Indham would live another night. Peoh was safe within his cell.

A soft voice whispered in his mind, telling him that going after Oswin was the right thing to do. Strangely, that voice belonged to Alfric.

32

EDOMA

EDOMA'S room was a mess, and yet there was no dragon
vial. Garments lay scattered about the floor. Dust
flittered through the air before settling.

As Edoma searched her room for the dozenth time, the
possibility that someone might have stolen the vial came to
her. It was a stupid thought. Why would anyone want to steal
it? They couldn't use it for anything. Selling it would provide
some coin, but wealth was becoming increasingly useless in
Indham. There was an aura of doom about the place. The
people were aware that the human blood from the dead
wouldn't last forever. Soon, there would be no more, and
what would Mother Superior Edoma do then?

She passed over her bed and paused. The chest seemed to
call to her, begging her to open it so that she could offer more
lifesoul to the scrying crystal. She knew it was merely her mind
desiring the otherworld. Using her foot, she pushed against
the chest until it was hidden beneath the bed's overhanging
sheets. Where the chest had been was a rope bracelet. She
grabbed it and slipped it onto her wrist. The knots had been
sealed with wax to look like precious jewels.

Idmaer had given her the bracelet. She had refused to

wear anything valuable. Ingenious as always, he had used rope and dyed candle wax to create a piece of jewelry that was simultaneously worthless and more valuable to her than anything in the world.

That moment, when he had given the bracelet to her, Edoma knew this was the man she would marry. And she did. That month, they were wed within the Basilica crypt. Later, they performed the old rites in their sacred room beneath the spire. She conceived that night, an awkward moment of bliss that she had wished would last forever.

Someone rapped on the doorframe. Edoma brushed away a stray tear and turned.

Mildryd stood within the doorway. The robes that tugged against her broad shoulders were clean, but her face still bore the wards from the night before, the symbols ebbed in crimson on her pale skin. They would remain until the magic within them was spent. She, like the other Daughters, had been helping paint the wards while Edoma spent most of the day traveling around the town to empower them.

"The wards are finished for this afternoon," Mildryd said. "There's no way for any of us Daughters to assist with the empowering?"

Edoma shook her head. "It's my burden alone." Every time she empowered a ward, Edoma considered the years of enslavement she would suffer to Mun when she passed from this life to the next.

Mildryd was one of the only people in Indham who knew that Edoma was Talented. Even Idmaer didn't know about that. Edoma hadn't drawn wards since she had come to Indham all those years ago. She had sworn never to practice magic again, but their dire situation made her break that oath. Talented were meant to register with King Beorhtel. Most didn't. And they were hunted down by the inquisitors. Edoma had thought her own secret was safe. From what the acolyte Ealstan had said, it seemed that her secret was now known to all. Of course, to think otherwise would have been to believe the people a collection of fools.

Not wanting to speak any more about magic, Edoma asked, "Still no sign of the vial?"

Mildryd shook her head. "The Daughters have upturned the entirety of the temple, and they haven't found it."

"How much blood remains?"

"Enough for another two weeks. We're slowly running out."

Maybe people will die, Edoma thought. It was a terrible thing to hope for, but it would provide for more wards.

"Then we'll need to ration it carefully," she said.

"Surely someone else might have dragon's blood? What of Idmaer?"

At the mention of Idmaer, Edoma realized that she was still wearing the bracelet. Making an effort not to be seen, she removed it and dropped it into her pocket. "Idmaer won't have anything dragon related. Especially after what happened with the dragon trade."

"A tragedy," Mildryd said. It was more than a tragedy. Idmaer had lost most of his influence after the people had learned the methods used to capture and enslave the dragons. He had allowed the use of suppression stones—barbaric devices that forced a magical creature to act against its will. According to Idmaer, the town had needed the money. After the fact, no one wanted to believe him. Suppression stones were one of the greatest evils of the past age. It wasn't only the stones that had turned the people against him. He had emptied most of the treasury to feed, clothe, and home the Fatherless. In some way, Edoma felt guilty. She had been the one to convince Idmaer to adopt the Fatherless. But an empty treasury didn't justify the dragon trade.

She sighed, trying to think of some possible way to resolve this predicament. Was there anyone else who might possess dragon's blood? Saega had a large collection of magical items and relics. If anyone were to have dragon's blood, it would be him.

"Saega," Edoma said.

"He's been unwell of late. Have you seen anything of him?"

"Not since the warriors went on their quest." It was only after saying it aloud that Edoma realized just how long it had been. He had been coughing and spluttering even a week ago. Perhaps he would have gotten over the sickness . . . but it could have easily gotten worse.

"After I empower the wards for tonight," Edoma said, "I'm going to pay Saega a visit. Hopefully he's well enough to speak." In truth, she also hoped he was still alive. It had been easy to forget how old he was. Even in the last month, he seemed to have worn away.

Edoma barked orders to the Daughters as she entered the carriage. She visited the various buildings important enough to ward. The inner buildings of the Basilica. Enlil's Temple. The Council Hall. Idmaer's Spire. Each ward she empowered seemed to take something from her.

By the time she was finished and back at the temple, she was aching. The sun still lingered on the horizon. She painted a final ward on her face and empowered it, filtering a small amount of spiritsoul into the symbols. Warmth rushed through her, and a soft reddish glow pulsed above her eyebrows.

Bidding the Daughters farewell, she made her way to Saega's home within the Basilica Quarter. He wasn't a priest of Aern, but because of his close relationship with Idmaer and the other priests, he had been given the small house.

When Edoma entered Saega's home, the scent of freshly cooked meat greeted her. Bones sat within a bowl on the table. Empty vials were arrayed in a neat line next to the chair Saega normally sat in. Edoma picked one up and sniffed it. She almost dropped the bottle from rearing back so quickly.

It was medicine. Potent and more likely to burn your insides than cure a sickness.

Why hadn't he come to her for healing?

Although Saega wasn't there now, he had definitely been here recently. That much was a relief. She couldn't imagine him dying. He was the only person other than Jaruman who had seen the terrors of the Scorched Lands. The Fatherless had journeyed from the Scorched Lands to get to Indham, but not one of them was old enough to remember what it was like. Thank Enlil for that.

The candles had burned away, now nothing more than disfigured clumps of wax. Had Saega been spending the nights in total darkness?

Glass figurines, ash wands—the room was overflowing with objects, most no more magical than a rock. Not knowing where to start, she searched for the likeliest place Saega might keep something as valuable as dragon blood.

The hunt took her to the storeroom in the back. Unlike the rest of the house, it was almost bare. A single table rested against a wall. Edoma removed the black robes that covered it. Large enough to be bedsheets, she held them in her hands. It still felt so soft after many years. It was Saega's runic device. He had worn it while they had traveled through the Scorched Lands. It had lasted the entire journey without a stain or a tear.

She put the robes aside. The only other items on the table were a suppression stone and Agnerod's Touch—Saega's fox-head staff. She reached for it but paused. A magical weapon of this sort bonded to its owner. Touching a foreign staff might lead to unforeseen consequences. They'd experienced that when they'd acquired the staves.

The suppression stone made her scowl. They were evil objects. Someone had made them with magic so that they could control magical creatures. Idmaer had allowed their use so the dragons could be captured. Now Beorhtel equipped his dragonriders with them so the magnificent beasts they rode were nothing more than husks, extensions of their rider's minds.

Disappointed, Edoma threw the robes back over the table and returned to the front room. The mess seemed to glare at her until she could take it no longer. She gathered the wax and dumped it outside. She replaced the holders with new candles. As she cleaned, she hoped that wherever Saega was, that he had made it to a warded building. Finally, she gathered the empty potion flasks. The smell that wafted from the washing basin was foul, but soon the flasks were cleaned and stacked in a corner.

Placing her hands on her hips, she admired her efforts. Even that little work had made the room look much cleaner. Out of breath, she sat on Saega's cushioned chair.

Sitting in the empty house soon made Edoma uneasy. There was something about the place and the absence of Bodil that made it seem wrong. Sure, she had remarried before her death, but, to Edoma, she had always been Saega's wife, even after she'd married Wulfnoth. They'd always seemed like two halves of a whole. But behind the closed doors of a home, much went on that outsiders weren't privy to.

Edoma could attest to that. She reached into her pocket and took out the rope bracelet. The touch of the fraying threads as she twirled it around her fingers unsettled her.

Through the window, she stared at Idmaer's Spire. It had once been her home as much as Idmaer's. The man she had once loved more than life itself had fathered her children. He'd fathered Alfric. He deserved to know what had happened to his son.

Edoma stood. *You mustn't*, she told herself. But her mind knew exactly what it would take to convince her to go there. Without dragon blood, the best thing she could do was enter the First Priest's tomb. To do that, she needed the First Priest's medallion to open it. All it would take was convincing Idmaer to give it to her.

33

IDMAER

"CONTINUE polishing the relics," Idmaer called out to the acolytes before leaving the Basilica's reliquary room. He made for his spire, glad to be away from the Basilica. There were only so many menial tasks he could demand of the acolytes. Without a Guardian, they were without purpose. Of course, they didn't know Aern wasn't within the altar at Tyme's Hill. Like everyone else, they had believed the lie that Aern had simply been weakened.

Many of them were asking questions about why Aern wasn't offered sacrifices, though. A few days had led to a few questions, but nine days led to many questions. Soon the Council would be asking them, too. He could handle the populace hating him for his lies, and even the acolytes, since he could simply hide within his spire. But it would be unthinkable for the Council to find out that he had lied to them; that would surely earn a death sentence, High Priest or not. He was more a king than priest, but even kings could fall.

He walked through the gardens and stepped over Edoma's wards that encircled the spire. They illuminated every night. Idmaer had often watched the wraith clouds attempt to breach the circle. Sparks flew as soon as they touched the boundary. As powerful as the spire was, it couldn't protect against wraiths. Only those mysterious wards Edoma drew were capable of that. Idmaer wasn't sure when he'd realized it, but he now knew that Edoma had been no librarian in Mundos. In fact, he was almost certain she'd been a mage. Thinking about it made him angry, that she would keep such a secret from him, but he soothed his fury by remembering that he'd also kept secrets from her. Their marriage, while good at times, had been a nest of lies and deceit. He was glad it was over.

As soon as Idmaer entered the spire, the customary comfort washed over him. It wasn't just a feeling of returning home after a long day; the spire offered him a genuine sanctuary that calmed his mind and rejuvenated his body. He hadn't slept more than a few hours a night since taking ownership, nor had he been bedridden with any sicknesses.

He grasped the medallion around his neck. The staircase shifted to meet him. As he walked the stone steps, he glanced at the portrait of his father. What would he think now? Aern's orb had been shattered. Surely he would castigate Idmaer for allowing it to happen. But what could have been done? There had been no sign of the giant nor any indication of his motives besides pure malice.

The staircase continued upward, stone shifting upon stone, until Idmaer reached his desired location—the spire's peak. For ten years, since his father had conducted the ceremony of transfer, Idmaer and the spire had been one in mind, if not in body. The spire transformed with his mental state—a magic that required constant meditation to control the passions. In a way, it had been good that he and Edoma had separated, since she tended to enrage him, and the spire mirrored that. During those days, it had been a volatile place where numerous injuries had been caused by disappearing steps or a servant crushed between walls that quickly narrowed.

Thousands of years ago, the First Priest had built the spire with godstone and an iron composition unlike anything else in the world. Its purpose was a mystery. Some said it was an act of hubris, a tower to spite the gods, whereas others suggested it was a means of entry into the Infernal City—the world of the gods. Regardless, the spire's magic was unlike anything even Beorhtel's inquisitors were capable of performing. Like the medallion around Idmaer's neck, the spire was passed down from High Priest to High Priest. Apparently, an unbroken succession extended from Idmaer to the First Priest, though there were arguments about certain links in the chain.

Idmaer spent the next hour within his study, opening letters and writing responses. He continued to correspond with King Beorhtel, who continued to reiterate that no one from Aernheim should cross the border. Idmaer daubed his initials on one particular letter to King Beorhtel. He cursed when he realized he had forgotten to address the king with the necessary titles he demanded of all correspondence.

The spire responded to Idmaer's mood with a sudden lurch that shook the overhanging beams. The desk rattled, sending letters from all over the continent to the floor.

Idmaer still couldn't believe King Beorhtel's outright refusal to help them. Indham's warriors were employed within Beorhtel's army as dragonriders. The dragons they rode upon had been captured by those same warriors. The suppression stones that forced the dragons to obey had come from the mines below Jagged Peaks. Everything the people of Indham had done for Beorhtel was now rejected.

Screwing up the vellum parchment, Idmaer tossed it onto a pile that was quickly becoming more expensive than any of the busts, tapestries, or relics haphazardly hung or mounted wherever there was space. He slid another parchment before him. Painstakingly, he rewrote the first letter. A knock came from the door, and he fumbled the quill, striking a crude line across the parchment.

His head shot up, ready to glare daggers at whoever had

interrupted his letter-writing. His anger pulsed through the spire.

Edoma's face peeked through the doorway, and Idmaer's tenseness dissolved. He had sensed a presence entering the spire earlier, but the last person he had expected was Edoma. The room seemed to expand as he exhaled, though it was impossible to tell whether it had actually increased in size or whether it was mere perception.

"Edoma, please, come in." He stood and beckoned her with a wave of his hand.

She shuffled into the room, the first time she had stepped through the doorway in many years. Her slight frame navigated through the mess to the rug beside the fireplace, where they'd once both lain, naked and satisfied. She had been prettier then, youthful and supple. Memories pained Idmaer, and he did his best to shun them.

The more pressing matter was why she had ignored their past grievances and come to the office? Perhaps she had come to apologize? Patches of dust and grime spotted her garments as if she had been in the middle of working and had decided to visit the spire on a whim. Glowing wards gave her face more color than it normally had. It gave her a wild look as if she were a witchdoctor from a barbarian tribe in Tygeheim.

Idmaer realized he had not spoken after inviting her in and said with a dry mouth, "The storms have cleared. Although without Aern, storms are something we must become accustomed to." The weather was always a suitable topic for conversation, no matter with whom you spoke, though the subject had become more interesting of late.

Her eyes lingered on the rug for a moment before she took a seat on the stool beside the fireplace. She appraised the room with a frown, staring at the portrait Idmaer had the spire construct from a compilation of godstone bricks of various shades. It was that artistic ability lurking within the spire's consciousness that made Idmaer think it was somehow alive and possibly even possessed a rational mind.

"I see this place is the same as always," Edoma said, turning up her nose. "Actually, I'd say it's worse than when I was last here." Her reaction wasn't a surprise. She had always hated how his office became the dumping ground for weapons, armor, books, and just about anything else he could get his hands on from outside Indham. In the years without her influence, the room had become nearly impassable.

"When did you become so negative?" Idmaer said in jest. In truth, Edoma had always been the kind of person to assume the worst. "You've come to condemn me for the bloodletting?" He had started the process himself. After hearing that the leeches would taint the blood, he thought that the mechanisms would be useful. Edoma was using similar ones to extract blood from corpses. Oswin had removed the mechanisms from the dungeons and taken them to the statuary behind the spire. There were only a few volunteers who'd come so far, but Idmaer hoped there would be more.

"As long as the people who give their blood are willing, I can't condemn you."

Satisfied, Idmaer smiled. There were a few he wouldn't mind taking to those barbaric devices. Most people, really. More likely that they would turn on him and he would become the first unwilling victim.

Edoma stared into the fire. She seemed to have trouble meeting his gaze, as though there was something she wished to say but lacked the courage to say it. "Do you think Hiroc will keep his tongue? I imagine a young man like him is chomping at the bit to talk with someone about what he saw."

Idmaer rubbed his beard, hiding his surprise behind gnarled fingers. He didn't think she would speak of Hiroc. "He will remain silent. He has his faults; reneging on promises is not among them."

"He saw a terrible thing. He cannot be blamed if he speaks."

"Oh, I won't blame him. I only hope this doesn't break him. We must guard our tongues. He won't take kindly to being pitied."

"He reminds me of someone I know," Edoma muttered.

Ignoring her, Idmaer returned to his desk and sat. Noticing a scroll out of line, he shifted it so that it was aligned at right angles with the other objects. Unlike the rest of the room, the desk had to remain immaculate. It was impossible to work otherwise. He caught himself before he adjusted the inkwell. Had he always been so fussy?

He looked at Edoma, and, for the first time in forever, he saw the woman who'd captured his heart long ago. Here she was, standing before him, something on her mind and yet too afraid to say it. He was ready for her apology.

"We're not competing sides, Edoma. If you have something to say, please say it."

She picked at the dust on her dress and flipped her braid over her shoulder. "I think it's about time we put aside our past. Indham needs us to be united. The warriors have been gone a week."

Idmaer smiled, glad he hadn't had to apologize. "They have likely arrived at Hurn's altar by now. Perhaps another week and they'll return. Unless something has happened to them . . ." Something unsettled him, though he couldn't place his finger on it. The topic appeared to unsettle Edoma, too. "Ah, it's probably just the weather," he said with a dismissive wave. "Cenred and Sigebert can handle themselves."

She stared into her lap. Unsettled by the strange way she was acting, Idmaer went over to the window. He didn't call the bricks away this time. More storm clouds had gathered over Indham.

"The gods have cursed us. Damn them, every last one."

"For a priest, you are an impious man."

"I stopped being a priest a long time ago. I'm more king than priest now."

199

Edoma shook her head. "Have you no trust in the gods?"

"You still believe in them? I'm afraid I've grown too old and weary for such notions."

"I thought you impious but not an atheist." She almost spat out the word as if it were horse manure.

"No, not an atheist. The gods exist beyond our plane, but do they have anything to do with us?"

"They gave us the Guardians."

Idmaer didn't respond. He didn't feel like arguing with Edoma about the finer points of philosophy. It wasn't that he thought her beneath him; it was the contrary. She would have been capable of rebutting every one of his claims, providing an answer to every stipulation. But in his heart, though she might defy it, he knew the gods didn't care about men anymore. Even during the plentiful times when Aern protected them, he had known this for truth. The gods had closed their ears to the cries of men, their eyes to the suffering of the poor. He knew the counterarguments. He could recite every one of them. But he wouldn't. He had long rejected them.

Idmaer wandered over to the fireplace to warm himself. While he stood there, neither he nor Edoma spoke. He couldn't guess what she was thinking. Perhaps it was of their shared memories, of bliss and paradise, suffering and sadness. He hoped she still remembered them.

He poured himself a goblet of wine, an import from five hundred miles down the Edin River, as far as the known lands reached. He poured another for Edoma. She had always appreciated good wine.

"No," she said, "I've given it up."

Idmaer raised his goblet. "Then surely the gods must exist, for that is a miracle!"

The jest earned him a sour look. She had been offended at his sacrilege. So be it.

"You don't happen to have any dragon blood in the spire?" Edoma said as she peered about the room. "I had a small vial, but I misplaced it."

It wasn't like her to lose something. Even if she had, she wouldn't admit to it. Narrowing his eyes, he said, "You think I stole it?"

Edoma raised her hands. "Of course not."

Idmaer swallowed. He couldn't help acting defensive. He still wished he'd never stolen from Edoma. He sighed. "No dragon blood here."

With a skeptical frown, she scanned the room again. "A pity." Her eyes settled on him. He followed her gaze to the medallion resting on his chest.

"It's good to see you still wear that, even though you no longer believe."

Idmaer lifted the medallion. Despite its small size, it was heavy. "I'll always wear it. Without it, I cannot control the spire." She had seen the medallion so many times before, so her apparent interest seemed unusual.

"May I?" Without waiting for a response, she grabbed the medallion. As she inspected it, a sweet scent drifted up from her hair, filling Idmaer's nostrils with a forgotten desire. She had always smelled so beautiful.

"I need it," she said, still clutching it in her hand. The determination in her face made Idmaer think that she might wring his neck with the leather cord should he refuse, but he had to. Smiling, he grabbed her wrist and squeezed slightly. She removed her hand.

She clutched her wrist, stricken as though he had squeezed her with more force than he had. "Could you not live without your medallion for an hour?"

"Never," Idmaer said. "It would mean separation from the spire. I haven't taken it off since my father gave it to me." He feared what that utter loneliness would be like.

Edoma grunted. "Then I will be going now."

He knew this wasn't the end of it. Still, he stood and followed Edoma out from his room.

34

EDOMA

E DOMA paused at the staircase, her fingers drumming on the handrail. She turned, biting her lip. "If you won't give the medallion to me, then come with me to the catacombs. I believe the medallion could be the key to opening the First Priest's tomb."

Idmaer gasped. The spire swayed, and the bricks lightened in color. It was always disturbing watching it change with his moods, but Edoma was more surprised this time. He'd never been all that interested in her quest to find the hidden tomb within the catacombs.

"No," Idmaer said, his face pale. "I cannot go there with you. Neither will the medallion leave my person. The warriors will return soon. Iurn will give us refuge. We don't need this grimoire." His gaze became stony. "I refuse."

From a height of forty feet, she glanced down. The foyer was filled with armored suits and shelves packed with histories of the known world. She looked everywhere except Idmaer's cold eyes. The entire evening, she'd been wearing the bracelet. Idmaer hadn't noticed it at all. Smugly, he'd sat, entombed in all that worthless dross he called collector's items, while she'd apologized. Instead of returning the apology, he'd gone on to claim the gods never helped mankind.

Why did it have to be him she needed help from? Any other person would have been better. The more she thought about it, the angrier she became. Balling her fists, she whirled upon him, her rage finally unfettered.

"You are a selfish man," she said. Her heart ached to the point of bursting as she thought of how they had once been so in love. While Idmaer's father was High Priest, inside this very spire, deep within the dungeons, they had frequently met in secret. Their love had been forbidden because she was an outsider. And now she saw Idmaer for who he had become—a conceited old man.

Despite her disgust, she still needed him. "Inside the tomb is the grimoire of the First Priest," she said, almost pleading. "With it, we could save Indham."

Idmaer's eyes widened. "Surely not. It is just a book."

But Edoma wasn't finished. "And yet you refuse to do me this small favor. You care only for yourself. Did you know that Alfric, our son, is now a skinwalker?" She didn't say that there may still be hope for him. That would only alleviate Idmaer of some guilt. And she didn't want that.

Idmaer shook his head. The ground shook beneath their feet. He had hardly seemed to hear her. "You say this grimoire can save us?"

She couldn't believe him. When he'd found out his son had become victim to the wraiths, he'd thought to care about everyone except him. Her left hand tightened around her staff. The knots in the wood pierced the skin of her palm. Blood dripped down the length of it.

Before she could swallow her anger, she lashed out. The staff slammed into Idmaer's midsection. "You're a despicable man," she said.

He groaned and clutched his stomach.

Edoma realized then her foolishness. The spire lurched. It seemed to groan along with Idmaer.

The stairs crumbled out from Edoma's feet. Letting go of her staff, her hands flayed as they grasped air. Her eyes bulged. She let out a breathless scream.

"Enough!" Idmaer cried as she fell.

At the last moment, before she would have fallen to her death, the ground became soft as cushions. The staff clattered beside her. Scrambling to her feet, Edoma grabbed the staff and stormed out from the spire.

35

HIROC

HIROC marched down the corridor toward Ealstan's room. He had searched for Oswin elsewhere but could find no sign of him. The runic glove fitted snugly over his left hand. Twisting the doorknob, he was about to push the door open when he heard a familiar voice— Saega the augur.

"Are you certain they were runes?" the deep voice droned from beyond the door.

"They were like ones the Daughters wear at night, except they reflected like metal does in the sunlight. He's being kept in Idmaer's dungeons with the skinwalkers."

Hiroc's heart skipped a beat. They were talking about Peoh. Kipp must have told Ealstan about him.

"Then he must be the mage I sensed," Saega continued. "I don't know why he's here, but it can't be good. I'll deal with him. In the meantime, you're going to find the missing page."

"There weren't any other pages."

"Do not make me a liar, Ealstan." There was a brief silence. "Take the book and find the page that's missing from it. By tomorrow evening, I want to know you've made progress. No more playing. Deal with that Fatherless. Make sure no one sees you."

"I can't yet," Ealstan said. "I'm using him for bait." He croaked, and a dry rasping sound followed, as though he were being choked.

"Cease your foolish games and do as I say," said Saega. "You did organize the priestly healer to look at my illness?"

"Yes, he'll take care of you tonight."

A thud sounded. The floorboards groaned as someone moved.

Hiroc rushed into the neighboring room. He shoved the door, but it wouldn't shut. He looked down. A fox skull's empty eye sockets stared up at him. He stumbled backward, falling over the wooden prayer stool.

Stars flashed before Hiroc's eyes. Saega's staff clopped as it hit the wooden planks.

"You have big ears for an acolyte," Saega said. His face was a sickly green with open sores. "Do you always listen at the doors of your fellow acolytes?"

Hiroc groaned as he stood.

Saega drew his cowl over his face and snarled. "What did you hear?" Hiroc had never seen the augur act this way. In public, he had always been amiable.

"Nothing," Hiroc said. "I mean, I heard a sound like someone choking, so I went to see what was happening."

Saega licked his lips. His tongue was blue and swollen. "Get on with you, acolyte. It's only because of your mother that I don't have you dealt with."

Hiroc bowed and walked past Saega when powerful fingers wrapped around his arm.

"It's best not to poke your ears where they don't belong," Saega said as his grip tightened, "lest you wake one day without them." His eyes fluttered. "Ah, so you've been called. I see now why Ealstan despises you." He released his grip. Hiroc watched as the man hobbled toward the staircase.

Everyone thought it a matter of time until Saega keeled

over. There was even an underground wager on the number of remaining days until he died. After feeling the man's strength, Hiroc thought he ought to live for a few more decades at least. Whatever the man was eating, it gave him strength enough to bruise Hiroc's arm with a grip. But those sores suggested he was deathly ill. How could a man be so strong and yet look like he was ready to pass through death's gates?

There was only one explanation—Saega was Talented. After all, he had known Hiroc was Talented after touching him. Edoma had done the same thing, and she was Talented.

When he was sure Saega wouldn't return, Hiroc entered Ealstan's room.

It was empty.

In the small amount of time Hiroc had been speaking with Saega, Ealstan must have escaped. A sheet of parchment lay on the bed.

"*If you wish to save your Fatherless friend, then come to the kitchen's cellars.*"

Night had already fallen, which meant Ealstan had to be within the dorms or the common room. He wouldn't go outside. The thought struck Hiroc that maybe Ealstan had left Oswin in an unwarded area, but he rejected it. He refused to think like that.

There would be no leaving the Basilica. Not for Hiroc. Not for Ealstan.

Hiroc just had to find him.

* * *

Hiroc watched as Ealstan lay sprawled over a bench, tossing his dagger in the air before catching it again. He continued throwing the weapon as if he hadn't noticed Hiroc in the room.

"Where's Oswin?" Hiroc said through clenched teeth.

"Getting some fresh air," he said without looking at Hiroc.

"You left him outside?"

Ealstan sighed. He swung his legs around the bench and stood. "He's a Fatherless. I couldn't bring him inside the Basilica. It would be an affront to the Holy Order."

"*I'm* a Fatherless."

"No," said Ealstan, sheathing the dagger, "you're not."

Hiroc narrowed his eyes. "I might be an acolyte now, but I came from the north just like everyone else."

"Your mother did, yes, but you were born here in Indham." Ealstan smirked. "I know all about your parents. Mother Superior Edoma and High Priest Idmaer."

"No," Hiroc said, shaking his head. "My mother died after she entered Indham's gates. Just like all the other adults." He didn't know who his father was, but he couldn't have been High Priest Idmaer.

"Quit being so naive," Ealstan snapped. "The only reason I didn't have you killed in your sleep was because you weren't a Fatherless. I almost tried before I knew the truth. Saega stopped me. He told me everything. Idmaer and Edoma gave you and your brother up." He grinned, as though he was taking great pleasure in revealing this to Hiroc.

What motive might he have for lying? Besides, there were probably better lies.

Hiroc found himself accepting Ealstan's words. Mildryd the librarian had said she was present at his birth. The only way that would have been possible was if he had been born in Indham. She had seemed crazy at the time, but he doubted that now.

"If you don't hate me because I'm Fatherless, why are you doing this? I haven't done anything wrong by you."

Hiroc focused on Ealstan, hoping that he might discern the truth.

Ealstan's face hardened and his nostrils flared. "Your very existence is an affront to me. You were called, and I wasn't. I've been devoted to Aern since I was able to utter my first prayer. You said Aern spoke with you, and unlike the others, I believed you. Every week I went to Tyme's Hill, hoping I might hear his voice, too. No matter how many times I cried out to him, he was silent."

"It wasn't Aern who called me."

"What?" Ealstan frowned.

"Enlil claimed me as his own."

"Then I have no reason to hate you," Ealstan said, seeming almost disappointed.

"You'll let Oswin go?"

Ealstan shook his head. "I can't do that. I'm not going outside to get him."

Hiroc gritted his teeth, his fears confirmed. If he had to, he would go outside to rescue Oswin. "Where did you leave him?"

Ealstan stepped in front of the stairs, blocking Hiroc's path. "I can't let you go."

"You said you don't hate me anymore."

"Saega doesn't want anyone alive who spoke with the tattooed mage."

Then Bertram was on Saega's list, too.

Hiroc could have told Ealstan that he wouldn't report back to anyone—but that would have been a lie. Ealstan would easily see through it.

"The mage can save us," Hiroc said.

"No one can save Indham. We don't deserve to be saved. You don't know what the First Priest did, do you? You don't know what the carcaern orbs really are."

"I don't care," Hiroc said. "What matters now are all those innocent people who will die unless the Council learns about the tattooed mage."

"No one is innocent," Ealstan said. "Every one of us is guilty of some sin or other."

This wasn't going anywhere. Hiroc could see there would be no reasoning with the other man. Whatever strange ideas he had, probably acquired from Saega, were like mental blocks to his mind. Ealstan's hand dropped to the knife at his belt. His fingers caressed the pommel bearing Aern's likeness.

Remaining calm, Hiroc bit his cheek until the taste of salty blood wet his tongue. "Enlil!" Blue fire wrapped around his runic glove, swirling like a flaming serpent.

Before Hiroc could launch the fireball, Ealstan's blade flashed into his hand, and Hiroc was thrown backward. He skidded across the ground and hit the wall. Pain knifed down his back as he fought for breath.

Ealstan's blade hadn't made contact, yet Hiroc had been pushed by a great force.

"You might be Talented," Ealstan said, knife held downward so the blade was beneath his hand, "but I'm Devoted."

Again Ealstan thrust the blade toward Hiroc. Although he was ten strides away, an invisible force punched Hiroc's face. The back of his neck hit the wall, and he blacked out.

36

FRYDA

"YOU did what you had to," Jaruman said to Fryda. "He lost an eye, but you could have lost far more than that. Don't worry about the hairpin. I'm just glad it helped you. I've said before that you Daughters should be given some kind of weapons. Especially if you're walking around the alley."

When she'd come to the Flaming Monkey, Fryda had scrubbed her hands until they throbbed. There was little blood on them, but she couldn't stop. When sleep evaded her in the cellar, she'd come to Jaruman.

"There've been plenty of stories like that of late," he said. "The Alley's gotten much worse. What were you doing there?" He sighed. "Sorry. I'm not blaming you. A woman should be able to walk where she likes without the scum trying a damned thing. Not all the victims were as lucky as you."

Fryda sipped from her mug and put it back down on the bench. The mead tasted stale. Weeks ago, she'd been unable to sleep until after midnight because of the clamoring drunks downstairs. But now, the inn was filled with families huddled together, most asleep.

The Flaming Monkey had been one of the few buildings

to be warded, and the inn had become home to those who weren't fortunate enough to be Daughters, members of the Holy Order of Aern, or warriors. Thankfully, Edoma had warded the storehouse in Alchemist's Alley, so there was unlikely to be a repeat of that afternoon's mishap.

"I just hope Edoma's thought of something more permanent," Jaruman said as he stared at the people sleeping.

"She said Sigebert and Cenred made it to Eosorheim." Fryda thought of telling Jaruman about what else Edoma had seen in the scrying crystal, but she couldn't. Jaruman would know immediately that she intended to find Alfric, and that would probably end with her being locked in her room.

"That's good," he said. "Hopefully they manage to convince Hurn to help us."

"She wants to send another party."

"That would mean she thinks they've failed. There's few others who Hurn wouldn't kill before they could enter Eosorheim. That pair were the best for the job."

Fryda scratched behind her ear.

"You intend to go," he said.

How did he guess? There would be no hiding anything from him now. "Not just to Eosorheim," she said. "Edoma seems to think that Alfric might still be alive."

"He's a skinwalker. His soul no longer inhabits his body."

"Edoma said he was different from the others."

"How does she know that?" Jaruman's eyebrows pinched together. "She's used that bloody scrying crystal again? I told her not to." His voice was growing louder. Some of the people stirred in their beds.

"I think she's right," Fryda cut in, hoping she might stop Jaruman on one of his tirades. "I have a feeling."

"Need I remind you what I think of feelings?"

Fryda shook her head. "It's more than just a feeling. Besides, Edoma wouldn't say that he was alive if he wasn't. She's seen skinwalkers. She knows the difference." She sighed, hoping Jaruman wouldn't be angry with what she said next. "I wanted to go after Alfric, but Edoma refused. So I stole her dragon vial."

"A stupid thing to do. It's useless to you without a mage."

"I came to realize that. I was going to give it back to Edoma when I saw a man outside the gates. The wards lit up beneath his feet, but he didn't look like a skinwalker. He looked like a regular man, except he had tattooed wards on his face."

Jaruman's eye widened. "Was there anything else?"

"The wards shimmered in the sun."

"Peoh," Jaruman said, gripping the bench with his large hands.

"You know the man?"

Jaruman nodded. "He was the Archmage of Mundos."

"So he *was* a mage," she said under her breath.

"More than that. He took a vow with Edoma and Saega before leaving Mundos. They were to pay the south back for the destruction of their orb. That vengeance was to shatter a southern orb, thereby bringing the wraiths to that region."

Fryda gasped. "Does that mean Edoma and Peoh are responsible for what happened to Aern?"

"They swore never to fulfill that vow."

Vowing not to fulfill another vow didn't make much sense. Still, Fryda agreed with Jaruman that they both loved Indham's people. And if Jaruman told her that they wouldn't have been capable of killing Aern, she believed him.

"Peoh's presence here must have something to do with Aern," Jaruman said. "I suspect he came to fulfill the oath where Edoma and Saega didn't."

"Hiroc said a giant was on Tyme's Hill. The man I saw at the gates wasn't a giant."

"Not all men are as they appear to be."

"I was going to ask him if he could ward me with the dragon blood, but Bertram had him imprisoned inside Idmaer's Spire."

Jaruman squatted behind the bench so that he was hidden from view. The clinking of metal sounded. When he stood, an ax was clipped to his belt. He held a short spear in one hand. It was the spear he had trained Fryda with ever since he'd adopted her.

He stepped out from the bench and handed her the spear. "Take this to bed with you tonight. In the morning, you will use what I've taught you. Bertram's probably imprisoned Peoh in the same cell as the skinwalkers. He's a resourceful man, though. Let's hope he lasts the night."

"But you said he shattered the orb. Why would we want to save him?"

"Because he might be the only man who can save Indham."

Fryda was surprised Jaruman was going to let her come with him to the spire. He must have known by now that she would have followed him.

Before she descended into the cellar, Jaruman brushed aside her hair with his calloused fingers. He'd never kissed her as a father did. He'd always said it wasn't right, him not really being her father. But when he touched her hair like that, she knew he loved her like a father.

"Don't fear tomorrow," he said. "Cut the head off a skinwalker and it stops living well enough."

Fryda gulped and nodded her head. It was a strange way to bid someone goodnight, but Jaruman had once been a great warrior, and that probably meant he didn't have nightmares. As she entered the cellar, the thought of nightmares brought Alfric to mind.

Where was he now? Was it true that his soul still existed within his body, sharing it with the wraith that now controlled it?

She pulled off her robes and fell onto the mattress. When she closed her eyes, she saw the man from Alchemist's Alley. He turned, the hairpin sticking from his eye like a lance, and pointed a finger at her. His face morphed and changed until it became Alfric. He scuttled backward and forward as he'd done in the clearing.

His mouth moved, and a strange voice came out. "You should have told me not to go on the quest."

Fryda clenched her fists and felt wood in her left hand. She thrust the spear at Alfric's face. The blade plunged into his left eye socket.

Alfric faded and became the man in the alley once more. He was lying dead on the cobblestones, the hairpin sticking out from his eye.

37

EDOMA

"I'M surprised you came so soon," Edoma said. She'd sent a messenger to Saega's home less than an hour ago. "I visited your house yesterday, but you weren't there."

"I spent the evening in the Basilica. It was fortuitous that your messenger saw my carriage this morning." He shuffled over to the desk and picked up one of the books. He flicked through the pages, turned up his nose, and placed it back down.

"What were you doing in the Basilica?"

"I have an acolyte keeping an eye on things." His face was swollen. Pus dripped from open sores along his cheeks and forehead. Every movement was mechanical, as though he struggled even to breathe.

She hadn't considered that Saega might be too unwell to come to her. After the way Idmaer's Spire had almost killed her, she wasn't making rational decisions.

With a groan, Saega placed a vial onto the table.

"Dragon blood," Edoma whispered, and picked it up. It was much smaller than the one she had lost. She held it up to the morning light coming through the windows. Only enough blood for a single warding.

"Mildryd told me you were looking for it." He smiled mirthlessly. His gums were a deep purple.

"Did she tell you what I saw in the scrying crystal?"

With effort, Saega walked over to her. He placed a bony hand on her shoulder. "You were a good mother to him. What you saw cannot be. He is lost. Don't hold on to false hope."

Edoma didn't know what to believe. She'd never seen a soul still inhabiting its body after a wraith had taken it.

"I can help you," Saega said, taking a seat beside her. "Ward me with the dragon blood. I can go to the enclosure and bring a dragon back."

"Even if I chose to ward you, you'd need a suppression—" She stopped. There had been a suppression stone lying on Saega's table, beneath the black robes and next to his fox-head staff.

"I'm the only person strong enough to take on a dragon by myself."

Edoma glanced at his frail body. Maybe he was still strong enough with Sulith's magic, however terrible he might look now. "Even so, a suppression stone can only control one dragon. There could be dozens down there."

"I'm Indham's only chance."

He was right. She could have warded more than one person with the vial of dragon blood she'd lost, but that could be anywhere. It could be broken, the blood spilt and unusable.

Saega's knees cracked loudly as he stood. "Now that that's sorted, you can ward me, and I'll leave for the dragon enclosure."

"There's something else," she said. She figured that while he was getting a dragon, she could find some other way to get the grimoire from the First Priest's tomb. "I found a statue inside the catacombs with its eyes closed. The riddle on the plinth spoke of a gift. There's a small ridge on the statue's chest. Those three things made me think that the statue is the First Priest and the First Priest's medallion is the gift that fits inside the ridge."

"That's excellent news. All you need is Idmaer to give you the medallion, then."

Edoma shook her head and clenched her fists. She fought back the anger.

"You already asked him," Saega said, reading her thoughts. He shuffled over to the pack he'd carried inside the temple. He removed his black runic robes from it and pulled them over his head. He touched a bleeding sore on his face and whispered an incantation.

Edoma realized then that his sickness must have been self-induced. He was using his own lifesoul to empower himself. It was like burning a candle at both ends.

Saega's sickness seemed to have vanished as he flooded his body with Sulith's magic. The sores were still there and his eyes were rheumy, but he had been energized. "Take me down the shaft."

* * *

Saega looked like a child during the Summertide Festival as he paced around the catacombs. His robes, much too big for him, trailed along the ground. "These are marvelous." His eyes widened upon seeing the luck charms of the First Priest. He held them against the torchlight. "Do they still work?"

"Everything in here has lost its magic to time." She took Saega to the room at the end of the corridor.

Saega passed the statues with his head bowed low. Much could be said about the man's contempt for just about everyone besides himself, but he truly revered the legendary heroes. They were renowned all over the continent, from the north to the south, the men and women who fought against the gods and won.

Saega strode over to the boy-statue and rested a hand on the stone claymore. "I'm not surprised that this statue is the key. I'm reminded of a certain apocryphal story. It said that the First Priest was not a man but a boy. His mouthpiece was a man of great age and a mighty beard. Everyone assumed the old man was the First Priest. That the First Priest was really the boy was a secret known only to his inner circle. His magic held the secret of youthfulness, but it came at a great price: he remained a boy for a thousand years, until his demise."

So the old man depicted on the godstone door wasn't the First Priest? She found that hard to believe. But Saega *had* been a scholar of great knowledge.

She had always thought the riddle on the plinth was a simple epitaph for the boy-warrior who had given his life to vanquish the water demons. She trusted Saega's words. Unlike her, he had actually been a librarian before Mundos fell. He had been visiting from the Isle of Sulith, lecturing on the ancient histories to the other apprentice mages. That same wealth of information had stopped them from succumbing to the many dangers of the Scorched Lands.

"*The gods granted me this boon.*" Saega read the riddle aloud. "This refers to the medallion. It makes sense, with the indentation on his chest. Legend has it that the gods provided the First Priest with the spire and the medallion to control it." He raised his eyebrows and grinned. The torchlight cast long shadows over his sunken eyes and gaping forehead, making him look like a goblin who'd discovered a cache of jewels. The effect was only greater as the secretions from his wounds glistened.

The shame Edoma had felt when Fryda had so easily pointed to the boy-statue came back tenfold. Her stomach fluttered and then clenched in anger. All this time she had overlooked such an easy riddle. It hadn't even been a difficult one. She hadn't thought a boy could be the First Priest. The elaborate tombs elsewhere had drawn her attention. Most of all, the godstone door. She had believed appearances weren't to be judged and to look beneath the surface. That same advice could have helped her years ago.

"It looks like we won't be needing Idmaer's medallion." Saega ran his fingers over the almost-invisible lines etched into the plinth between the statue and the base. "It seems that someone has already opened the tomb."

As Edoma gasped, Saega removed a dagger from his robes and slid it across his palms. "Sulith, grant me strength." His form shifted and his robes grew tight around his limbs. He wasn't any taller, but he was much wider. He still looked like an old and sick man, but every muscle on his body now bulged through the black fabric.

"Whoever entered the tomb last failed to close it properly." His massive hands gripped the statue's edges. Grunting, he heaved with such power that the walls trembled, showering Edoma in dust. The statue screeched as it slowly shifted aside, revealing a marble staircase.

The grimoire! It was the first thing that came to Edoma's mind. Maybe it would hold information that might save Indham. There was no guarantee, but being so close ignited her hopes.

She stepped onto the staircase. Saega stood beside her, the magic still coursing through his body. Beneath translucent skin, tiny blue lights swam through his veins. He shrank to normal size as the magic left him, the lights fading. "After you."

Edoma stepped over the stone lip and descended the stairs. She pricked her finger and drew a ward on her palm. She infused it with a fraction of spiritsoul, and it burned with power. The ward was designed to provide healing, but all wards glowed with a certain light. This one in particular was brighter than any torch, ample light to illuminate the dazzling brilliance that presented itself at the bottom of the stairs.

Every surface was pure gold, immaculately molded with a precision that took Edoma's breath away. She heard Saega gasp behind her. "Amazing," he said before sitting on the steps, breathing heavily. "I'm afraid I cannot maneuver past the wards."

Etched into the square stones at Edoma's feet were wards she had never seen before, curving things that depicted a preservation magic that buzzed with power. As far as she knew, there was no creature with blood powerful enough to sustain magic for millennia. But here it was.

Careful not to penetrate the protection fields on the floor, she stepped on one stone and another. She paused at one brick with wards that no longer glowed. The magic here was too expert to have stopped working. The ward must have been triggered.

Twenty paces later, she saw three golden pedestals lining the far wall.

Heart racing, she approached the first pedestal. It housed a scrying crystal made from glass of the deepest black. A gauntlet sat upon the second pedestal, made from a material equally black, but nothing like glass.

With bated breath, she moved to the third pedestal. A crystal stand that looked like it might have once held a book reflected her ward's light.

Once held a book. There's no book within the stand.

"It's not here," Edoma whispered. "Someone has taken it."

38

IDMAER

IDMAER awoke with a gnawing guilt that wouldn't subside. Rather than immediately going to the hidden room the night before, he had drunk firewine. The alcohol had only served to make the spire dangerous to walk in, so he hadn't gone to where he'd hidden the book.

Now, he oiled and braided his beard, preparing himself for the conversation he would soon have with Edoma. The truth would be easier for her to swallow if he delivered it with the book. The consequences of revealing the truth to her would be great, but a clear conscience was something he had been without for so long that he had almost forgotten what it was like to have one. People tended to think old men were stuck in their ways, but he liked to think he could go against habit. How he handled the business of giving Edoma the book would be evidence of that.

He breathed a frosted sigh and looked around one of the spire's many halls. He owned one of the only buildings constructed with godstone in the known world, and it was all for nothing. He had lied to Edoma all this time. If he had told her all those years ago that he had found the book, she might have even forgiven him. But it had been too long for forgiveness now. But at least he might absolve a guilty conscience.

As he walked up the staircase, he heard a warrior bringing in another skinwalker. The sounds had become too frequent of late, and he wanted so desperately to drown them with firewine. But there was a matter to attend to first.

He made his way up the staircase until he came to the fourth floor. A painting of Aern hung on the hallway wall. The artist had depicted Aern as a giant imp, humanoid, except for the deep purple skin, scales like a serpent, and giant wings. The painting showed Aern beating his wings to generate twin hurricanes. Below him was a decimated city, torn apart by the violent winds. Idmaer had always been amused by the painting—for him, the gods were mere forces rather than personal entities. The Talented thought themselves "called" by the gods. Idmaer had other theories.

Maybe there were various energies, and some people were granted access to these energies for no other reason than because it was passed down their bloodlines. This passing, he surmised, was akin to the various aptitudes a child might inherit from their parents.

Those same energies that people called the Guardians were contained in great concentration within the carcaern orbs. The wraiths—and other entities that gained their sustenance from another plane of existence—were kept away by this great energy.

Of course, this was all conjecture. He could prove none of it. Still, such philosophizing kept his mind busy where it might once have been filled with prayer. He had found people would worship anything they saw as more powerful than themselves. For most of Indham's existence, that powerful concept had been Aern. Now, Enlil fought for that place within the common mind. Idmaer had once been a staunch supporter of Edoma's reinstitution of the Daughters of Enlil, but that had been before.

Edoma's rejection of him and the love they'd shared had made him lose faith in all things he couldn't see. He knew the carcaern orbs kept the wraiths away, but that didn't mean they contained gods. The picture before him now—a fantastical creature that mimicked the reality of an imp—was simply a figment of the artist's imagination.

Idmaer ran his hands over Aern's wings. The wall rippled. He stepped back. A moment later, the painting opened. He stepped through the revealed doorway.

The secret room was home to precious items, hidden from prying eyes and thieving hands. The spire could hide almost anything from anyone, but he was particularly cautious about the things within this room. The special nature of it meant the spire didn't have full knowledge, as it did elsewhere. It was useful should the following owner enter the room. He didn't want them to know the things he had hidden there. If there were no gods and no afterlife, then all that would live on after Idmaer's death was his legacy.

The only other place within the spire where it lacked eyes was beneath the ground. Idmaer was thankful for that. His curiosity often made him do foolish things—and he'd often wondered what the skinwalkers were up to within the dungeons. *Better not to know that*, he thought. Besides that, the dungeons and the corridors surrounding them were museums of a gruesome history that had once been. The bloodletting devices were just one among many of the terrible things down there.

Even as a young man, Idmaer had only ventured into the spire's depths to visit Edoma in their special room. Oftentimes, she had entered the tunnel from beneath the candlemaker's shop and met him there. It had been the place where they'd consummated their forbidden marriage. While they lay upon the old rug with nothing but stone beneath it, she'd conceived their sons.

Idmaer was surprised at the singular tear that trailed from

his left eye. He had no time for reminiscing or to mourn over something lost. Now was the time for confession, to give the grimoire back and apologize. After that, Edoma would deal with him as she saw fit.

Maneuvering around the shelves and precariously stacked crates, he came to the reading nook. He plopped into the armchair and slid his hand beneath it. A tug of the hidden latch and the secret compartment clicked open. He stretched a little farther and felt cool wooden walls, but no book. Pulse quickening, he knelt down and reached into the compartment with his whole arm. Still nothing.

His mind raced to remember if he had placed it anywhere else, but nothing came to mind. The book had been within the compartment ever since he had taken it from the First Priest's tomb, only removed when he checked on it every so often. He brushed the dust from his robes and pulled the armchair away to reveal the compartment. Still nothing.

He remained calm, remembering the last time he had been inside this room. Three months ago. He'd been searching for a suppression stone, thinking that it would be a good idea to have one at hand should he ever need it. That search had come up empty, but he had remained within the room, drinking a particularly strong firewine. Not long after, he'd taken the book in hand and flicked through its indecipherable pages. Maybe he had placed it somewhere other than the secret compartment?

No, he recalled pinching his thumb on the armchair when he'd put the book back. Afterward, he'd stumbled back to his chambers. But the book had definitely been put back.

Blunt realization came swiftly.

It was gone. The book had been stolen.

Terror seized him. Even though he couldn't read the words on the pages, every time he opened it, he had sensed a great darkness. What had he unleashed?

The ground trembled as he fought to remain calm. The

225

floorboards churned up and down like the tides of the ocean, tripping him.

On his hands and knees, as the floor swayed, Idmaer forced himself to take deep breaths while bile crept up his throat. The ground slowly solidified until it ceased moving. He'd almost lost control. Even he wasn't invulnerable to the spire's malformations, should he lose focus.

Focusing on his breathing, Idmaer scoured the room. The spire assisted where it could until finally, he found a single page beneath a bronze shield. It was certainly from the book. He now remembered tearing the pages out in anger when Edoma had told him she no longer loved him. Even though he had stolen the book from the tomb, thereby preventing Edoma from ever fulfilling her quest, it hadn't been enough to quench his anger.

But where was the rest of the book and the other pages he'd torn from it?

Idmaer opened his mind to commune with the spire. Communication with the spire was primitive at best. It afforded him glimpses into the things it had seen in the places it had eyes. It would be unable to tell him who'd been inside the room, but maybe that wouldn't matter.

He saw an acolyte, his face hidden beneath a cowl, carrying the book. The image faded. He tried to bring it up again, but the spire wouldn't grant him another look.

Idmaer stood. In his mind was the steady resolve that something had had happened or was about to happen. He couldn't help feeling that somehow this theft was tied to the shattered orb.

Without the book, it would be much harder to admit to Edoma that he'd stolen it. Nevertheless, he would have to tell her what he'd done and how it had been stolen. But first, he needed wine.

39

FRYDA

"WE can't wait any longer," Jaruman said. It was late afternoon. He had refused to enter the dungeons until Idmaer had left the spire. Unfortunately, Idmaer didn't seem to be going anywhere.

Fryda carried the short spear, and Jaruman's ax shone in the sunlight as they walked through the spire's courtyard. They'd received a few strange glances earlier, but not as many as they might have a few weeks ago. Tension was increasing in the town, and it seemed like every second person was wearing a weapon of some kind.

The spire's entrance hall was empty. Fryda had been expecting Oswin to greet them. Alfric had been a much better porter.

"Remember, the skinwalkers aren't real people," Jaruman said. "As soon as you forget that, you're vulnerable."

"Aren't they in cells? We shouldn't have anything to worry about."

"If something can go wrong, it will. Thankfully, we can kill them and not worry about becoming hosts. The spire is warded. The wraiths cannot remain within a warded zone."

"Do they die?"

He smiled mirthlessly. "Nothing can kill them. They return to the Scorched Lands. If Peoh's still alive when we get in there, don't listen to a thing he says." He opened the door to the dungeons. Fryda followed behind him, the spear held in both hands.

Jaruman lit a torch, and they marched down the steps behind the staircase and through a tunnel until they came to a corridor with prison cells on either side. The first thing Fryda noticed was the deathly stench.

The skinwalkers reached through the iron bars, their talons clawing at them as they passed. Although their talons couldn't reach her, Fryda hunched her shoulders together to make herself narrower.

"They're decomposing," Jaruman said with a grimace. "They feed on lifesoul to remain within this world. Without it, the bodies fade away. If any of them get too close, put your spear through its skull."

Just the day before, she had skewered a man's eyeball, and now she was expected to kill people? No, not people. She had to remind herself of that. Still, she couldn't shake the niggling feeling that some might be like Alfric—still human in some way.

Fryda noticed a charred patch of brick in one cell. It puzzled her, but she didn't wait around. At the end of the corridor, past a dozen skinwalkers, was a cell where the tattooed man sat.

"Never thought I'd see you again," Jaruman said to him.

"Ah, this is quite the surprise. I knew Edoma and Saega made it through the Scorched Lands, but I never suspected you would survive."

"I'm hard to kill."

"Evidently."

Something snarled. Fryda jumped, realizing that she'd come within an inch of being grabbed by a skinwalker. Behind her, a gangly skinwalker was reaching through the bars. Its eyes bulged from their sockets. Thin skin pressed against angular cheekbones. It looked like it was starving. Fryda almost felt sorry for it.

"Who's the pretty lass?" Peoh said.

"Never mind her," said Jaruman. He gently nudged Fryda's back so she was farther from the reaching skinwalker. "What are you doing in Indham?"

"I heard about what happened to Aern. I've come to help you all."

"Did you have anything to do with it?"

"Not a thing. I have my suspicions about who did it, though."

Jaruman's face didn't soften. He seemed to be studying Peoh.

As far as Fryda could tell, the man was telling the truth. But Jaruman had said that he was an excellent liar.

"You look familiar," Peoh said to Fryda. He got up and walked to the iron bars.

"Not too close," Jaruman said, clanking the bars with his ax.

Peoh rolled his eyes and looked back at Fryda. "Your mother was from the North?"

"Yes," she said. "She lived in the Scorched Lands."

"This is quite the reunion. I freed the people who came to Indham from there. The orcs had been holding them captive. They suffered terrible things. It's not a wonder they died."

Before Fryda could react, the walls shook. The floor tilted, and Fryda lost her footing. Arms flailing, she fell backward. A skeletal hand gripped her tunic and pulled her backward. She screamed and reached for her spear, but it was too far away. She gripped the fingers and tried to peel them back, but they pressed into her shoulder, the blade-like nails sinking into her skin. Her screams became terrified shrieks.

Jaruman slammed his ax down and excised the hand at the wrist. He pulled her upright and away from the skinwalker. It snarled but now lay out of reach.

With a grimace, Fryda tore the severed hand from her shoulder and threw it against the wall. It clattered onto the stone floor.

"Idmaer must be in another of his moods," Jaruman said, peering up.

"Take me with you," Peoh said. "The lad named Hiroc told me he would tell the Council, but he hasn't returned."

Jaruman eyed the trembling rooftop as dust flittered down from it. "Even if I wanted to, I don't have a key for your cell."

"We can't just leave him here," Fryda said. "Not with the skinwalkers. You said he might save us."

"As long as they're in the cells, he'll be fine."

"You said if something can go wrong, it will."

Jaruman gave her a hard look. "Don't use my words against me."

The door opened at the other end of the corridor. Bertram marched toward them with a torch in hand, followed by two other warriors carrying a skinwalker. The skinwalker snarled and snapped its lupine jaws. Neither warrior seemed pleased to be carrying the monster.

Jaruman gripped his ax. He didn't tell Fryda to pick up her spear, but she did it all the same.

"What are you two doing down here?" Bertram said. Though his face was still in accusation, his eye twitched as he focused on Jaruman. He seemed to be trying in earnest not to look inside the cells. Hanging around his neck was the dragon vial.

Fryda was surprised to see him back in the spire. The way he had been talking when he stole the dragon vial, he should have received passage out of Indham by now.

"That's Edoma's dragon vial," Fryda said to Jaruman, pointing at Bertram's neck. "He stole it from me."

Bertram sneered. "And you stole it from Mother Edoma."

"Give it back to her," Jaruman said.

"No," said Bertram. "I might not be able to sell it, but it's mine all the same."

They stared at each other. It was just like the way they'd looked at one other outside the gates. This time, however, Bertram seemed more worn down.

"I've had just about enough of your insolence," Bertram said. He surveyed Fryda and smiled. "You know, if I can't leave Aernheim, I might as well have a little fun while I'm here." His sword swung free of its scabbard. It met Jaruman's ax with a resounding clang.

The two warriors behind Bertram looked at each other, puzzled, and then gripped their own swords in hand. One darted toward Fryda, but the skinwalker inside the cell grabbed his ankle. The man hit the ground, a taloned hand dragging him to the cell. Blood burst from his neck as the skinwalker tore it open. The other warrior turned to run, but a falling boulder crushed him beneath it.

Suddenly, the dungeon shook again. This time, the tremor was much greater. There was a thunderous sound, and the corridor shifted. The stone floor split with a deafening crack.

A skinwalker leaped from an open cell and attacked Bertram. He turned and drove his sword through the skinwalker's chest. He left the sword and bolted for the entrance. Jaruman reached for him, but only grabbed the necklace holding the dragon vial. The necklace snapped, and Bertram got away as the roof above collapsed, blocking the exit.

A sound like the twanging of a bow came from the cell beside Fryda. The iron bars buckled until they snapped. The skinwalker crawled through the broken bars.

Fryda wasted no time. Gripping the spear with both hands, she thrust it into the skinwalker's chest. She pinned it against a few unbroken bars. She gritted her teeth and twisted the blade, but the skinwalker didn't die.

A sound like rushing wind came from behind her, and

the skinwalker's head exploded, showering her in blood and brain matter.

Standing behind her was Peoh. The tattoos along his right arm glowed red. "We'll go through there," he said, pointing at a hole in the wall behind her.

"Why not go the other way?" Fryda saw why that was impossible. Rubble covered the exit.

She gasped. Someone was trapped within the rubble. All she could see was an arm clutching at the air, the rest of the body buried by rocks and debris.

"No," Peoh said, grabbing her arm. "The other skinwalkers will be out of the cells soon."

Fryda tore away from him and leaped over the crack in the floor. By the time she reached the buried arm, tears trailed down her cheeks. She pulled the rubble away until she saw him—Jaruman. His face was covered in cuts and bruises. His eyes were half-open and his breathing was ragged. A giant rock pinned him from the waist down.

"Fryda . . ."

Placing both palms beneath the massive rock's edge, she heaved. Jaruman bellowed with pain, but she ignored him. No matter how hard she pushed or from what angle, the rock wouldn't budge.

Weeping, she turned to Peoh. "Do something. Use your magic."

Peoh shook his head. Blood ran down his arm. "I can't. There's nothing I can do." He glanced anxiously at the cells beside him. A skinwalker burst from one. He extended a hand. The skinwalker's head split open as if an invisible ax had cleaved it in two.

"Quickly," he said, breathing heavily. "I can't fight them all."

"Go," Jaruman croaked.

Fryda cried out as Peoh dragged her away from the only man she knew as father.

40

HIROC

"YOU said you weren't called," Hiroc said. He had awoken in the cellar not long ago, the runic glove missing, and his hands and feet bound. Despite how much anger he felt, he wanted answers about the magic Ealstan had used. "How, then, did you use magic?"

It wasn't the best time to ask, but he wasn't going to get a better chance. For all he knew, Ealstan was dragging him to his death. Some unseen force had struck him. It had to be magic.

Ealstan paused and wiped sweat from his brow. "Saega taught me that one doesn't have to be called to use a god's magic. I still needed a runic device. He gave me this." He spun the dagger around his fingers. He tickled Hiroc's neck with the blade. "With it, and with my devotion, Aern grants me his power. He might not have called me, but I use it."

"Aern is dead," Hiroc struggled to say as the dagger's edge pressed against his skin.

Ealstan laughed.

"Why are you laughing?" Hiroc asked. "You said you're devoted to him."

"You really know nothing at all. The carcaern orbs are

prisons. Aern was trapped within it. The shatterer *freed* him."
He cackled again, sheathed his dagger, and kicked Hiroc.
"Get up."

Taking his time, Hiroc staggered to his feet, a difficult
task with his wrists and ankles bound. It took an inordinate
amount of time to reach the top of the stairs. Ealstan pushed
him through the doorway opposite the door leading to the
kitchens.

It was dark outside. Hiroc's head throbbed from hitting
the wall, but he couldn't tell whether he'd been unconscious
for a few hours or an entire day.

The dumping grounds smelled like rotten meat and sour
milk. Mangy dogs sniffed at the piles of filth. Beyond them,
red wards glowed. It was the border of the ward circles that
protected the Basilica from the wraiths. A few paces away,
Oswin was sitting below the signpost, well outside the warded
zone.

Hiroc turned to Ealstan. "You have to bring him inside.
The wraiths will get him."

Ealstan nodded with a smile. "That's the plan."

Kipp came from the doorway. Bags sat beneath his eyes,
as though he hadn't slept for days. His usual smile was absent.

"Sorry I'm late," he said.

"Yes, yes," Ealstan said, frustrated. "Just make sure you tie
him up properly."

"What if the wraiths come while I'm out there?"

"Then you'd better be quick." Ealstan handed Hiroc over
to Kipp. "I've got somewhere to be. It won't be long now
until your little friend in the spire's dungeons ends up like
you. Then where will Indham be? Judgment is coming." He
whistled as he went back inside.

"Kipp, you can't do this. You've seen the skinwalkers.
Don't let me become one."

"I have to take you out there. Ealstan said he'd use his
magic on me unless I do."

"You're taking me to my death," Hiroc pleaded as Kipp dragged him over the piles of rotten food.

"Aye," Kipp said, as though he had made the decision long ago.

When they passed over the wards, Hiroc yanked against the bonds, trying to free himself of the other man.

Kipp hit him over the head, hard enough that his vision became peppered. "Don't make this any harder than it has to be."

Kipp dragged Hiroc to the signpost. Oswin lifted his chin. His once handsome face was purple and clumpy, his one visible eye bulging and bloodshot. He licked his swollen lips as he looked at Hiroc. "So they got you, too? Looks like you and I are going to meet these wraiths everyone is talking about."

"It doesn't have to be like this," Hiroc said as Kipp knelt and tied the bonds to the signpost.

"It does." He stood and glanced toward the Basilica. "But I brought something for you." He removed something from his belt pouch and then knelt down again.

Hiroc felt Kipp playing with his hand and then something slipped over it. A glove.

"Ealstan told me to destroy it, but I couldn't. I know you and I haven't always got along, but I don't think you and Oswin deserve to become one of them skinwalkers."

"Then why not bring us inside?"

Kipp shook his head. "I can't do that. Ealstan will kill me."

He obviously hadn't thought this through. Ealstan would probably kill Kipp for giving Hiroc the runic glove. But if he did manage to get away without becoming a skinwalker, maybe he could stop that from happening.

As Kipp ran back into the Basilica, Hiroc realized he wouldn't be able to return there. He needed to get help, someone who could stop Saega from harming Peoh. He couldn't explain why, but he knew with certainty that Peoh had to be kept from harm.

"How tight are your bonds?" he called over his shoulder.

"Too tight to get out of."

Hiroc's were the same.

"They've come," Oswin said.

Hiroc was facing the opposite way so he couldn't see what Oswin referred to. But he didn't have to see it. He knew that Oswin was looking at the crimson wraith clouds.

For his life, Hiroc couldn't think of a way out. The wound on his head had scabbed over, so even if he wanted to use magic, he didn't have any blood to draw from. Not unless he made himself bleed.

Heart racing, he moved his hands up and down, feeling the ropes bite into his skin. Ignoring the pain, he continued until his skin was slick with blood. The clouds were now close enough for him to see. They swirled and tumbled through the air.

"Enlil, hear me," Hiroc whispered. His hands grew hot, and he pulled against the bonds. They melted away. He quickly removed the ropes around his ankles.

When he turned around, his heart almost leaped from his chest.

A hand made of mist extended toward Oswin. It reached into his open mouth and disappeared. The night suddenly became dark. There were no more crimson clouds. The wards were too far behind them to give off anything more than the faintest light.

Hiroc started as Oswin coughed and gargled before making a retching noise. His eyes burst with crimson light as he screamed. The screaming stopped. Oswin's eyes burned like hot coals. He turned his head toward Hiroc and grinned. Red light glowed through his teeth.

Hiroc raised a gloved hand to his friend. He closed his eyes. "Enlil, hear my prayer."

41

EDOMA

E DOMA dipped a cloth into a bucket of water and began washing Saega's face. The water soon became murky from his sores. He seemed to have aged greatly in the last week. Even the threads of white hair that once clung to his head were gone. He looked like death would come for him at any moment. But he had said he would be capable of bringing the dragon back. She believed him—she didn't have a choice.

She considered using healing wards, against his will, but thought otherwise. Doing so, even if it was for a good cause, was too much like what the mages in Mundos had done with their magic.

"I'll begin the warding process. Try not to move." The dragon blood was more precious than anything else. Now that Sigebert and Cenred had been gone for so long, she was sure they had perished. It was only Saega who could save them now by bringing back more dragon blood.

She glanced up and caught sight of Idmaer's Spire, creeping over the other buildings in the eastern part of the town. Cursing herself for allowing Idmaer to enter her mind, she tried in earnest not to think about what they'd found in the First Priest's tomb. Or rather, what they hadn't found.

She had wanted so desperately to storm over to the spire and demand Idmaer return it to her. When she was younger, she would have done exactly that, but age had brought her wisdom, and she knew not to act while in the throes of anger. Perhaps she had remained here because of a sliver of hope that Idmaer hadn't stolen the grimoire.

Edoma removed a brush from her pocket, dabbed it into the blood vial, and dragged the first line across Saega's cheek. His expression remained placid until she finished. She tapped spiritsoul, channeled it through the runestone, and navigated it along the bloodied ward. The magic penetrated the ward and illuminated it.

A great darkness washed over her. She shivered. The feeling had never come like that before when warding. She reasoned that the dark feeling was because Saega was a mage. But Hiroc hadn't felt like this. It felt wrong, evil. Like a disease. Could it have come from his sickness? It would explain why he hadn't wanted healing—healing wards would be unable to treat a magical disease.

"This is strange," Saega said, as though he hadn't noticed Edoma's sudden fear. "Sulith's magic is less…uncomfortable."

His voice brought her back to reality. The wards glowed crimson, illuminating the open wounds on his face. They festered and dripped with pus. "These sores don't look good. Are you sure I can't construct a healing ward?" She hoped he would say yes, if only to see whether his illness was indeed magical.

"No," Saega said, getting to his feet. "I don't have much time. As long as the wards last the night, they'll be sufficient." He pulled the cowl of his black robes over his head. "Before I leave, there's something else. I have been thinking of a way to broach the subject for most the day."

"You're not dying," Edoma said, refusing to believe what her eyes had been telling her every time she'd looked at him that day. "You must let me heal you."

He shook his head. "It's a simple fever. But that's not what I've come to tell you. Peoh is in Indham."

Edoma's vision wavered. It couldn't be true. She'd seen Peoh die in the Scorched Lands. Vigash, the orc chieftain, had given him to a wraith. She looked down at the runestone. It had been Peoh's parting gift to her. He had been a great devotee of Mun and had infused the runestone with much devotion. He had also been her first love. He couldn't be alive.

"He hides within Idmaer's dungeons," Saega said. "The acolyte, Ealstan, told me."

"Are you sure?"

Saega nodded. "It wasn't just Ealstan who spoke of a man with ward tattoos. Bertram advised me that he arrested a man bearing tattooed runes. The ward circle activated outside the gates when the man stepped on it. You don't believe me? Inspect the energies, and you'll feel it, too."

Edoma hadn't opened herself to the other-realm since she'd seen Alfric as a skinwalker. She didn't know whether she'd survive a second time. But she wasn't willing to take Saega's word for it. Not with this. If Peoh was inside Indham, then they might have finally found the person responsible for shattering Aern's orb.

She went to her chambers and flipped open the chest. By the time she had sat on the floor with the scrying crystal in front of her, Saega had come. He remained silent and watched as she cut herself and palmed the crystal with her bloody hand.

Her vision shifted until the room became gray. Her heart seemed to relish the return to the other-realm, as though it had been yearning to taste again of the strange sensory experiences.

She shifted focus to Saega, who burned with a gray light and smelled of honey. All mages smelled of honey. There was something else beneath that scent, though, a rancid odor that made her shiver.

She rose above the town, not flying, but something else entirely, a rapid shifting like someone blinking. In a moment, she was surveying all of Indham from a hundred feet above. Her stomach plummeted, and not from the height. Her power in the other-realm was weak from the other day, and she had reached the zenith of her abilities. Any longer and she might lose control entirely. She dropped a little, just to be safe.

She scanned the town for any fluctuations in her other-senses. Everything remained the same until she came upon a trail from the gates. Honey. As soon as she focused on it, the sweet scent burst. The feeling was euphoric. The golden trail led from the gates to Idmaer's Spire. Without realizing, she had drifted and was losing her grip on her other-self.

The other-realm whispered to her with sweet promises. She could remain here and keep an eye on Indham. Everything she had done so far had failed. She was an enemy of the man she had loved. One of her sons had become a skinwalker. The people she had adopted as her own would soon perish.

Nothing mattered. Not anymore.

Another figure materialized beside her. The necrotic stench almost overwhelmed her as she was torn from the other-realm.

Returning to her body, she rolled over and vomited. She wiped her mouth and looked to Saega. "You saved me."

"Nothing you wouldn't have done for me. When you were gone for so long, I thought you'd been trapped." With effort, he picked up the scrying crystal and put it back in the chest. "I see now why you were so hesitant to go there."

Edoma beckoned Saega out from the room and asked a passing Daughter to clean her chambers. They stopped outside where she had done the warding. She didn't want to waste any more time than she had to since his wards would only last a day, but she had to know more.

"Why would Idmaer be hiding Peoh within his dungeons?" she asked.

Saega shrugged. "Perhaps he has been consorting with the Archmage of Mundos."

"Idmaer wouldn't know how to do that. He would need a scrying crystal."

"Maybe he has something like a scrying crystal? There are many mysterious things within his spire." That was true. Edoma had barely been able to walk in Idmaer's room with all the obstructions. And there were many other rooms, some even more cramped than Idmaer's private chambers. "Or maybe he found a way to speak across great distances from the book he stole."

"It might not have been him," Edoma said. "We don't know for certain. Someone could have stolen the medallion."

"You truly believe that? He has not removed it once since it was first placed around his neck. He treats the spire like a lover. Giving the medallion away would be like committing adultery."

Edoma couldn't argue with that. Idmaer treated the spire better than he had ever treated her.

But none of it made sense. If Peoh had shattered the orb, why had he returned? Why would Idmaer give him refuge? Maybe they had conspired together, but what would Idmaer have to gain from bringing destruction upon Indham?

There was much she didn't know about his intentions. After all, he had stolen the grimoire from the catacombs. She couldn't think of a reason he might have done that, and yet he had.

"Idmaer and Peoh must pay for their crimes," Saega said.

"That can wait," Edoma said. "Go to the enclosure now. We'll give you the fastest horse." She paused. Saega didn't look like he would be capable of riding a horse. "The fastest carriage."

"I will go, but the people need to see justice done. As soon as possible. They've been talking. I've heard them in the streets. They know that Aern no longer protects them.

They might not know he's dead, but they think someone has done something to him. Some have sneaked past the guards at Tyme's Hill. They've seen the fake orb Idmaer's placed within the golden hands. They've seen the dull wards and the fallen pillars. Unless something is done soon, there'll be a riot. If the wraiths don't destroy Indham, the people will. I was wrong about justice not being important. I see the truth now. Justice will give our people life, at least until we find more permanent means.

"While I'm gone, you'll draw Idmaer out from the spire. Far enough away so that it cannot intervene on his behalf. Then we will force him to transfer ownership. Then we can bring Peoh to account for his crime. We just need someone he would be willing to leave the spire for . . ." Saega gave Edoma a meaningful look.

"You think I should be used for bait?"

"Can you think of any other reason he would leave?"

"He won't leave the spire for me."

"I wouldn't be so sure."

42

HIROC

HEART pounding, Hiroc stumbled toward the gates of Enlil's Temple. He looked about him constantly, to the left, to the right, above. Everywhere, he searched for that crimson glow.

"Go no farther." Bertram was standing atop a makeshift palisade within the temple gates. Torches flickered next to him, illumining a dozen other warriors with their light. They all had arrows nocked to their bows and pointed them toward Hiroc. It was just his luck to have Bertram guarding the temple. Why wasn't he at the town gates?

"I'm not a skinwalker," Hiroc cried. When they didn't let down their bows, he stopped walking and glanced nervously behind him. There were no wraiths. For now. But the way Bertram held his bow suggested that he might let the arrow fly at any moment.

Hiroc needed to get inside the temple's warded zone. His heart couldn't take being outside any longer. He'd walked for an hour to get to the temple, constantly watching for wraith clouds.

Bertram glanced behind him. He said something to the other warriors, and they all dropped their bows.

Edoma appeared at the gates. "Come forward, Hiroc," she said.

As soon as Hiroc's feet planted on the wards, a cool energy rushed through him. The wards throbbed with a crimson light.

"Stay there," Edoma said. She nodded at Bertram, and he put another arrow to his bow.

The feeling suddenly became invasive. Ephemeral fingers crawled across Hiroc's flesh and reached into his mind. As soon as it had begun, it was over.

Edoma let out a long, drawn-out sigh. "Well, I'm glad you're clean. I wouldn't have liked to kill you." She spoke evenly, as though she truly meant it.

He considered this woman, who so readily suggested she might have killed him. She was his mother, according to Ealstan. Seeing her now with new eyes, he realized the truth of it. He didn't think he looked much like her, but Alfric did. Had Alfric been born with black hair rather than blond hair, they would have shared an uncanny resemblance.

Hiroc's throat had become unusually dry. He didn't know whether to hug her or yell at her. He decided to do neither.

Edoma's gaze flittered down to the runic glove he was wearing. "Come inside and tell me where you've been."

Hiroc followed her into a small room with a table and cushioned armchairs. She lit the candle on the table and sat on a stool. "Why were you outside a warded zone?"

Still standing, Hiroc bristled at her accusatory tone. He couldn't stop what he said next. "Why did you lie to me about being Fatherless?"

Edoma's face paled. Her hand cupped her gaping mouth. "I . . ."

"I know everything. You and Idmaer are my parents. You lied to Alfric and me."

"We did what we had to," she said. He'd never seen her so afraid, but that didn't cool his fury.

"I don't want excuses. I'm not going to forgive you." Things would have been so different had he been raised as the child of Edoma and Idmaer. Alfric would never have gone off on that stupid quest. Hiroc wouldn't have been despised by the other acolytes. In fact, he probably would have one day seceded Idmaer as High Priest. He would never do that now. Even if Edoma told the truth, he was known as Fatherless. No one would believe her.

"I don't expect you to forgive me," Edoma said. "The past is done. Now, tell me why you risked the wraiths to come to the temple?"

The swiftness with which she had composed herself angered Hiroc further. How could she so quickly change the subject? He expected an excuse, even if it were a meager one. But she'd given nothing.

Hiroc looked down at his hands. He remembered the blue fire shooting from his palms. "I watched a wraith take Oswin. He changed immediately. I saw hatred in those eyes. I killed him myself."

"You killed the skinwalker?" She seemed to purposefully avoid calling it Oswin.

"With Enlil's fire." Hiroc pulled on one of the glove's fingers and removed it. "What will happen to his daughter?"

"I'll take her in. She can become a Daughter of Enlil, if she pleases."

"I killed her father."

Edoma shook her head. "That thing wasn't Oswin—no matter what it looked like. You cannot carry this weight on your conscience. You still haven't told me what you were doing outside a warded zone."

Edoma was the last person he wanted to speak with right now, but he had no one else.

"When I came back to the Basilica last night, I overheard Saega and Ealstan speaking. Saega said to 'deal with' the Fatherless. Later that night, Ealstan attacked me. He bound

Oswin and me to a signpost. Evidently, that's how Saega wanted us dealt with."

"You must have misheard," said Edoma.

"I know what I heard. Saega and Ealstan are responsible for Oswin becoming a skinwalker. They're responsible for me . . ." There came the image of Oswin burning alive, his skin bubbling like hot soup. Hiroc tried to tell himself that it wasn't Oswin anymore, but it had looked so much like him.

"You did what you had to." Edoma placed her hand on Hiroc's.

Hiroc snarled. "Don't touch me." He despised Edoma for lying to him, but he had to tell her about what Ealstan had said.

"Before he left me for dead, Ealstan admitted that he and Saega wanted to kill a mage within the spire."

"Who?" she asked.

"Peoh?"

"Did they tell you that name?"

Hiroc told Edoma about how he had spoken with Peoh in the dungeons. He didn't tell her about his lesson in magic, but he did say how Peoh had offered them salvation.

"If Ealstan hadn't taken Oswin," he said, "I would have come right to you." *And I never would have found out that you are my mother.*

Edoma shook her head. "I believe Peoh is responsible for the shattering. Idmaer likely had a hand in it, too. There was a book within the First Priest's tomb—a grimoire. Idmaer stole it. Inside were spells capable of destroying a Guardian."

"Idmaer wouldn't do such a thing," Hiroc said. He didn't know why he was defending Idmaer, but Idmaer had always been kind to Hiroc and encouraged him to become an acolyte. Edoma had always been stern and remote.

"He hides Peoh within his spire."

Hiroc was about to explain that Idmaer likely didn't even know about the existence of Peoh, when Edoma raised her hand to cut him off.

"Many years ago, I was born in Mundos. It's a city far to the north, beyond Babon's Pass and beyond the Scorched Lands. We had our Guardian, Mun, who protected us from the wraiths as Aern once did in Indham, but someone from the south came and destroyed Mun's orb. With Mun's protection lifted, eventually, the wraiths came.

"Peoh was the Archmage of Mundos. He gathered the few survivors—Saega and I were among them. We all swore to take revenge upon the south by destroying one of their orbs. Peoh gave Saega and me each a grimoire. We were to use it to destroy a southern orb. Jaruman tried to stop us from swearing the oath, but we didn't listen. But when we came to Indham, it wasn't long before we fell in love with its people. Saega and I abandoned our vow and burned the grimoires."

"So you think Peoh shattered Aern's orb because of a vow made years ago? That still doesn't explain why Idmaer would help him do it."

"Idmaer is a man of many secrets."

"That explains why you married him."

Edoma sighed. "Living alone in that spire has changed him. He doesn't care for Indham."

"He wouldn't kill Aern. Not if it meant the wraiths coming."

"Do you have any other explanation? Tell me what makes you trust Idmaer and Peoh so much?"

Hiroc couldn't say why. Maybe he was just hostile toward Edoma because she had lied to him all these years. He *did* have a habit of holding grudges. Idmaer had lied, too, but he couldn't be blamed. It was only through his intervention that Hiroc had been accepted into the Holy Order of Aern.

Bertram knocked on the door. Edoma turned and beckoned him into the room. He smiled at Hiroc. "Almost got yourself killed out there. You're lucky I didn't slip on my bowstring."

Edoma cleared her throat. "What is it, Bertram?"

"I wanted to ask you for healing." He pulled down his collar. A vicious wound slashed from his collarbone to his left shoulder.

Edoma stood and inspected the injury. "A skinwalker did this."

"Aye," he said. "There was an incident earlier today in the spire's dungeons. The spire was moving about, and the cells broke. The skinwalkers got out. One of them did this to me." He grimaced as Edoma touched the wound with her finger.

She studied her finger, sniffed it, and reared back. "We'll have to treat this right away." She ushered Bertram onto the floor.

Hiroc went to leave, and Edoma said, "Stay here. It'll help for you to see some wards."

He sat down again. Edoma took a jug of water from the table and washed the wound with it. She then pressed the cuts so fresh blood seeped out from them. Using the blood, she drew wards onto Bertram's flesh. She grabbed the runestone around her neck and whispered an incantation.

Bertram groaned and thrashed about. Hiroc rushed to the floor and pinned him down. Edoma smiled at Hiroc. Finally, Bertram passed out. Where the flaring wounds once had been were now day-old scabs.

"He's going to be out for a few more hours," she said. "Would you like to walk with me?"

They walked through the temple halls, neither speaking. Although it was past midnight, Daughters dashed about, administering to people. Many of those who weren't able to stay within other warded zones had taken refuge inside Enlil's Temple. Seeing them all invading the holy places Edoma loved made him reconsider things.

"Why did you not raise Alfric and me as your sons?" Hiroc said when he couldn't take the silence any longer.

"When you were first born, there was no dragon trade.

Idmaer and I were in love, and we couldn't imagine anything more perfect than two beautiful boys. But our perfect life was interrupted when the caravans arrived a few weeks after your birth. The Council wanted to send them away—by force if necessary. Idmaer was inclined to agree with them, but I convinced him otherwise. I encouraged him to use the money in the treasury to employ the people. The Council thought it reckless—few of the adults could even speak—but Idmaer held the power of veto. Soon after, the parents of the Fatherless died. All that food and money wasted, the Council had said.

"It wasn't wasted, though. So many children had lived because of that money. We'd built homes for them all and fed them. But the treasury had been bled dry. Fearing an uproar, Idmaer took a party of warriors to the abandoned mines. He had hoped to find some wealth there. What he found were suppression stones. With the stones, he could command the minds of any magical creatures. He considered selling the stones, since they were very valuable. Instead, he decided that dragons would be worth far more than the stones. The warriors were more than capable of capturing dragons with suppression stones. So that's what they did. They entered Eosorheim and stole a hundred dragons from Hurn."

"Durwin," Hiroc said. Even though most of what Edoma had said was new to him, he'd been able to follow along. He knew what had happened next. "Durwin and his small band of warriors tried to stop the dragon trade. They couldn't, and he despised Idmaer because of that."

"Yes, and that's why we let you and Alfric be raised as Fatherless."

"You thought Durwin would have killed us to get at Idmaer?"

"For certain," she said. "But that didn't make the decision easier. I wanted so desperately to tell you both the truth. But by the time Durwin was executed, you were already known as Fatherless. There were so many Fatherless children that it was simple to have you raised as one of them. They were, after all, mostly living within Enlil's Temple. None of them were old enough to remember who was Fatherless and who wasn't."

"You could have told us. It's not like growing up as a Fatherless was good."

"It was initially. Many of the people thought the Fatherless lovely. They baked food and let their children play with them. But as the Fatherless grew older, they began to turn to crime. Public perception grew cold, and that only worsened things. Idmaer and I couldn't parent them all. We had done our best. The stress of it soon caused Idmaer and I to separate. After that, we never spoke about you two again."

Hiroc still couldn't understand Edoma's reasoning. It still seemed too much like an excuse. "How did you convince an entire town that we weren't your sons?"

"The Fatherless entered the gates only weeks after you were born. Because of the many deaths and misplaced children, it was simple. It was simple. Had it been harder, we might never have done it."

Before he could ask any more questions, Mildryd came.

"Ah, Hiroc. What a pleasure to see you here." She beamed at him and turned to Edoma. "Bertram has awoken."

Edoma had said it would be hours until he awoke. Had they really been walking the temple for that long? As if answering him, the sun crept over the horizon, sending its light through the windows.

Hiroc followed Edoma back to the room where Bertram had passed out.

After making sure that Bertram was feeling better, Edoma asked him, "You said the spire was moving?"

"More than I've ever seen it. Something has Idmaer riled up."

"I wonder if Idmaer knows," Edoma said under her breath. "Retrieving him will be difficult with the dangers the spire poses in such a state."

"Retrieving him?" Hiroc said.

"The Council is putting Idmaer to trial for Aern's death."

"You can't do that! You don't know for certain he did it."

"That's what a trial is for. Evidence will be put forward. He will have a chance to defend himself."

43

IDMAER

THE next morning, Idmaer commanded everyone to leave his spire. It was a good thing he did, because the spire was mirroring his rage. His one chance to reconcile with Edoma and clear his conscience had been stolen from him. In a way, it was ironic. He had been a thief, only to become a victim of theft.

A pang of deep regret churned his stomach. Once again, his past was coming back to haunt him. Why was it that the fates never let a misdeed go unpunished?

He pushed open the door to his room. A singular thought might have opened the door, but doing so in his present emotional state could lead to chaotic consequences.

When he sat in his chair, he ran through the laws of self perfection. Those laws had been passed down to him by his father. They enabled a High Priest to control himself. The first law was one of acceptance. He accepted the return of theft and allowed nature's circle to comfort him.

The rage subsided and the spire stilled.

Idmaer placed the paper from the grimoire on the desk in front of him. The sheet was worn and tattered, though the writing was still legible. The grimoire had been smaller than most tomes, almost pocket-sized. He distinctly remembered its leather surface, untarnished from time because of the gilded wards.

Without those wards, the page in front of him had browned. Idmaer had thumbed the grimoire's contents a number of times. He only knew a smattering of the old tongue, so it was mostly undecipherable.

He held the page up to examine it, his old eyes failing him. The paper slipped from his hand and fluttered to the floor. He bent to pick it up and whacked his head on the desk. Groaning, he rubbed the injury. His hand came away bloody. He wiped the blood on his robes, but not all of it. His fingers pressed into the grimoire's page, leaving bloody fingerprints.

He stared at the loose sheet for a while as if the foreign symbols would materialize into a language he could understand. Strangely, they did just that. The harsh lines swirled and connected into the common tongue until each line was entirely translated. He rubbed his eyes, swearing that his senses were lying.

After the God Wars, our lands were barren and desolate. The ground yielded no vegetation. Our livestock were born monstrous and defiled. Even our children came forth strange and light of mind.

So we entered the Infernal City, hoping to request help from the gods. Instead, they rejected us. Their memories are long, and they do not easily forgive. So I thought of a way. Their world was luscious, filled with beautiful trees that gave forth wondrous fruit. The beings living within the city were strong and produced many offspring, none of them born without the ability to speak or hear.

Emboldened by the fruitfulness of the city, I returned to the mortal realm and gathered those left of all the races. Together with the greatest mages, wizards, warlocks, and sorcerers, I fashioned crystal orbs of great power. With those orbs and an army of desperate mortals, we entered the city. At the height of a long and costly battle, I entered the Bargaining Plaza with thirty orbs. Soon after, I returned to the mortal realm with thirty incarcerated gods. Those orbs became known as the carcaern orbs. The gods became Guardians.

We didn't learn until later that the gods had their own punishments in mind. Whoever had held an orb became afflicted with a terrible disease. It was only the pool within the spire that prevented me from becoming a husk like the others. They turned into walking dead men, decaying until only their spirits remained. They tried to enact their vengeance, but the orbs kept them out.

It's been five hundred years. Altars have arisen throughout the known lands, and I've sent an orb to each of them. New cults have emerged to celebrate the protection these new gods provide. With those orbs, none of the original spirits can enter the realms. They now roam the lands defiled after the God Wars. Some call them wraiths. But I still call them friends. They wish vengeance upon me since I did not share the pool with them. I still visit that pool every day, fending off death's call. Mostly I fear what will happen when I pass from this world to the next. Will the gods have their vengeance then?

Idmaer turned away from the page, disgusted. This wasn't a grimoire. Grimoires depicted magical spells and their properties. This was the personal diary of the First Priest.

He had never seen a pool of youth in the dungeons, but that didn't mean it wasn't there.

Idmaer returned to the page, but the words had become their previously indecipherable state. Whether his mind had conjured a fantasy or whether the words had truly been in the common tongue was impossible to tell. He slipped the page into a secret pocket inside his coat. It seemed not even his spire was a good place to store things; on his person was the only place he could trust to keep thieves away.

A commotion from outside drew his attention. He crossed the room and peered out the window. A number of warriors were waiting below, staring straight at him.

Idmaer hadn't the slightest idea what they wanted with him, but he left his room and traipsed down the stairs. The spire responded by moving the spiral staircase so that it plunged straight down, providing a more expedient trip to the entrance foyer.

A dozen warriors stood at the spire steps. They were garbed in full armor, sunlight reflecting off chainmail shirts peeking through green tabards. Fastened to studded baldrics looped over their shoulders were swords and axes. None of them had unsheathed their weapons, but they stood with their arms folded across their chests in a united front of menace. At the front stood Bertram, captain of the warriors. Unlike the rest of the men, his weapon wasn't sheathed. He pointed a longsword toward the spire in open contempt of Idmaer's office as High Priest.

Realizing that this was an assault, Idmaer communed with the spire. The iron gargoyles on the walls transmogrified, becoming liquid metal. The blobs of metal slithered to the windows and double-doors. Iron bars formed in crisscrossing lines over them.

"To what do I owe the pleasure of a visit from the warriors?" Idmaer called out, his words dripping with conceit.

Bertram stepped forward, still pointing his sword as if he would storm the spire with his men. "You are accused of deceit against the Council. You are commanded to attend a trial."

Well, this was an interesting development. More people had gathered behind the armed men outside. It looked like half the town had come to watch the warriors draw Idmaer out.

But there was no chance whatsoever he would be going to the courtroom. Those trials were only for appearances. The people wanted blood—and they wanted his.

"You are welcome to enter my spire and we can discuss this command over a meal," he said. "You cannot wait out there forever. The sun will fall tonight, and you'll have to return to warded premises."

Bertram scowled. He would know how futile it would be

to enter the spire with harmful intent. "You can come out now, or you can come out later."

Idmaer laughed, loudly enough so each of the warriors could hear him. "I assure you the spire's storehouse has ample supplies to keep me satiated until I die of old age." And that could be a long time if he found the pool of youth the First Priest had written about.

Bertram sheathed his sword. Turning, he waved his arms, and a cart crested the hill. It stopped just outside the spire's gardens. The warriors began removing a number of tools from the cart—shovels, pitchforks, barrows, and the like. They each took a tool and started digging.

Idmaer's smile faltered. They were removing the wards.

Closing his eyes, he concentrated on the stone bricks that formed the outside steps. He imagined them flying of their own accord, shooting through the air and crushing the warriors. He heard yelling and crashing. When he opened his eyes, he peered outside. A half-dozen warriors lay beneath stone bricks, but more warriors had taken their place. It wouldn't be long until they'd removed the wards.

What crime did they think he had committed to make them so willing to give their lives to capture him?

Idmaer extended his hand toward the iron bars that crossed over the windows. He twisted his palm, and the bars became liquid metal again. With little time, he fashioned them into crude iron spears. A volley of spears shot through the window, each one finding a mark.

Bertram had retreated outside the spire's influence with more warriors. They were no longer digging.

Idmaer smiled. He had done it.

"You may kill us all," Bertram yelled from a place of safety, "but you'll be a wraith's victim tonight."

What did he mean? Had the final ward been removed?

Sweat trickled down Idmaer's forehead. He didn't wipe it away as it ran down his cheek. The spire trembled.

"No more killing," he heard someone yell from outside. That voice. It was Edoma's. "You are only adding more crimes to your tally."

Her voice struck him through the heart. If she was here, then she believed the charges. His conscience wanted nothing more than to tell her that he'd stolen the book, but doing that would only incriminate him further.

He couldn't remain in the spire. Soon, darkness would come, and he would become a skinwalker. The spire would be lost then.

The doors opened at his command. They lurched free of their hinges, flying toward the warriors. They stumbled out of the way, but one of the doors clipped a warrior on the back of his knees. His legs exploded, and he dropped to the ground, screaming. The doors could be replaced; Idmaer's pride, however, would be harder to repair.

Idmaer didn't look at Edoma as he strode out into the courtyard, hands tucked into his coat pockets. "So, you've decided to destroy the wards around my building. I guess you're happy, now? I must say you—"

Someone came from behind and slammed him into the ground. The gravel scraped across his face, and pain surged along his shoulder. He felt shackles cinch around his wrists. He called out to the spire a final time. The medallion burst with light and a great screeching emitted from the spire, like the chorus of a thousand dying souls. Too far to do anything but watch on, the spire bucked before straightening again. It, like Idmaer, knew they were defeated.

Bertram threw Idmaer inside a waiting carriage and chained his arms to a plank. Edoma came soon after.

"I know that you're a mage," Idmaer said. "It all makes sense now. I suspected something all along. Both you and Saega. But I never allowed myself to believe it. I thought my wife would never lie to me about something so great. But the wards, the scrying crystal you spoke of, the grimoire, the staff you carry . . . All those things can only mean one thing."

"And you are a god-killer," she said without emotion. Dark eyes glared at him, and he was unable to speak. There was no love between them anymore—he could see that now. She spat on the ground and slammed the carriage doors shut. The lock sounded with a clank. The carriage lurched and bucked as it left the spire.

44

EDOMA

THROUGH the wicket, Edoma stared at Idmaer's crumpled form. Gargled breaths were the only confirmation that he still lived. He had been arrested a few hours ago. She closed the hatch and turned to Wulfnoth, who was seated on a chair just outside the cell. "Has he been given any water?"

Wulfnoth dropped the waterskin from his mouth, guilt plain on his face. "Before Saega left, he said Idmaer wasn't to receive any until tomorrow morning."

"For the gods' sake, man!" Edoma reached for the waterskin in Wulfnoth's hand. He looked on as she grabbed it but made no move to stop her. She sniffed the skin and threw it back at him. "Wine? What kind of guard are you?"

Wulfnoth shrugged. "It's not like he'll be going anywhere."

Edoma couldn't believe it. The greatest tracker in Aernheim had been reduced to this drunken fool. Sure, he'd had his moments of sober usefulness, but those were infrequent at best. Saega would have told Wulfnoth to guard Idmaer out of spite. They'd once been great friends.

"Do you think he did it?" Edoma asked.

Wulfnoth seemed to calculate his answer. "I'd rather wait

for the trial."

"You have information?"

He swallowed under her gaze. He fumbled on his belt and unclipped a second skin. "This is water."

Edoma tore the waterskin from his grip. She peered through the grates again. Idmaer hadn't awoken. His chest rose and fell in fragmented jolts. He'd been taken straight from his spire to the warrior's barracks to await his trial. That had been done on Saega's orders. It seemed that Saega had been planning Idmaer's arrest for some time.

In the meantime, Edoma had tried to gain access to the spire. It seemed that she was no different from everyone else— an iron rod had come a fraction from pinning her to a tree in the spire's garden. Since then, she'd commanded the warriors to cease their attempts to gain access. It had become clear that another approach was needed.

She wouldn't have visited Idmaer had she another chance. She needed to get into the spire. If the trial was to be fair—and that was necessary given the blood the people now yearned for—Peoh needed to be present. Wulfnoth's lack of an answer troubled her. What information did he have that he wasn't willing to reveal to her?

Unsettled, Edoma glared at him. "Well? Are you going to open the cell?"

"Saega said—"

"I don't give a damn what he said! Open the bloody cell!"

Wulfnoth fumbled the keys and unlocked the cell door.

"Get someone to relieve you," she said. "You're a drunken mess."

Wulfnoth gave her the keys and stumbled off.

Edoma soaked the hem of her dress with the waterskin and wiped Idmaer's bloodied face. He moaned, but his eyes didn't open. She grabbed either side of him and felt fresh wounds. Scourging. Someone—or many people—had presumed to punish him without a trial. Had that been on Saega's orders too, or had they done it of their own volition?

Seething, she turned him over, careful of the lesions. The lightness of his body came as no surprise. She remembered when he had been well-muscled with a thick layer of fat, but that had been before stress and old age had taken its toll. Now he was frail, and beaten besides. With his body already weak, he might not survive the day. If that were the case, there would be no trial.

Edoma wasn't sure whether she believed he had done it. He'd definitely played a part. Peoh's presence in the spire and the stolen grimoire made her sure of that. But was he capable of deicide? In her anger, she had accused him of it.

Had she not seen him use the spire to kill dozens of warriors, she might have controlled herself.

Why would he have killed men who'd fought to defend Indham unless he were guilty?

The wounds on his back were fiery and swollen, begging to be dressed. She needed him to survive for the trial. He cried out as she washed them. Pieces of gravel fell from the cuts.

She peered out into the passageway. No one had come to relieve Wulfnoth yet. She and Idmaer were alone for now. Palming the runestone, she used Idmaer's own blood to ward his back. When she was finished, he awoke, eyes half open. Even her magic couldn't bring a man back from the brink of death completely. He might never recover fully.

"Edoma . . ."

"I have come to request something from you."

"What is it, my love?" he whispered.

She reared back. How long had it been since he'd called her that? It should have made her angry. Instead, all she felt was pity. She looked down at her weathered hands, Idmaer's blood caked into every crease. Throughout the years they had spent as lovers, she had thought of this moment—Idmaer's final hour. Now her magic had extended his life beyond where it might have ended. She slowly fed Idmaer the remains of the waterskin. By the time he had finished drinking, he had mostly returned to his senses.

"You came for me," he said.

"No. I need you to relinquish control of the spire."

"I cannot." Idmaer slumped against the brick wall.

"You must!" Edoma wanted to throw the waterskin in his face. Only sheer force of will prevented it. "No one can enter it. Everyone who tries is killed by the spire's magic."

Idmaer laughed dryly. "A loyal friend to the end. Nothing like Wulfnoth." He raised his voice. "You still out there, old friend? Care to give me another lashing?" Confused, he looked at Edoma. "You can't enter it?"

"I almost died trying."

"It must have been the way I felt when I left. Now, no one who has enmity with me can enter the spire. And it will be difficult finding someone who doesn't, now that you've convinced them all that I killed Aern."

Half-truths. Always half-truths. He could never speak a word without infusing it with some falsehood.

"You might not have killed Aern, but you helped the archmage do it."

"What archmage?" he said, seeming confused. Edoma knew the confusion for a lie.

She narrowed her eyes. "I do not know why you helped Peoh, but at least make penance for your sins by granting me this."

"It is true that I stole the grimoire. I was angry and wanted to spite you. I meant to tell you but never found the right occasion." Idmaer's gaze settled on Edoma. His gray eyes were stalwart, not wavering in the slightest. "The book was stolen from me. I know not how long ago, but it is not where I kept it."

"Why must you lie?" Edoma balled her fists, willing herself not to cry. She couldn't understand why he would tell the truth about stealing the book but not the truth about Aern. Perhaps he thought they didn't have condemning evidence.

"I did not kill Aern." Idmaer reached for her, but she pulled away. "Please, trust me."

Edoma closed her eyes. She so desperately wanted to believe him. She could believe that he was a thief, but not a murderer, especially of Aern. But the evidence said otherwise. He might not have shattered the orb with his own hands, but he'd assisted another to do so.

"Release the spire from your control," she whispered. "Unless you do so now, Saega will torture you when he returns." She knew it for certain now. No one would heed his cries for mercy here. The warriors had beaten him to the point of death, and they would return with more forms of punishment before the trial began.

"Let Wulfnoth do his best. I've already been punished for a crime I did not commit. Whoever is responsible has turned the woman I once loved against me. I will not lose the spire, too."

"No one else turned me against you. You did that yourself." Edoma left the cell, determined now to find someone who might be able to enter the spire. She could only think of one person.

45

IDMAER

IDMAER tried to keep a cool head while he waited in the dank cell. He was the lone occupant of the cells in the warrior's barracks. The stench of mildew filled the air, and the only noise was his own breathing. The presence of the spire lingered in his mind, even though he was a mile away from it. In that sense, he wasn't completely alone. The spire didn't speak with human words, but it did offer comfort. He hadn't left the town in years because he couldn't take being away from it for extended periods.

Edoma's visit had done much to ignite his spirits. Even though she believed him to be Aern's murderer, she had healed him. That had to mean something.

She was the only person he could count on to save him. Wulfnoth had seemed to take pleasure in striking him. When Idmaer had asked why, Wulfnoth hadn't answered. Instead, the next lash had come harder, and the one after that even harder.

In one corner of the room were the tattered remains of his cloak. They'd torn it to shreds before beating him. Exhausted, he slipped his hand into his coat pocket and removed the page of the grimoire. The bloody fingerprints were dark now.

The letters were still indecipherable. It made him wonder if he had indeed seen them translated.

Struck by a strange idea, Idmaer bit his thumb until he drew blood. He pressed his now bloody thumb onto the page. The letters danced until they formed the common tongue.

Blood magic. He should have known.

He read over the text again. If it was accurate, he had been wrong about the Guardians. They weren't simply forces as he'd philosophized. The thought made him ill. Over the years, he'd been so consumed with his own vague theories about the nature of gods, Guardians, and existence itself, that he'd missed his life.

Where were his sons now?

For the first time, he truly considered Alfric's misfortune. A skinwalker. And Hiroc? It had been revealed that he was Talented. If Indham ever survived the wraiths, he would be taken by Beorhtel's inquisitors. If Idmaer lived through the trial and Indham survived, he would ensure Hiroc would be hidden somewhere the inquisitors couldn't find him.

The passageway door outside his cell creaked open. Idmaer quickly searched the cell for somewhere to hide the page. The steady clinking of falling boots drew near. Idmaer found a loose brick from the cell's left wall and removed it. When the brick was replaced, the page was hidden behind it. The cell's lock clicked and the door opened. Torchlight burned Idmaer's eyes before his vision settled.

Wulfnoth stood in full armor at the cell's opening. He had never worn such gleaming steel before.

"Good to see you've dressed well for the trial," Idmaer said.

Wulfnoth's gloved hand smashed into Idmaer's face, rocking his head back.

"I've been waiting a long time for you to get what you deserve." He gripped Idmaer's wrists and cinched chains around them and then did the same with Idmaer's ankles.

Idmaer still couldn't understand why Wulfnoth suddenly hated him. "I didn't kill Aern." He wiped his bloody mouth with his shoulder, the chains preventing him from using his hand.

"You sent my son away. You could have protected him."

"Garmund? He was Talented. Beorhtel's inquisitors came for him. There was nothing I could have done."

Wulfnoth wrapped his fists around the chains until Idmaer's face was a fraction of an inch away. "I hear your son Hiroc is Talented. Tell me, if it had been him, would you have let him be taken?" When Idmaer didn't answer, Wulfnoth grunted. "I thought so. After Bodil died, my son was everything. I blamed Saega, but he wasn't responsible. He and Bodil didn't see eye to eye, but he told me all about how you showed the inquisitors where to find Garmund. He told me you even had a word with Bodil before she killed herself. Tell me, what did you say to her?"

Idmaer couldn't believe it. Had the one man he'd called a friend hated him all this time? Idmaer had been the one to convince Bodil to remain with Saega. Not long after, he had told her that if she must be with Wulfnoth, it was better to marry him. "I told her to make your marriage official. That I would officiate the ceremony myself. I wished happiness for her. She was my cousin. We were family."

"You never cared for family." Taking the chains over his shoulder, Wulfnoth dragged him through the passageway. Idmaer stumbled, unable to stay on his feet. The chains pulled him nonetheless, until they came to the open air.

Wulfnoth allowed Idmaer to stand. There was no carriage waiting to escort them to the courthouse. There was, however, a retinue of the warriors, equipped as if for battle in full armor and the customary three blades of the warrior's watch.

"We will walk to the Council hall." Wulfnoth nudged Idmaer on with a fist to the back.

The onlookers gaped as they passed. The majority

muttered curses under their breath, while the braver few yelled obscenities. Idmaer tried to ignore them, but the accusations cut deep. They called him Guardian-killer, desecrater, and much worse besides.

The sun was at its zenith, and it baked his skin. Sweat poured down his face, making the cuts sting. He thought the people had grown tired of cursing him, when something cracked him over the head with a splat. Fruit after rotten fruit pommeled him until he arrived at the sanctuary of the courthouse.

Wulfnoth locked the end of Idmaer's chains to one of the posts outside the courthouse. "You'll wait here until the Council calls you in."

When Wulfnoth had gone into the hall, Idmaer closed his eyes, not wanting to look upon the masses of people any longer. He concentrated on the spire, feeling its faint presence even now. The exercise allowed him to deafen the taunts and curses of the people.

Screams flooded his ears. His eyes shot open.

The people clamored as a forest dragon flew above them.

Idmaer gaped as the dragon landed in the middle of the parted people. Men and women ran in all directions, trying to escape the terrifying creature.

Wearing robes black as midnight, Saega stumbled down from the dragon's back. In his hand shone a stone of pure white—a suppression stone. Under the stone's haze, the dragon's eyes were filmy and white. It was a large dragon, with magnificent green scales and three-pronged antlers. It had probably been nothing more than a pup when the enclosures had been abandoned. Its wings were small from little use. But the magic that allowed dragons to fly cared not for the size of wings.

The crowd parted as Saega walked toward the hall. He moved with a long and painful-looking gait. His staff pulled him along like a rower would an oar.

He stopped in front of Idmaer. The cowl covering his face couldn't obscure the sight of leprous skin. Before Idmaer's eyes stood a dead man walking. He was reminded of the First Priest's words about those who touched carcaern orbs.

"You . . . you killed Aern!" Saega's eyes shifted to the people behind him, as though he had yelled in order for them to hear. He steadied himself on the post and coughed. Globs of black mucus fell from his mouth, some landing on Idmaer.

Saega lifted the fox-head staff. He trembled as it came above his waist. Idmaer was unable to do anything as Saega jabbed the end of the staff into his jaw. Idmaer's head rocked back. He spat blood.

Idmaer's eyes widened. That staff. It was magical. The incision running down Aern's altar at Tyme's Hill . . . Saega's staff could have been used to do it.

It was plain now. Saega was afflicted with the disease that had tormented the people who had touched the carcaern orbs. He had framed Idmaer for his own crime. He'd also convinced Wulfnoth that he was responsible for Bodil's death and Garmund's capture.

Saega reached for the medallion at Idmaer's neck and tore it away. Immediately, the spire's presence became dull. It was still there, but Idmaer could no more communicate with it than someone would hear him whisper from a thousand feet away.

But Saega still wouldn't have full ownership. Not until Idmaer spoke the words of transferal. And he would never do that.

"High Priest Idmaer is responsible for all your grievances," Saega called out to the crowd and pocketed the medallion. "The wraiths have come because of him. But he will be dealt with. Justice shall be swift."

46

HIROC

"HELP me move this." Edoma put down her staff, the runes on its tip glowing, and grabbed the edges of a rack filled with candles and cobwebs.

When they'd entered the shop, the candlemaker wasn't surprised at all to see them. He had simply opened the door and led them to the back. Hiroc had asked Edoma whether Idmaer's trial had started yet. When she'd answered no, there seemed to be a deep sadness lurking behind her eyes.

It was understandable. She had obviously once loved Idmaer enough to marry him and father two children. Hiroc still couldn't believe they were his parents. It had started to make more sense the more he thought about it. Although Idmaer had never acted quite like a father, he'd always favored Hiroc and Alfric. Hiroc had been able to enter the Holy Order. Alfric had been the head porter of the spire.

"We don't have all day."

Stirring, Hiroc got beneath one end of the rack while Edoma took the other. It shifted with their combined strength. Where the rack had been was a frayed rug. Edoma peeled it back, revealing a trapdoor. Hiroc's eyes widened. Suddenly, Edoma dragging him to this place made sense. Earlier, he'd asked her why they didn't simply enter through the spire's front door. "There's no door anymore," she had said. "The spire has removed it. Now there is only smooth stone at the tower's base."

"Let's hope the spire hasn't changed this entrance," she said now as she opened the trapdoor. Holding her staff, Edoma illuminated the darkness. A staircase crept downward. "Thank Enlil. It hasn't changed."

Hiroc shook his head. "How many secrets are there that I have no knowledge of?"

"This town is a relic of the First Empire. There are many places beneath the earth where no one has ventured for years."

"How did you know about this entrance?"

"In my younger days," Edoma said, a distant tone dampening her voice, "I used to visit Idmaer. It was best to keep our meetings clandestine, and these tunnels made that possible. Not from his father, of course, since he had the spire for eyes. But from those who didn't want us to marry." She cleared her throat. "Remember what I told you. Do not reveal our intentions to Peoh. Tell him you're taking him to see the Council. If he knows what we intend, he won't agree to go with you."

Edoma guided them through the tunnels, her staff's tip glowing in a small sphere that lit their path a few paces away. Writings lined the walls in a language Hiroc couldn't read, as well as images of creatures he had never seen before. He wanted to pause to look at them, but every time he slowed down, he received a curt demand from Edoma not to tarry.

The tunnels grew smaller and smaller. He hunched so low that it would have been almost better for him to crawl. He breathed a sigh when the tunnel came to an end and opened into a small alcove. The alcove was furnished plainly with a plaid rug, a wooden chest, and a cabinet. A wooden door was at the other end.

Edoma walked over to the chest and rummaged through its

contents while Hiroc paced around the room. He stopped at a crude etching in the wall beside the rug. Edoma and Idmaer's names were each in separate, but linked, circles. In the middle of the intersecting circles were two smaller names—Hiroc and Alfric. He recognized the formations. It was the old ritual of marriage. A magical warding that was said to keep the couple together. Feeling like he was intruding upon a sacred space, he turned back to Edoma.

She inserted a key into the door, and it swung open. He thought that it was strange to keep a key in the same place as the lock, but then he realized she probably hadn't come through here in years. "Go now," she said. "The door leads to the dungeons."

"Bertram said the skinwalkers had escaped."

"You have your glove. I'm afraid that's the best we can do."

"Why risk my life to bring Peoh?" he said. He was her son, after all.

"Peoh might be a liar. He might be the one responsible for shattering the orb. But he also might be able to save Aernheim. He has knowledge beyond anything I've known. You are my son." She touched his shoulder affectionately. "If you do not wish to enter the spire, you can walk away now. I will not think less of you."

He looked at his feet. A little over a week ago, at a moment's notice, Alfric had conjured a plan to help Indham. He'd risked everything. Where was he now? Alive? Dead? He wasn't here. This time, it was Hiroc Indham needed.

"I'm the only one," Hiroc said. "You said that yourself."

Edoma smiled. "You have the glove. You have your knife. Draw blood when you need it, just a small cut. Call upon Enlil, and he will keep you safe." She removed a small vial from her robes. "This is the last of the human blood we have. We used the rest of it for this evening's wards. Tomorrow, we will have to make difficult decisions to keep warding the town, unless Saega brings back a dragon. But he might not return. It's up to you to save Indham. Go now. May Enlil's hand keep you from harm."

Hiroc was about to leave when he caught sight of the etching on the wall. "I think Idmaer is innocent," he said.

Edoma shook her head. "The grimoire of the First Priest was stolen from the tomb. Idmaer's medallion was the only thing that could open it. He isn't the man you think he is. Once, he was just, kind, and devout. But no more."

"The Council might find him guilty. What then? Will you allow the man you once loved—the man who once loved you—to be executed? Will you allow my *father* to be executed?"

Edoma's face clenched, as though she were fighting back tears. "That will only happen if he's guilty. He will have a fair trial."

47

EDOMA

TWO hours before sundown, the Council gathered for the trial.

Edoma had raced from the candlemaker's shop to the Council Hall and taken a seat beside Saega at the high table.

"Is it wise to have the people present?" Edoma whispered to Saega.

Wherever there was space to stand or climb, there were people. Fatherless, warriors, priests, acolytes, and Daughters of Enlil. There were even some pilgrims who had remained in Indham rather than seek their luck elsewhere. The only empty space was behind the Council member's table and a section in front of it, where Idmaer knelt.

The Council sat on the high table. Edoma had purposely sat directly behind him, where he would be unable to see her. There were scant few Council members who had been amicable with Idmaer before today, but now, every one of them looked on with scowls. Edoma hoped their minds weren't already determined. She had promised Hiroc that Idmaer would have a fair trial.

"Everyone knows the charges," Saega said to Edoma. He

was wearing his black runic robes. The wards on his face still glowed faintly. "I was outside. They chanted god-killer."

Edoma sighed. She had been unable to think of anything except the trial since she'd visited Idmaer earlier that morning. Her anger had since subsided. In its place was a calm readiness to accept whatever happened today.

"I'm not going to mention Peoh to the Council," Saega said. "Better that we deal with him ourselves. Should the Council learn of the oath you and I made with Peoh, we would suffer a similar fate to the real killer."

Edoma didn't like lying, but she accepted it with a nod. It wasn't their trial today, but Idmaer's. Not only that, but she wanted Hiroc to find Peoh before Saega did. She suspected Saega wouldn't wait to question whether Peoh could help them. She still had hope that, even if Peoh had shattered Aern's orb, he might be convinced to restore them. She had, after all, once been close to him.

Saega's body shuddered, and she caught sight of blood beneath his sleeve. The ends of his fingers were black with rot. He must now only be sustaining himself with Sulith's magic.

Not a single person spoke as Saega stepped out from the table. A hood obscured his face. "Esteemed members of Indham's Council, I bring before you a charge of great weight. You were informed by Idmaer, High Priest of Indham, that Aern was weakened. This, however, was a lie."

Saega nodded to Wulfnoth, and he stood. He opened a small wooden box and held it in an outstretched palm. He strolled behind each seated Council member, and they turned to gaze inside the box. Horror struck their somber faces. Edoma was last to discern the box's contents—the broken shards of Aern's orb.

If there had been any doubt in the Council's mind until this point, it was gone now. Aern's orb had been shattered. Idmaer had lied to them.

Edoma grimaced. This wasn't the best way to start a fair

trial. Seeing that he had lied to them would make them more likely to condemn him for shattering the orb. Had it been her who had addressed the other Council members, she might have admitted that she had also known the orb was broken. But that would have been foolish. If Idmaer was condemned, they might have condemned her, too.

Edoma hoped that if they did rule against him, more evidence would be put forward. If not, she would have to testify on his behalf, revealing that she had also known that Aern had been killed.

Wulfnoth placed the box on the table, still open. The shards caught the sunlight through the windows. Everyone in the room was now able to look upon the fractured remains of their beloved protector.

Saega nodded to Edoma, and she stood. It was her turn now to question the witness. Now she would learn what Wulfnoth had refused to tell her.

"Where did you get this box?" Edoma asked.

"I've owned it for most my life."

Her question had been a test, and Wulfnoth had answered truthfully. That was good. He wasn't intending to lie to the Council.

"And the shards?" she asked.

"Idmaer told me to collect them from the altar. They are, as you can see, those that once formed Aern's orb."

With not nearly enough information for a verdict either way, Edoma pressed on. "What else did he tell you?"

"He said to scrub the blood clean so that no one would know what really happened to Aern."

"What really happened?" Edoma said, holding her breath.

"Idmaer stole a grimoire from the First Priest's tomb. He used the dark magic inside to destroy Aern's orb."

Edoma felt her legs weaken. She grasped the table's edge with both hands.

"Do you wish to continue?" Saega asked her.

She nodded. Taking a deep breath, she asked her final question. This would be the one to determine Idmaer's guilt or innocence. "Did he tell you why?"

"He wanted to prove that Aern didn't live within the orb. He wanted to show that there was nothing but energy within it. He called it an impersonal force."

Edoma found herself nodding. It was all making sense. The motives rang true. Idmaer had spoken these diabolical philosophies with her before.

"And this book?" Saega leaned heavily on his staff and groaned as he removed a tome from his pocket. It was small and blackened from burning. "Is it true you gave this book to me?"

Edoma gasped as Wulfnoth answered, "Yes."

"And where did you get it?"

"Idmaer told me to dispose of it as he said to dispose of the shards. He had been unable to burn it completely. It is what remains of the First Priest's grimoire."

A dry laugh broke through the shocked gasps of the people. The laughing continued, followed by a slow and pitiful clapping. Idmaer's chains clinked as he continued to applaud. He didn't speak, but he seemed to be taken with a hysterical bout of laughter.

Edoma looked away. She clenched her fists beneath the table.

Saega thrust a black-tipped finger at Idmaer. "This man before you, a so-called *High Priest*, has spoken heresy. The Guardians he calls nothing but *forces*. This is madness." Saega sneered down at Idmaer. "Do you believe these things?"

Idmaer had remained silent for the duration of the trial. Edoma hadn't looked at him once during her questioning, but she did now.

He smiled, eyes heavy-lidded. "Does it really matter what I tell you? How can you sentence a man to death for his beliefs?"

"Answer the question," Edoma said through gritted teeth.

His smugness infuriated her.

"No, I don't believe that now. This grimoire you speak of taught me otherwise."

She had known he'd stolen it. And now he'd admitted he'd read it before the Council and before Indham's people.

"There is no defense I can give," Idmaer said. "Since I will be leaving you all soon, I'd like to confess the only sins I am guilty of."

Saega looked at Edoma, and she forced herself to nod. She braced herself for what might come next.

"You may speak," Saega said to Idmaer.

"Firstly, I failed in my duties to my family. As husband, I heeded not the advice of my wife, and when I did, I did so begrudgingly. I manipulated her into giving up our only sons. When she sought separation from the marriage bed and our home, I entered the catacombs beneath Enlil's Temple. In a stroke of pure luck, I happened upon a statue that contained a perfect fit for the High Priest's medallion. With it, I opened the tomb and stole the First Priest's grimoire.

"But I spurned more than just my wife and my sons. My cousin, Bodil, was taken by men whom I suggested she court. The first betrays me now before you all; the other stands in condemnation of me. Both I counted as friends, but I see now that they are scorpions who preyed upon my dear cousin and now conspire to have me killed.

"And to Indham's people—" He tried to turn his head to face them, but the chains made it impossible. "My father handed down the office of High Priest, thinking that I would do it justice. I didn't. I failed to lead the people as I ought. I convinced you all that the dragons were to be captured and enslaved. Those of you who opposed me, I ensured were silenced. Durwin, the man who made his opposition most clear, I framed for stealing an object from the Basilica. He was executed for a crime he didn't commit. And now, the gods, whom I have denied for so long, have seen fit to mete out justice. I did not kill Aern, but I shall suffer the punishment of death for the crimes I have committed."

There was silence.

Edoma barely noticed the tears running down her face. She rubbed them away with her sleeves, scowling at Idmaer as she did. He refused to meet her gaze. She wanted to storm over to him and strike him.

How dare he admit to all those things and yet not tell the truth about Aern?

"The charge is deicide," Saega announced. "Does the Council perceive the accused guilty?"

Edoma considered things as hands shot up around her. Hiroc had spoken of a giant. Where was the giant in all of this? She supposed it wasn't unbelievable that Idmaer had hired a giant from the northern mountains to remain at the hill while he made an escape. And Peoh? The events described by Wulfnoth had left him out completely. Still, it was clear from Wulfnoth's testimony and the evidence presented that Idmaer—even if he hadn't struck the killing blow—had played an instrumental part in Aern's murder.

Steeling her resolve, Edoma lifted her hand. She could see from the corner of her eye that every other Council member had a hand raised. Although only the Council's judgment could send a man to the chopping block, all over the room hands were lifted. Not a single person, Council member or otherwise, showed themselves to disagree with the charge.

"The decision is unanimous." Saega wandered over to Idmaer. He nodded at Wulfnoth, who removed something from his girdle pouch. Idmaer's eyes widened at the whip Wulfnoth was unraveling.

"Idmaer, you are stripped of your title as High Priest."

A lash descended, breaking skin. Idmaer didn't scream.

"You are stripped of your blood-right."

Another lash, and still he didn't scream. He bit his lip.

"You are stripped of your humanity. You are stripped of

your eternal reward. You are stripped of your name."

Three lashes this time, and on the last, he cried out. He lay on the cold stone, breathing heavily.

"You will be executed at daybreak tomorrow," Saega said. His sandaled feet walked away, dotted with blood. The whip clattered to the ground inches from Idmaer's face.

"Return the desecrater to the dungeons," Saega said.

Edoma looked away as Idmaer was dragged out. He had admitted to all those things, and yet he hadn't admitted to killing Aern.

"You got the dragon," Edoma said as Saega approached her. His faded habit obscured his face. A deathly stench filled the air.

"Indeed. It was not easy, but it is done. After the execution, you can begin the bloodletting."

"You commanded that Idmaer be tortured," Edoma said.

"I needed him ready to give up the spire. You spoke with him, didn't you?"

"Wulfnoth told you?"

Saega nodded. "And you were unable to convince him to grant you ownership."

"No," she said.

"There are . . . *other* means by which Idmaer would transfer ownership." He drummed his fingers on his staff. They were, as she had seen earlier, black around the fingernails.

Edoma couldn't believe that she was considering what Saega was implying. But Idmaer had stolen the grimoire and used it to murder Aern. He was entirely responsible for Indham's current plight.

"Do what you must," she said.

48

FRYDA

FRYDA continued through another sequence of corridors, following closely behind Peoh. She still held the short spear in her hand. The only light came from Peoh's tattoos. He'd removed his tunic so that the tattoos glowed brighter. She couldn't help looking at the strange woman depicted on his back. Was that what his Guardian looked like? He had come from Mundos like Edoma, so his Guardian was probably Mun. From the little Edoma had told her, Mun was a terrible Guardian who took pleasure in suffering. But this woman seemed to have a caring expression, her hands pressed together in a prayerful posture.

They'd been traveling beneath the spire for hours. There was nothing unique about the stone walls or the sconces jutting out from them—everything looked the same. Were it not for Peoh's constant encouragement that they were almost at the exit, Fryda feared she might have gone insane.

"Through here," Peoh said.

Fryda stepped through a narrow doorway. Had he not pointed it out, she might have thought it was merely an inlet in the wall. She gasped at what was inside.

In the middle of the round room was a pool. The spire's

constant shaking caused the water to move about. A green light emanated from the center of the pool. Water trickled from a fountain on the wall behind it.

"This spire is a magnificent place," Peoh said. He knelt beside the pool and ran his hands through the water. "It is said that godstone, the material used to build the spire, was mined in the realm of the gods—the Infernal City." He pointed to a symbol like a number eight that was carved onto each of the four stone pillars that held up the domed ceiling. "That is the symbol of the divine city."

Fryda recognized it from the catacombs at Enlil's Temple. It had marked the giant door Edoma had thought the First Priest's tomb lay behind.

Peoh nodded to a doorway left of the pool. "And that's the way out."

"How can you be sure?" They'd traveled through a dozen doors that led into more rooms with more doors. Although, none of the rooms had been quite like this one.

"Can't you smell it? The air is fresh."

Fryda shook her head. All she could smell was dust.

"Trust me," he said with a smile. He went to walk through the doorway, but Fryda stopped him.

"We can't leave yet," she said. "Jaruman is still out there."

"He was a good man," Peoh said. "We grew up together. He became a soldier and I a mage. The world is a lesser place for having lost him."

"We left him trapped beneath the rubble, still alive. Don't speak of him like he's dead." The spire shook and the pool's water splashed onto the stone outside of it. "It's not just Jaruman we need to retrieve. The warrior dropped a vial of dragon blood."

Peoh looked at her with a hard gaze. "Why do you need dragon blood?"

"I want to be warded." When his eyes narrowed, she prayed that this strange man who could command unseen forces had a heart. She doubted it, but she had to try. "Alfric was a man I loved. He went with two other warriors to Eosorheim."

"We don't have time for this," he said.

She grabbed his arm and immediately let go. His skin had scalded her palm. Ignoring the pain, she said, "Please, hear me."

Peoh looked sympathetically at her burned hand and nodded.

"Before Alfric got there, the wraiths came. They possessed him and made him into a skinwalker. I saw him. I thought my horse killed him, but it didn't. I want to find him."

"Forget it," he said. "He's more lost than Jaruman. There's no coming back once a skinwalker takes you." He stopped, as though he was about to correct himself. "No coming back," he repeated.

"Alfric is different," Fryda insisted. "Edoma said she saw him in the scrying crystal. His soul was still in his body, even while the wraith was controlling it."

Peoh suddenly grabbed her shoulders and stared her in the eyes. "Are you certain?"

Fryda winced, realizing that a man who had punched a hole in a wall was now gripping her tightly enough to break her arms. "I'm certain!"

He let go of her. He scratched his chin in thought. "We must find this dragon blood. I'll ward you myself. I'd come with you to find this Alfric, but saving Aernheim is more important. At least for now."

"Why are you willing to go back for the dragon blood when you weren't willing to go back for Jaruman?" Fryda almost regretted asking the question, but she needed to know.

"There's something important about this Alfric, if what Edoma saw was true." Without saying any more, he walked past her. He went to one of the walls and pressed his ear against it.

"What are you doing?" she asked.

Raising a hand to silence her, he rapped against the wall with his fist. The sound came back hollow. "I was looking for this," he said. "The water pipes that make the fountain work lie beyond this wall."

Peoh extended his arm, and the wards along them glowed. Fryda gasped as blood leaked from the tattoos. He widened his legs and turned from the hip, twisting his arm. His fist shot through the wall. Water trickled out from the new hole. "Well, we know where the pipes are." He wore an expression of concern as he crammed the broken bricks into the hole. Despite the obstruction, water continued leaking from it.

Brow furrowed, he walked farther along the wall, pressing his ear against it. He punched a few more sections, his fist blasting through the stone. Each time more water gushed out. Cracks started to appear along the wall. What would happen if it caved in? Fryda shuddered at the thought. They would be buried like Jaruman.

Peoh put his fist through the wall again. This time it came out dry. His knuckles were bloodied, and it looked like bone had broken through the skin. He turned back to her. "Care to help move some bricks?"

A tearing sound split the air. Above her, two cracks raced along the wall, meeting each other. She dropped her spear and scrambled to remove the rubble from the hole. When it was large enough to fit through, she grabbed her short spear. Hunching her shoulders, she squeezed through the hole. Peoh followed, and not a moment too soon. He grabbed her and they dived. A thunderous crash boomed.

For a moment, Fryda could hear nothing except white noise. When her hearing returned, there was the soft trickle of water.

Peoh's tattoos afforded her some light. The wall had collapsed outward, into the pool. With the wall now removed, the strange pipe system that circulated the water could be seen. It was now destroyed, Peoh's punches having burst a number of the metal cylinders.

"This water system must run through the walls. I heard the same trickling while I was in the cell. It drove me near mad. Wherever these pipes lead, we'll eventually come back to where we left Jaruman."

And the skinwalkers, Fryda thought. It had been easy to say that they needed to return to find the dragon vial, but now that they were doing it, all she could think about was the skinwalkers that had been freed from their prisons.

"The integrity of this tunnel is damaged," he said, eying the ceiling nervously. "One moment and we'll get moving." A puddle of green water sat near the rubble. He knelt before it and washed his hands. The water seemed to glow, even as it touched his broken knuckles. When he'd finished cleaning them, his hands were completely healed.

Fryda rushed over to the pool and submerged her burned hand. In seconds, where Peoh's tattoos had left blisters, there was fresh skin. Her mouth dropped as she turned the hand over, unable to believe what her eyes were telling her. "How?"

"Magical properties," Peoh said, admiring his own hands. "I didn't know for certain they would heal me. But I suspected this water, like the spire that contains it, came from the Infernal City."

Fryda followed Peoh into more narrow tunnels. They used the strange pipes as guides.

"You said you could save Aernheim," she said. "You really shouldn't be risking your life to help me." She now realized that her desires were selfish. Saving Jaruman. Getting the dragon blood. Going after Alfric. None of that mattered compared to the thousands of people who would be saved if Peoh survived.

"Remember when I said I knew your mother?" Peoh said.

"I thought you were deceiving me." Fryda remembered what Jaruman had said about Peoh being a great liar.

"I knew her," he said. "She was a beautiful woman. In

more than just her appearance. She was kind and caring. I removed the bonds shackling her wrists. She had been enslaved by the orcs who live beneath the Scorched Lands. All the Fatherless had come from that city. Their trip beneath the earth and out through Babon's Pass must have driven the adults mad. Thankfully, you children survived. And what a blessing that is." He smiled at her. "Your mother taught me that vengeance means nothing. It's forgiveness that cleanses. I was so consumed with getting across the Scorched Lands and fulfilling my oath to destroy a southern orb, but she convinced me otherwise. It's for that reason that I'll help you. Don't worry, a skinwalker will not kill me. And I'll make sure you come to no harm either."

He spoke with such sincerity that Fryda couldn't help but believe him. Jaruman had warned her against trusting Peoh, but he hadn't known this man. He had known the old Peoh who wanted only to destroy a southern orb.

Footsteps sounded from around the corner. Fryda gripped her short spear above her head, poised for stabbing. Beside her, Peoh readied himself in a fighting stance, his tattoos glowing brighter.

As a figure rounded the corner and came into view, Fryda almost jabbed but stopped. Hiroc leaped back. He raised a gloved hand into the air and held a knife in the other. The sleeves of his robes were torn, exposing his forearms. Blood dripped from a recent cut on his left hand.

"Hiroc," Peoh said, letting down his fists.

"You know each other?" she said, looking from one man to the other.

"What are you doing down here?" Hiroc said to her at the same time.

49

HIROC

"LET'S leave the spire now," Hiroc said. "The Council is ready to meet with you."

Peoh eyed Hiroc strangely, as though he knew that Hiroc was lying to him. He seemed strangely distant, different from the talkative man he had met in the spire's dungeons.

Furrowing her brow, Fryda looked at his glove but didn't say anything. "We can't leave yet. Jaruman is still within the cells." She had just finished explaining to Hiroc what had happened to her and Peoh in the spire. She looked so different, her hair flowing down to her shoulders, and the short spear in her hand. She was lucky he hadn't burned her with Enlil's fire.

Hiroc considered waiting in the current room while they went to find Jaruman. Sighing, he decided he couldn't let them go alone. "I'll come with you."

"You've changed," Fryda said before leaving down the right corridor. Peoh followed after her.

Hiroc heard something strange in the passageway to the left. Rather than follow the others, he decided to seek it out. He would be able to catch up with them. The passageway ended in an open room. It was filled with bloodletting mechanisms.

Many differently shaped blades hung from metal arms. A half-dozen coats were hanging from hooks against the far wall. A figure stepped out from beneath them.

Hiroc gasped as he recognized the person holding a runic dagger. He wasn't surprised to find Ealstan in the spire. He had expected him to be here. After all, the last he'd heard was that Ealstan was looking for the missing page in the spire. He must have gotten in before Idmaer was arrested and the spire closed itself off.

"Hiroc," Ealstan said.

Hiroc wasted no time in removing his own dagger. Blood still dripped from the wound he had made earlier, but he wanted to be sure he would have enough. Grimacing, he slid the blade across his forearm.

"I'm surprised you're still alive and not one of those skinwalkers. I suspect Kipp showed himself a craven."

"Aye," Hiroc said, "Kipp saved us, but he was no craven. Because of you, Oswin died."

Ealstan chuckled. "A good end for a Fatherless. Tell me, did you strike him down with Enlil's fire?"

Screaming with rage, Hiroc called out for Enlil. His hand ignited. At the same time, Ealstan invoked Aern. The two fists met each other, one bursting with blue fire, the other shimmering with an invisible shield. Sparks exploded from the meeting of powers. A second time, Hiroc called upon Enlil. His fist met Ealstan's own again. The sound of contact ruptured the ground beneath them, sending shockwaves rippling along the stone.

Ealstan swept his knife downward. Hiroc blocked it with his own. "Enlil, hear me!" He brought his flaming fist onto Ealstan's face. Skin seared beneath the blow's heat.

Hiroc doubled over as an invisible force plowed into his stomach. Winded, he called out to Enlil, but nothing happened. Ealstan's magic pounded into Hiroc. He spun through the air and crashed into one of the bloodletting mechanisms. He groaned as he stood. Pain flared in his right side. He lifted his arms. A serrated blade had embedded itself between the ribs. Gritting his teeth, he pulled himself from it.

"Enlil!" Hiroc cried. Still, nothing came.

Ealstan barked a laugh. He strolled among the mechanisms. Hiroc took the knife in hand. If he wasn't going to have magic to fight with, he would at least have a knife.

Another force threw Hiroc backward. He smashed against the mechanisms. Again and again, he was thrown around the room. Each time, a new blade cut into him.

Hiroc lay on the ground. He tried to stand but couldn't.

He whispered Enlil's name. He wished only to have Enlil respond. He had spoken to him before, on Tyme's Hill, thinking it had been Aern. Why now was Enlil silent? He had never needed a runic device to speak with Enlil then.

"It seems that Enlil is no god at all," Ealstan said. "Aern is far superior."

While staring at the rooftop, hearing Ealstan drone on, Hiroc remembered what Peoh had said about spiritsoul and how some Talented could use magic without runic devices. He thought that if Enlil gave him power this one time, he would give every drop of spiritsoul he possessed. Hiroc yelled at the top of his lungs, unable to form any other words except, "Enlil."

Hiroc burst into a conflagration of blue flames. It seared away his pain and filled him with strength.

He stood, power flowing through him. Ealstan thrust his hand forward. A dull thud hit Hiroc's chest. It was nothing more than a feeble prod. Ealstan continued throwing invisible punches. He cried out, and the bloodletting mechanisms lifted from the ground and flew at Hiroc. He tossed jets of blue flame, and the devices melted in the heat, even before they fell to the ground.

Hiroc concentrated on Ealstan's hand that grasped the dagger. Flames fired forward. Ealstan yelped as his hand burst into flame. The dagger clattered to the ground.

Hatred clouded Hiroc's vision, and Ealstan cowered against the wall. He slid to the ground, eyes wide. "How . . . you're the burning man."

Hiroc snarled and held out his hand. He could see Ealstan's face reddening beneath the heat. Sweat balled on his forehead and atop his mustached lip.

Through the anger, Hiroc remembered Fryda's words about Jaruman. Buried beneath rubble. Hiroc closed his eyes and exhaled. The flames vanished. He stood naked, healed of all his wounds, his clothes burned away.

Ealstan still cowering, Hiroc picked up the man's dagger. He grabbed Ealstan by the collar and lifted him to his feet. He pressed the dagger against the other man's throat. "You're going to start making amends."

50

IDMAER

THE sound of the passageway door opening drew Idmaer to his feet. He hadn't slept long, a few hours at most, although it was impossible to tell with no light inside his cell. The only thing that made him aware of the time was Saega's constant visitations through the night. He'd come at least a dozen times. Maybe he stayed a minute, maybe an hour. All Idmaer knew was that those dozen visits had been filled with pain, unlike anything he'd felt before.

Beyond the agony, Idmaer licked his lips, the very action making his head whirl as wetness filled the cracks.

The cell door creaked open, and Saega entered. He inserted a flaming torch into the sconce beside the cell door and rested his fox-head staff on the wall next to it. He wore those deep black robes he'd been wearing all night.

"Good morning, Idmaer. I trust you slept well?" Saega seemed to exert intense effort merely to remain standing. "I'm looking forward to obtaining the spire today." He turned and smiled, the torchlight revealing the leprous sores overwhelming his face. Along his cheeks were lacerations that looked to be a result of scratching an itch without satisfaction.

Idmaer quaked at seeing the fox-head staff. Somehow,

that weapon had crushed his bones without crushing them, made him bleed without ever bleeding out, snapped his spine without crippling him. It was no ordinary staff, that was for certain.

Saega looked from the staff to Idmaer. "You have become well-acquainted with Agnerod's Touch." He picked up the staff and ran his hands along the fox-head. "It is the king of staves, a relic from the First Empire. It can make a man feel pain without inflicting grave wounds. A pity, really, since most of the enjoyment in torture is in seeing a weapon's handiwork."

"Did you do it? Did you kill Aern?" Idmaer had asked those questions a dozen times. Each time Saega had treated the question with a blow from Agnerod's Touch. Wincing, Idmaer waited again for the coming pain. But there was none.

"Aye," Saega said. "I shattered the orb. This illness is my reward for touching it. I freed Aern from his imprisonment." He thrust a finger at Idmaer. "But I did it for more than that. It was your decision to allow the Fatherless into our walls that poisoned my adopted home. Had you not done that, Bodil might never have spent her evenings outside of my home. She might never have been taken by that barbarian, Wulfnoth. I might never have slain her by mine own hand."

Idmaer gasped. "You killed Bodil?"

Saega scowled. "A year after she left me to marry Wulfnoth, I went to their home after drinking too much firewine. I wanted to watch her from the window. Just to see her face again. But I found something else. She had mounted Wulfnoth, riding him like a wild animal. There was more passion in her lovemaking with him than I'd ever shared with her. I was filled with wrath, and it didn't subside. I waited there within the shrubbery until morning. Wulfnoth took Garmund tracking, leaving Bodil alone. I went inside the house and crushed her neck between my hands. I made it look like a feeble attempt at taking her own life. But anyone who knew her truly would have known she would never commit suicide. Wulfnoth had his suspicions, I suspect, but I convinced him to despise you. What he might have felt toward me was channeled toward you."

"Bodil didn't deserve that," Idmaer said, shaking his head.

"She didn't. But I blame you and your Fatherless. It was only care for Edoma that stopped me from moving against you. But when an ally presented himself and Ealstan found the grimoire within your spire, I knew I had to act. For justice. For vengeance."

"You've harbored hatred against me this whole time?"

Saega grunted. He no longer seemed willing to talk. "Relinquish ownership of the spire. This mage you are hiding cannot stay there forever."

"I don't know anything of this man," Idmaer said. Edoma had mentioned him, too.

Saega frowned. "Is that so?"

A cold sensation drifted across Idmaer's ribs. It was the touch of the fox-head staff. Then came pain. A shooting tendril made him cry out in agony. An ephemeral blade twisted. Flesh churned and skin shredded. He knew it wasn't real, but it felt like fire and ice intertwined into a single sensation of terrifying agony.

"Maybe I will chain you outside where you are unprotected. By morning, you will be a skinwalker. Then I will bring you back here with Edoma. I'll chain her to the other side of the cell. How long before the wraith within you grows so hungry that it tears itself from the chains, heedless of the damage it does to your hands, and rips Edoma apart?"

"You can't do this," Idmaer said, his voice muffled from the swelling.

Saega's expression was cool. It was the look of a maniac who committed atrocities without batting an eye. He approached slowly, every footfall echoing in the stone-walled chamber. "I shattered the orb. I am more than capable of bringing her here."

Saega dropped the staff. He swept the black cloak over his shoulders. Strange mutterings came from his lips, and his body shuddered. It continued vibrating while his body expanded, his muscles inflating. The transformation was over as quickly as it had begun. The robes that had hung loosely over his small frame constricted around a body of a monster. A giant.

The force of an anvil crushed Idmaer's face. A garbled cry fell from his mouth. Even had he wanted to recite the incantation to transfer ownership, it would have been difficult through the broken teeth and cut gums. With a grand tug, Saega tore Idmaer's beard. His other hand struck again and again. Pain surged beyond sense. All Idmaer could see was white.

"You will relinquish ownership of the spire to me," Saega said, his voice deep and menacing between wheezing breaths. "If you do not, I will make you a skinwalker and bring Edoma to this chamber."

"You wouldn't . . ." Idmaer said, coughing up blood.

"Test me."

Idmaer saw in Saega's eyes a resolve that would not waver. Unless Saega received ownership of the spire, Idmaer would become a skinwalker. Edoma would be torn apart by his own hands. That was something he couldn't endure.

"Say it," Saega said. "My father was Alesand," he added, and held out the First Priest's medallion.

Drool fell from Idmaer's chin. With the shackles restricting him, he couldn't have wiped it even if he had the energy to. "I relinquish . . . ownership of the First Priest's Spire to . . . Saega, son of Alesand." Touching the medallion, Idmaer channeled what remained of his will into the words. He had been taught the transferal from his father, and he had intended to use them for his own sons. In many ways, preparing Hiroc as an acolyte had also been his way of preparing a son for the spire one day. But that would never be. As the last of Idmaer's will left him, Saega gained control of the spire.

"That wasn't so hard, was it?" Saega's body trembled again until it was the frail old man he had always appeared as. "I apologize if I got a little carried away. Obtaining the spire is far more important than you can imagine."

"What is it you're planning?"

Saega smiled. "You're not going to live to find out. But I can assure you that the world will suffer much before we're finished. The gods have been imprisoned for too long. The petty oath I made all those years ago means nothing now. We have a greater calling."

We? Who was the other person? And what was this oath he spoke of? The questions lingered in the back of Idmaer's mind, even as he wanted to collapse onto the floor and die. He fought to stand, arms hanging like anchors, dragging him down despite his best efforts. He dropped to his knees.

Saega crossed the room and hesitated at the door. "Ah, the spire is a wonderful gift. I feel it now, although afar off, telling me secrets." He went to the wall where Idmaer had hidden the grimoire's page. Smiling, he shifted the loose brick out and took the page in hand. "Thank you for keeping this safe for me."

Idmaer lost control of his body. His face hit the floor first. His body came after.

As he drifted in and out of consciousness, his mind whirled through many things. Principal among them was justice.

Justice had come, at least for his crimes. Perhaps it would soon seek out Saega, too.

Unsatisfied with this most meager end, Idmaer struggled to his knees. For the first time in years, even as he wrestled with the darkness of exhaustion, he murmured the Ode to Enlil. In a voice barely above a whisper, he asked forgiveness from the gods and readied himself for death.

51

FRYDA

FRYDA impaled a skinwalker with her short spear. She planted her foot against its chest and pushed it off the blade. Beside her, Peoh twisted his hand. A few feet away, a skinwalker's head crumpled. It stopped halfway through a charge and dropped. All around, crimson mist floated before vanishing.

Heaving, Fryda leaned on her spear. There were no more skinwalkers. They'd killed them all. The split in the ground was much wider than it had been before. The spire's constant shaking must have opened it farther. It was now a chasm.

On the other side, Jaruman was still beneath the stones. She couldn't see whether he was breathing. Enlil grant that he was. Eying the distance, she figured it was too large to leap across.

"It's too far," Peoh said, confirming her thoughts. His entire body was now slick with blood. Most of the tattoos were covered by it. He'd killed eight skinwalkers where she'd killed only two. So many times she had come close to being slashed by their talons, and he had saved her.

"Not for him," a voice said from behind them. Wearing a cloak, Hiroc entered the room through the hole in the wall and threw a man at their feet.

Ealstan looked up at Fryda.

"How did he—?"

"There's no time," Peoh said. He grabbed Ealstan and pulled him to his feet. "You're Devoted to Aern, aren't you?"

Scowling, Ealstan nodded.

Hiroc held out a dagger with an imp on the pommel. "Will this runic device work if it's not in his hand?"

Peoh inspected it and nodded. "Hold it on his flesh when he invokes Aern."

Hiroc grabbed Ealstan roughly and pressed the blade to his back. "Take her across. Start making amends."

Fryda didn't ask what he was meant to be making amends for, or why Hiroc was clothed in a cloak.

"I can't take her all the way," Ealstan said. "I can only push her farther."

"She dies," said Hiroc, "you die."

Fryda didn't like the sound of that. Not when Ealstan looked like he wanted to kill them all. Still, she had to get to Jaruman. They cleared the path of rubble and skinwalker corpses. Beginning at the other side of the walkway, she took a running start. Pumping her arms, she sprinted as fast as she could. When she got to the edge of the chasm, she jumped. A great force pushed from beneath her feet and propelled her forward.

She landed on the other side. Not waiting to catch her breath, she bounded over to Jaruman. His breaths were so light as to be almost non-existent. But he was alive.

She tried again to push the block of stone from Jaruman's legs but failed. It was far too heavy. It was the same predicament that had forced her to leave him here before.

"How do I remove the rubble?" she called out to the men across the chasm.

Hiroc shoved Ealstan again. With the dagger at his back, Ealstan pointed his hand to the giant slab of stone holding

Jaruman down. The slab shook. A soft groan left Jaruman's lips. It only moved a fraction, and that had been toward Jaruman's top-half. If it slid forward, it could finally kill him.

"It's not enough!" Fryda cried. She squatted and put both hands beneath the slab. Gritting her teeth, she heaved. The slab shifted and finally slid away. Fryda knelt and lifted Jaruman's head.

She heard yelling and looked up. Ealstan was now pointing his knife at Hiroc and Peoh.

52

HIROC

"AERN, grant me power," Ealstan said.

Hiroc jumped back as Ealstan pushed the dagger toward him. He was expecting another wave of force, but nothing happened.

Hiroc narrowed his eyes. Somehow, Ealstan had disarmed him. Thankfully, it seemed the other man's luck had finally run out.

As Hiroc marched forward, Ealstan swung the dagger through the air. "Aern!" Cursing, he rushed Hiroc. Before he could get within striking distance, his head seemed to cave in. It burst in a fountain of blood. Dropping the dagger, he fell to his knees, his eye hanging from its socket by a thread.

Hiroc kicked Ealstan's chest, and he fell backward, descending into the chasm. Hiroc shuffled over to the precipice. There was no sound that indicated Ealstan had hit the bottom. The drop looked endless. But that wasn't saying much, considering the only light in the room was coming from the wards on Peoh's body.

Ealstan's dagger lay on the chasm's edge. It was a miracle it hadn't fallen its owner had done. Hiroc picked it up.

"We can't get across," Peoh said as he came alongside

Hiroc. Fryda was on the other side, nursing Jaruman's head in her lap. "She's trapped with Jaruman."

A sound penetrated Hiroc's ears, like a single chiming of a giant bell. He clutched both ears. The sound stopped. There was an explosion of light as every stone along the walls seemed to burst with the brightness of a sun.

When the light faded, the chasm was gone. The hole in the wall was repaired. The original entrance was no longer blocked with rubble.

Peoh grabbed Hiroc's shoulder. "The gods have seen fit to save us. That explosion of light was the spire transferring ownership."

Idmaer had given up ownership. Did that mean he was dead, condemned by the Council? Hiroc refused to believe that until he knew for certain.

As they stepped across the stone where the chasm had been, Hiroc marveled at the spire's power. Magic seemed an impossible thing. Only moments ago, Hiroc had been a man of flames. Ealstan had called him the burning man—a reference to the depictions of Enlil. How had the fire come without a runic device? He didn't know the answer, but he feared it might have something to do with giving all his spiritsoul to Enlil.

Jaruman's legs were mangled and bloody. White bone stuck out from below his left knee. A pool of blood lay beneath him.

"Can't we take him to the pool?" Fryda said to Peoh. She frowned. "I forgot that it was broken by the falling wall."

"It will have been restored." Peoh stopped and thought for a moment. "Who is most likely to own the spire now?"

"Edoma," Fryda answered.

Hiroc shook his head. "Not Edoma. She hated the spire. It will be Saega." His eyes widened. "Saega wishes to kill you. I overheard him speaking."

Peoh bristled. "Then we cannot waste any more time. It

will take too long to heal such wounds in the pool. If we don't leave before Saega learns of our presence, we will be trapped again."

Not wanting to be in the spire another moment, Hiroc got beneath Jaruman and lifted him up. Peoh took the other side. They ventured out from the spire, through the entrance.

As they stepped through the doors, they suddenly clanged shut. Every window along the spire's surface vanished.

"Not a moment too soon," Peoh said.

They carried Jaruman through the streets. Surprisingly, there was almost no one around. Hiroc was thankful since now that his adrenaline was gone, he realized he was naked but for the cloak pinned around him.

When they arrived at The Flaming Monkey, Hiroc saw why the streets had been so deserted—the chopping block was being readied in the courtyard.

53

EDOMA

THE ax fell. Idmaer's head fell after it.

Edoma forced herself not to look away. Idmaer had been guilty. Wulfnoth had condemned Idmaer with his testimony.

What was left of the town—those who hadn't become skinwalkers, victims to skinwalkers, or victims to one another—watched on as a great fire burned at the center of them.

Two warriors took Idmaer's body. It slumped in their arms, limp and lifeless. Another warrior picked up his head by his silver braid.

The warriors tossed Idmaer's head and his corpse onto the fire. It spit and crackled. The smell of burned flesh was overpowering. Edoma held her breath and walked to the fire. Bracing the heat, she fished the multicolored bracelet from her pocket and cast it into the flames. She watched the flames lick it up, the threads curling and disintegrating. She walked backward until a familiar voice spoke.

"Justice is done," Saega said.

"The people seem satisfied with justice."

There was an air of silence about them. Many had likely suspected that the absence of Aern's protection was more than just a weakening. But he was dead. They knew that now. And the man who had a hand in killing him had seen justice.

Edoma felt nothing. She had expected to flee after the execution, unable to stop herself from crying. Instead, all she could think about was their next step. Hiroc hadn't returned from the spire with Peoh yet. But Saega now controlled it. It would be simple to extract them.

The dragon Saega had captured looked on. Within its veins ran the blood that would keep Indham safe for at least a little while. Long enough to send another party to Eosorheim, or even to think of a more permanent solution. Indham would stand where Mundos had fallen. She was sure of it.

"I'm sorry, but we must act soon." Saega's voice sounded strange, and when he smiled, it was clear why. Only a handful of teeth remained in his mouth, and his gums were black. A poultice covered his face, but the stench of death overcame even the smell of Idmaer's burning body.

"Now that you're back, I can heal you. I'll not let you refuse."

"There will be time for that," he said. "I must retrieve Peoh from the spire."

"You cannot go in your condition. He will kill you."

"Ha, I can assure you that with the spire, even Peoh cannot harm me."

Edoma couldn't argue with that. With Peoh inside the spire, he was at the mercy of its owner—who was now Saega.

"You don't have to go alone. I'll come with you."

As Saega shook his head, the sunlight shone onto his face. The skin of his cheeks seemed translucent, as though his head had been dipped in a single film of wax. The sores were black now. "You must harvest the blood from the dragon." He handed her the suppression stone. "Nightfall will be here soon." She let him stagger into his carriage.

As the carriage took him up the hill toward the spire, she realized he had been decomposing before her eyes. She would have to keep an eye on him. When he returned, she would get to the bottom of it. There were rumors about dark magic and how it could take its toll on a person. She feared that, like Idmaer, Saega might hold secrets. Could he be using more than just his own lifesoul to power his magic?

If he didn't get well soon, she would know that he had dabbled in dark things.

She glanced at the Daughters behind her. "Tie the dragon down with more ropes. Make sure its jaws are closed."

The Daughters swarmed the dragon, throwing ropes over its massive form. They tied the ropes around nails and hammered the nails into the ground.

The dragon remained placid, Edoma controlling it with the suppression stone. She felt its pain and fear, but it could do nothing. This dragon would die to save thousands.

She faltered. Had Idmaer once thought the same thing?

The dragon screeched. Realizing she'd let her mind waver, she returned her focus upon the beast. She drew her knife and steadily walked toward it. She stroked the scales. They gleamed in the light. She saw her reflection in them. So old. So frail. So burdened.

"Forgive me," she whispered as she plunged the knife into the dragon.

54

FRYDA

FRYDA stood beside Hiroc and Peoh as the fire became embers. She had watched the execution through the window of her room in The Flaming Monkey. Jaruman rested in the room nearby. Peoh had performed healing magic on him, but it was nothing like the waters of the spire's pool. Jaruman was still unconscious, but his bones had been repaired. Peoh had said there might be bleeding inside him. She hoped not, because she wouldn't be in Indham to see whether he returned to health.

She had spoken with another Daughter about what was happening. Idmaer had killed Aern. Now the whole town knew that their Guardian had fallen. What would happen now? From the somber atmosphere, it didn't seem like anything good could come from it.

"It is a great crime against nature for a man to suffer for a sin he didn't commit," Peoh said.

"You don't think Idmaer did it?" Fryda never liked him, but to think that he'd killed Aern was...unthinkable.

Before Peoh could answer, Hiroc said, "The Council must know what you intend to do to save them." Although his eyes were dry, it was clear that Idmaer's death had affected

304

him. He seemed colder, harder, more unlike Alfric than ever. The clothes he now wore had been from Jaruman's room. Although large, they were cinched tight with a belt. On one side of the belt was Ealstan's dagger, his own knife on the other. Without his robes and with two blades, he looked more like a warrior than an acolyte.

"The Council cannot know." Peoh had taken a poleax from Jaruman's room. She didn't know why he needed a weapon—he had fought well with just his fists and his magic. "Saega holds the spire. It is too dangerous to remain in Indham. The thing that must be done must be done alone."

"And what about me?" Fryda asked. She hoped he hadn't forgotten about his promise.

Before Peoh could answer, the dragon outside moaned. It was a terrible sound, filled with despair. The Daughters fixed another of the bloodletting devices beneath it, and it moaned again. Edoma stood beside it, a white stone in her hand. The stone shone brightly, and the dragon quieted.

"Dragons shouldn't be used for such things," Fryda said.

"It is the way of the Guardian's magic. Some gods refuse to take blood not given freely. But not Mun. She will take whatever blood is given to her."

Fryda forced herself to turn away. Was it right for her to ask Peoh to ward her with the dragon blood? She could now see the terrible price it had cost.

"Sometimes we are forced to make difficult decisions. Is it right? Is it wrong? I'm sure there's a correct answer, but in the moment, we can only do what we think best. To use this blood could mean saving the man you love. It could also mean so much more."

Fryda didn't know exactly what Peoh meant by that, but she took consolation in his words. She didn't know whether using the dragon blood was the right thing to do, but she did know she loved Alfric and would do anything to find him. She might not be able to remove the wraith from his body and return him to normal, but she'd never be able to live with herself if she didn't try.

"Where are you going?" Hiroc asked.

In the madness of the past few days, Fryda hadn't had to tell Hiroc about Alfric. Swallowing, she said, "I'm going to find Alfric."

"In Eosorheim?" As he looked at her, his expression became confused. "Somewhere else?"

Fryda nodded, her bottom lip trembling. "Alfric is a skinwalker." She burst into tears. When she brought herself under control, Hiroc was looking through the window with vacant eyes.

He turned to her, face as cold as before. "I blame myself," he said. "I betrayed him. Maybe with Enlil's fire, he might have stood a chance. Deep down, I think I knew Alfric was lost after the warriors didn't return."

"He's not lost," Fryda said. Hiroc's placidness made her feel ill. When she had found out, she had broken into a fit of tears. She feared what might happen to a man who couldn't grieve properly. Elated, she realized she hadn't told him about the things Edoma had seen through the scrying crystal. He would have hope if he knew that. "Edoma said Alfric might be different. He might still live."

"Go on your quest if you must, but I know my brother is lost. I've seen what happens when a skinwalker takes someone." He turned and walked back inside The Flaming Monkey.

When Fryda and Peoh went inside, Hiroc wasn't there. He had probably gone to one of the rooms.

"Hand me the dragon vial," Peoh said as he took a seat.

Fryda sat across from him and handed him the vial. He removed the stopper. He dabbed his finger with the blood and began tracing wards on her face.

Finally, after so long, she was being warded with the dragon's blood. Exhaustion sapped at her energy. She couldn't rest, though. Not when she would be able to find Alfric. She had to leave before Edoma found out what she was planning.

"Mun, protect this woman," Peoh said. All along his body, the tattoos flared with color. At the same time, Fryda felt heat surge along her face and down through her limbs.

"It is done," he said. "You'll have a week. If you don't find refuge before then, you'll be prey for the skinwalkers. Tell me, this man you seek, was he Talented like his brother?"

Fryda shook her head. "Not that I know of."

Peoh frowned. "Strange. Did he have any other gifts?"

Recalling what Jaruman had said about dreamers, Fryda nodded vigorously. "He used to dream about dragons."

"Ah," Peoh said, as though something had clicked inside his mind. "Then you must be especially careful. Much rests upon you finding him and restoring him."

"Restoring him?"

"There are ways to bring someone back who still shares their body."

"Do you know how?"

Peoh shook his head. "I only know it's possible. Because someone did the same to me."

Fryda's eyes widened. Peoh had once been a skinwalker? But he looked like an ordinary man—well, except for the tattoos. Her chest filled with hope. Alfric could be saved.

"Who helped you?" she said. "Perhaps I can visit them and they might tell me how to do the same for Alfric."

"It was your mother," Peoh said with a forlorn smile.

Fryda stood and walked to the window. Outside, a crowd watched while the Daughters continued their work on the dragon. She could see Edoma barking orders to them. Edoma had refused to send someone after Alfric. Her own son. Fryda wouldn't abandon him like that. Even if she didn't know how to save Alfric, she would try.

She grabbed her cloak and clipped it over her shoulders. Pulling the hood over her head, she turned to Peoh. "Will you say goodbye to Hiroc for me?"

Peoh nodded. "May the gods keep you safe."

"Which one?"

"All of them."

Without her Daughters robes, none of the Daughters seemed to notice her in the crowd as she passed the courtyard and went to the gatehouse stables. Flight whinnied when Fryda came to her. With a sigh, she stroked the horse's silky hair.

"You didn't kill Alfric," she whispered to the beast. "We're going to find him now."

After Fryda had saddled the horse, she galloped through Indham's gates.

55

SAEGA

SAEGA allowed the two men to help him down from the carriage. The closer he had gotten to the spire, the more he felt the power of it. He breathed in its consciousness. Mucus and blood burst from his mouth as he battled a coughing fit.

He had read the grimoire's page many times overnight. He had even tried to find the pool that morning. Unfortunately, he had been called to the execution just as he'd discovered the room beneath the dungeons.

"Do you need assistance getting up the stairs?" one of the men said.

Saega chuckled, wiping his mouth. He extended a hand toward the spire. A brick as large as a tower shield lifted from its place on the outside staircase and floated into the air. It drifted toward Saega as the men watched with wide eyes. It dropped before Saega's feet. He stepped on top of it. "Idmaer hadn't the slightest idea how to use the spire's magic," he said to himself.

A mental command and the brick flew back to the staircase while Saega stood on it. The staff kept him upright, and the trip was slow enough to keep him from losing balance. The brick didn't stop at the staircase, though. Saega flicked his hand, and the double doors flung open. Another flick of the hand and the door to the dungeons opened as well.

He continued on the flying brick, through the corridors and chambers beneath the spire, until he came to the room with the pool. The grimoire's page had spoken of this pool, confirming Saega's suspicions about its existence.

As soon as his aching feet touched the cool waters, he sighed. He continued down, wincing with each step. Before long, his entire body was submerged.

He sat there for a while, beneath the surface, fighting off the urge to breathe in. The feeling was pure elation.

The First Priest had built this pool to restore himself to health and youthfulness. Where all those who had touched the carcaern orb had died, the First Priest had lived. And now Saega would live, too.

When he stepped out from the pool, he gazed upon his image in the pool's reflection. Not only had the waters healed him, but they'd also restored him to youthfulness.

This, he thought, *will be hard to explain to Edoma.*

He knew she suspected something, since his illness had worn well beyond what might kill a person. But now what would she think? That would be something he would have to deal with later.

Donning his runic robes, Saega took the brick again to the spire's entrance hall. Rather than use the staircase, he commanded the brick to take him to the peak. He rearranged the room, morphing it until it suited his desires. Everything was pure white. Gone was the dark stone that Idmaer had desired. This was no longer a place of darkness, but light.

The gods had their savior, and his name was Saega, son of Alesand.

A knock came from the door.

Startled, Saega bolted upright.

Wulfnoth walked through the doorway. He glanced

around. "I see you've made some changes already." His eyes
fell upon Saega and his mouth dropped. "How...you're *young?*"

Saega grinned. He had been looking forward to this.
"Thank you for upholding your end of the bargain."

"I'm pleased to finally have Idmaer pay, but it doesn't feel
good." Wulfnoth shook his head. He staggered, obviously
drunk. His eyes were encircled with dark pits as if he hadn't
slept for days. "I don't know who really killed Aern, but I
know Idmaer didn't. Have I condemned a man for something
he didn't commit?"

"Indham's fall came long before Aern was killed," Saega
said. He wanted to hear nothing of Wulfnoth's pitiful guilt.
What had Bodil ever seen in this man?

"I thought vengeance would feel better."

"Oh, vengeance can feel so very good." Saega flicked his
hand. The fireplace surrounded Wulfnoth. He tried to escape,
but bricks encircled him until it was enclosed like an oven.
His screams filled Saega with a deep pleasure as he sampled
Idmaer's firewine.

He could get used to this.

But that was not to be. There was much more to do before
he would ever be able to simply live within the spire.

Saega commanded the spire to bring him the scrying
crystal. It obeyed, the scrying crystal sitting atop a godstone
brick that levitated toward him. There were shortcomings to
the spire—for one, he could only command the godstone that
had been mined in the Infernal City and the special iron that
had been forged there.

Saega laughed. *I am a fool. That is hardly a shortcoming.*

He smiled and leaned back into the couch as he drew a
blade across his palm and touched the scrying crystal.

The otherworld greeted him. Across the room, standing
beside the fireplace, was Hurn's image. It was shrouded behind
a cloaking magic—a strange mist in the form of a man but with
nothing distinctive to make him out. Saega only knew it as

Hurn because this was how he'd always met with him.

"As you can see," Saega said, holding out his arms, "the spire is now mine."

"Congratulations." Hurn's voice was like the crumbling of old earth, ancient and gravelly. "The missing page?"

"In my possession."

"The Archmage of Mundos?"

"Escaped." Saega grimaced. He had been trying to enjoy this day without thinking of the single failed aspect of his plan. When he'd first gone to the spire, it was the early hours of the morning. Peoh had no longer been there. The spire provided a mental image of three figures, but they had been little more than shrouds.

"This displeases me," Hurn said. The mist grew darker. Saega waited to feel pain, but none came. "Our mission must go ahead regardless. The skinwalkers are searching now for the dragon soul. As soon as they find it, they'll destroy it."

"Shall I proceed as planned?"

Hurn dipped ethereal fingers into Saega's chest. Icy tendrils seized Saega's heart. "Everything you have has been given to you by me. I serve the Guardians, but you serve me. Remember that." In a flash of light, Hurn vanished.

Able to breathe again, Saega returned to the mortal realm. Hurn was right. Saega did serve him. But only for as long as doing so was expedient.

THE STORY CONTINUES IN
THE DRAGON SOUL

The wraiths have come to Aernheim. A powerful sorcerer is calling them to his forest stronghold. Only a skinwalker and a dragon-riding priestess can stop him.

Fryda sets out from Indham to find the man she loves. The only problem is that he's a skinwalker capable of tearing her limb from limb. And outside the safety of Indham's walls, she's just one woman against a tide of skinwalkers.

When a blood-hungry skinwalker hunts Fryda, two forest dragons come to her aid. But their price is far greater than she could have imagined. What the dragons desire could doom not only her, but all the land.

Get your copy on Amazon today.
http://gen.ius/dragonsoul

Signup for the mailing list for information on new releases, promotions, and exclusive offers. You'll receive a high-definition electronic file of the World of Vagrant Souls. You'll also get a free eBook—*Fall of Mundos*—which tells the early history of Edoma when she was a mage apprentice in Mundos.

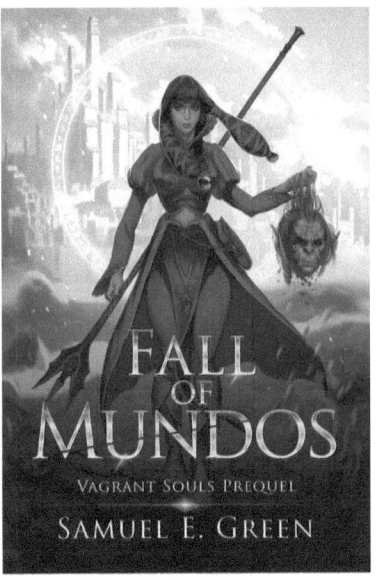

After the wards around Mundos are destroyed, the city is taken over by wraiths. The orcs from the Desolate Lands strike at the same moment, a bargain with the wraiths giving them the city. Edoma is taken as a slave, and she must convince the orc chieftain to set her free. That's no easy task, especially when the orc wishes to use her magic for his own purposes.

Sign up to the mailing list and get your
high-def map and free eBook today!

www.SamuelEGreen.com/MailingList

Samuel E. Green is an author of dark fantasy. A lover of tall tales from a young age, the muse struck after reading the works of Joe Abercrombie, Brent Weeks, and Brandon Sanderson. Inspired by these and many others, every story is filled with mysterious magic, dark heroes, and new twists on old tropes. His debut fantasy novel, *The Shattered Orb*, was published in March 2017.

www.SamuelEGreen.com

www.Facebook.com/SamuelEGreenAuthor

Author@SamuelEGreen.com

www.ingramcontent.com/pod-product-compliance
Lightning Source LLC
Chambersburg PA
CBHW021459110726
47899CB00001BA/215